**Praise for the C:**

"A high-speed chase of ⌐ characters, a timely plot, and writing so compelling that readers will be unable to turn away from the page."
— *Kings River Life Magazine*

"Will keep you turning pages late into the night and make you think twice about the dark side of the Hollywood Dream."
— Paul D. Marks,
Shamus Award-Winning Author of *Vortex*

"Radio host Carol Childs meets her match in this page-turner. Her opponent is everyone's good guy but she knows the truth about the man behind the mask. Now Carol must reveal a supremely clever enemy before he gets the chance to silence her for good."
— Laurie Stevens,
Award-Winning Author of the Gabriel McRay Series

"A story of suspense, raw emotion, and peril which builds up to a satisfying climax...Silverman has given us another book where we can sit down and get our teeth into, and I look forward to the next in the series. Highly recommended."
— *Any Good Book*

"Fast paced and cleverly plotted, an edgy cozy with undertones of noir."
— Sue McGinty,
Author of the Bella Kowalski Central Coast Mysteries

"A thoroughly satisfying crime novel with fascinating, authentic glimpses into the world of talk radio and some of its nastier stars... The writing is compelling and the settings ring true thanks to the author's background as a newscaster herself."
— Jill Amadio,
Author of *Digging Too Deep*

"The author gives us a terrific story building up to a climax that will please the reader. The old saying regarding 'people are not always what they seem' fits perfectly in this case...Readers will be waiting impatiently for the next installment."

– *Suspense Magazine*

"Silverman provides us with inside look into the world of talk radio as Carol Childs, an investigative reporter, finds herself in the middle of a Hollywood murder mystery...A hunky FBI Agent and a wacky psychic will keep readers guessing from beginning to end."

– Annette Dashofy,
*USA Today* Bestselling Author of *Lost Legacy*

"Silverman creates a trip through Hollywood filled with aging hippies, greedy agents, and a deadly case of product tampering. Forget the shower scene in *Psycho*; *Shadow of Doubt* will make you scared to take a bath!"

– Diane Vallere,
National Bestselling Author of *Pillow Stalk*

"Carol is a smart, savvy heroine that will appeal to readers. This is a cozy with a bite."

– *Books for Avid Readers*

"Crackles with memorable characters, Hollywood legends, and as much action behind the mic as investigative reporter Carol Childs finds in the field."

– Mar Preston,
Author of *A Very Private High School*

"I loved the tone, the pace, and the drama which pulled me in immediately...All the while I suspected something was amiss, and when it came to fruition, I knew the author was going to pull a fast one, and yes, she did, and bravo because now I must read the next book to see how it all plays out."

– *Dru's Book Musings*

# ROOM FOR DOUBT

ROOM FOR DOUBT
A Carol Childs Mystery
Part of the Henery Press Mystery Collection

First Edition | July 2017

Henery Press
www.henerypress.com

Copyright © 2017 by Nancy Cole Silverman
Cover art by Stephanie Savage

Trade Paperback ISBN-13: 978-1-63511-235-1
Digital epub ISBN-13: 978-1-63511-236-8
Kindle ISBN-13: 978-1-63511-237-5
Hardcover ISBN-13: 978-1-63511-238-2

Printed in the United States of America

# ROOM FOR DOUBT

## A CAROL CHILDS MYSTERY

# NANCY COLE SILVERMAN

To Sarah,
    So happy to
get to know you,
        Nancy Cole
        S

**HENERY PRESS**

**The Carol Childs Mystery Series
by Nancy Cole Silverman**

*To My Family*

## ACKNOWLEDGMENTS

I have to thank my grandmother, Marjorie Childs, for *Room For Doubt*. When I was a young girl, she told me a story about an odd woman who had lived next door to her when she was first married. That would have been back in the early 1900s. Frequently, the police had been seen coming to the woman's door and then leaving. Then one day, the police returned to her home, and so did the coroner's van. After that, my grandmother said no one in the neighborhood ever saw the woman again. They were all certain she was still living in the house. But for whatever reason, she became a recluse. The story always haunted me. Whatever happened in that house remained a mystery, but for me, and my overactive imagination, it was fertilizer for a story I would one day write. And while the names, location and time of events in no way resemble those from the story she told me, I do credit her for the idea. Thanks, Gramma.

I would also like to thank my publisher, Kendel Lynn at Henery Press, who took a chance on the Carol Childs Mysteries and has made this dream of mine a reality. My editors, Erin George and Rachel Jackson. It takes a team for a writer to create a novel, and these two women with their keen eyes and understanding of story structure help me to look good on the page. Stephanie Savage, who designed what I think is my favorite cover yet, and Art Molinares, who keeps the Hen House clucking.

And, finally to my friends and family who are too numerous to mention, but most importantly, my husband, Bruce. You make this all possible.

# CHAPTER 1

"Excuse me, miss? Are you a model?"

I was in the cereal aisle at the grocery store with a box of bran flakes in my hand when I heard the voice behind me. It had been years since I'd done any modeling, and I wasn't feeling particularly glamorous. My hair was in a ponytail, and I was wearing a pair of sweatpants and a ratty old KCHC t-shirt with a cartoon of a dead chicken on my chest. The words Radio Road Kill blasted beneath it. Not exactly the type of thing one wears to make a good first impression.

"Not in years." I laughed and turned expecting to find a friendly face. Grocery stores these days topped bars for places to meet men. Despite the fact the line was an obvious come on, I was, unfortunately, once again in the market.

Instead, the voice belonged to a nice-looking, well-built gym-rat with a neatly cropped beard. He was about half my age, and worse yet, he wasn't talking to me. Not at all. He had cornered a young girl directly behind me; a twenty-something darling dressed in a skin-tight running outfit that looked like it had been painted onto her body.

I smiled apologetically and turned to read the label on the cereal box. Not that they noticed. Lately, I felt as though I'd become the invisible woman.

My name is Carol Childs, I'm a single mom, and I work as a reporter for a talk radio station in Los Angeles. I was one of those faceless voices on the airwaves people heard every day. Perhaps that, and the fact I'd recently turned forty, explained why I was beginning to feel I blended into the background like wallpaper paste. Few of my listeners could identify me, and in LA, women over forty simply weren't on anyone's radar. Out of the corner of my eye, I watched, while I listened to their exchange.

Gym-rat, with muscled arms like watermelons bulging from beneath his t-shirt, pressed a business card into Running-girl's hand. "You ever want to get into the club, just call."

Gym-rat was making a big impression. Running-girl glanced at the card, hugged it to her chest like she had just won the lottery, then kissed Gym-rat on the cheek as she tucked the card into her sports bra.

At that point, I tossed the cereal box into my cart and started up the aisle. I didn't give it another thought.

Until the next day.

My bedroom was still dark when the phone rang. With my head barely off the pillow, I squinted at the digital clock next to my bed: 5:55 a.m. *Dammit, Tyler, it's not even five o'clock. New record.* I fumbled for the bedside phone—a requirement the station demanded of all its reporters—and knocked it to the floor before grabbing the handle. Nobody else, not even a phone solicitor, would dare to call before sunup.

"Please, Tyler, tell me this isn't becoming a habit with you."

"Sorry, Carol. I need you."

On the other end of the line was my boss, Tyler Hunt, a twenty-one-year-old whiz-kid who referred to me as the world's oldest cub reporter.

"No," I begged. "Absolutely not. Please, Tyler, not today."

Tomorrow was my son's birthday, and Tyler had promised me the day off to prepare. On Saturday, Charlie, my youngest, would officially be sixteen, and I had planned a big surprise party to celebrate. My daughter, Cate, was coming up from San Diego State. My best friend, Sheri, her son, Clint, and fourteen members of Charlie's football team would all be here. Plus, my ex, Robert, planned stop by with *the wife* and Charlie's new step-brother. No way was I about to get caught up in anything that would distract me.

"I need you to take this, Carol. There's a body up on the Hollywood Sign."

I sat up in bed and pushed the hair out of my face. He had to be kidding. The Hollywood Sign? Recently a prankster had climbed to the top of the sign and with tarps and tape lettered it to read Hollyweed. A pro-cannabis statement for sure.

"Tyler, if there's a body on the Hollywood Sign, it's got to be a publicity stunt. Something one of the studios is doing for a movie maybe."

"It's not a stunt, Carol. The police are reporting a man's naked body hanging from the sign. It's for real. I need you up there. Now. Go!"

# CHAPTER 2

I reminded myself, as I stumbled into my closet and grabbed a pair of jeans and a sweatshirt, that when it came to news reporting, I didn't have a lot of options. The station had recently gone through a format change, dropping our old KCHC Chick Lite call letters and adopting a new hard-hitting, male-dominated format. KNST News Sports and Talk. Every reporter on staff, including me, was under review, and since I was still the new kid on the block, when Tyler called, I jumped. On my way out the door, I stopped in the kitchen, took a box of Cheerios from the cabinet for Charlie, and scribbled a quick sticky note. *Tyler called. Hope to be back before you leave for school. Xoxo, Mom.* I drew a happy face at the end and placed it on the refrigerator door where I knew he wouldn't miss it.

In the car, I programmed my GPS for a popular lookout directly beneath the Hollywood Sign. At night the grassy field was used by kids to park and do those things they didn't want their folks to know about. Daytime, it was busy nonstop with tour vans and snap-happy day-trippers grabbing selfies from beneath the sign. At this hour, I figured the police would still be securing the area, and with a little luck, I might be able to get in and out before the cops closed it off to everyone, including the press. I glanced at my watch. It wasn't yet six-fifteen. GPS said I was ten minutes away. I pressed the accelerator and speed along the canyon road. If I got there early enough and met with the police, I might be able to file my story live from the scene and still be home in time to see Charlie off for school. Any follow-up Tyler could handle, at least for today. No murder or late breaking story was going to interfere with my prep plans for Charlie's party. Tyler owed me that much.

\*    \*    \*

I squinted into the early morning sun as I drove east along the canyon road. The sun was just starting to rise above the Santa Monica Mountains. With the first rays of daylight on the hills, the city glistened below. It looked like it was going to be one of those picture-perfect sunny California days. Too glorious for anything bad to happen. And then, as I rounded the bend, I saw it. Hanging like a crucifix, from the center of the Hollywood Sign, was the body of a nude man.

I hit the brakes. With my eyes fixed on the sign, I nearly skidded off the road.

My front fender kissed the guardrail. I pulled the steering wheel hard to the right and came to a stop next to the grassy field, directly below the sign. No time to panic. Two police cruisers and an unmarked car were already on the scene, their lights flashing. I grabbed my reporter's bag off the seat next to me and ran towards the action.

"Hey, miss. Stop. You can't go over there." A young cop blocked my approach to the investigating officers in the field. He looked to be a rookie, barely old enough to be out of school, much less dressed in an LAPD uniform. "Sorry, but I'm cordoning off this area." He gestured with a roll of yellow crime scene tape in his hand, then stood back. "Gotta secure the site. Keep everybody behind the line."

"I'm a reporter." I reached into my bag for my ID, hopeful my credentials would allow me a few questions before he finished stringing up the yellow tape and I was denied permanent access. Behind him, several plainclothes officers appeared to be searching a late model gray Tahoe, its doors and tailgate open. "Somebody around here I can talk to? A detective, maybe?"

He glanced over his shoulder. "Look, I'll tell my sergeant, but for now, I need you to stand over there." He pointed in the direction of several early morning hikers huddled in a semi-circle behind crime scene tape. "Everybody stays behind the line, including you."

I approached the group of hikers, three older women who looked to be anywhere from fifty-five to sixty years old. They were all dressed similarly in sweats, t-shirts, and tennis shoes and appeared to be in good shape. I figured them for regulars and was hopeful one of them might have seen something. I asked how long they had been there. They looked at me, a critical evaluation from head to toe, then spotting the reporter's bag on my shoulder appeared to soften.

"You a reporter?" The tallest of the three, a woman of about sixty with salt-and-pepper gray hair, stepped forward.

"Yes, my name's Carol Childs. I'm with KNST. Anything you can tell me?"

"Bessie here called it in." The woman nodded to her friend, a shorter brunette with a warm smile.

She answered. "We were hiking the canyon like we do every morning 'fore sunrise when we noticed the body."

"Awful, isn't it?" A third voice came from behind them both, a smaller-framed woman with thick gray hair in a ponytail. "Good-looking young man like that."

"And you ladies never saw anyone else in the canyon?" I asked.

"No." The three answered in unison, then stared back up at the sign.

I grabbed a small pair of field glasses from my reporter's bag and focused on the pale, bulky white hulk hanging limply against the sign. I estimated the man's age to be in his late twenties, maybe early thirties. Young and fit. Tied around his neck was a rope, like a hangman's noose. I zeroed in on the face, hidden by the position of his left shoulder and something else.

"You see that?" I pointed up at the body, unsure what was partially blocking his face.

"His nose?" Bessie appeared surprised I hadn't noticed before.

"Yeah, what is it? It looks like a—"

"A red clown's nose," she said. "We've been wondering about it too. Who'd do such a thing?"

If it weren't for the number of rescue workers who were now scaling the sign and police helicopters in the sky above me, I would swear this whole gruesome scene had been staged for some macabre feature film. But I knew it wasn't. And as I looked back at the body, I knew why. I had seen this man before. The short dark curly hair. The reddish beard. I knew him, or at least I knew of him. Hanging from the center of the Hollywood Sign was the gym-rat I had seen in the grocery store yesterday.

The sound of helicopter blades in the sky overhead made it almost impossible for me to continue my conversation with the women. News choppers from the local stations were beginning to join them, and soon all of LA would be waking up to the news there was a body hanging from the Hollywood Sign.

I looked back for the young cop who had shooed me away from the investigating officers. He was standing just feet from where they were searching the abandoned gray Tahoe. I took my microphone from my bag and waved to him. I couldn't wait any longer. If I was going to get this story, I needed to talk to someone and fast. If not, my news-chopper brothers in the sky would grab the story out from under me.

"Hey, remember me? The reporter. I need to talk to someone, can you help me?"

The peach-faced young rookie approached, then glanced nervously over his shoulder as though he were questioning his orders to keep everyone, including reporters, at bay.

I prompted him. "I do a lot of work with LAPD. You remember the Hollywood murders...those missing girls a couple months back?" He stared back at me. He had to know the story. In the end, our radio reports made the cops and the FBI look like heroes. I could see he was weighing his decision. "I worked that case. Couldn't have done it without you guys."

Whatever I said, it worked. He punched the two-way radio on his shoulder. There was a brief exchange. I couldn't hear a word due to the heavy sounds of chopper blades buffeting above my head, but finally, he lifted the yellow crime scene tape and waved me through.

"You can talk to Detective Riley." He pointed to the center of the field where a group of cops was checking out the gray Tahoe. "He's the old guy in the tweed jacket standing next to the police cruiser. He'll talk to you."

Riley was a paunchy, gray-haired detective who looked like he had spent too many hours behind the desk and not enough time in the gym. Or the field for that matter. Judging from the lack of sweat on his brow, I doubted he had been up the mountain to check the scene out for himself.

I introduced myself and asked if he had any idea who the victim was.

"Cops up the hill found a driver's license, but you know the drill. Can't say anything. Not 'til the family's notified, and we have a positive ID."

"Any idea how he got there?" I gestured with my mic to the top of the hill.

"No, but I'd say it was a suicide."

"Suicide?" I glanced back up at the sign. Rescue workers had already removed the body, and cops in black uniforms were all over the hill, like ants at a picnic. "You think that guy just climbed up there and killed himself?"

"It happens. Wouldn't be the first. Guy wants to off himself, believe me, he'll find a way."

"Did you even see the body?"

I could feel myself growing irritated. The fact that Detective Riley hadn't moved three feet from his unmarked car since I'd arrived and the body was already being removed caused me to wonder. What was the rush? Was it just a courtesy to a possible suicide victim to remove the body before commuters spotted it on their way to work, or were the police trying to cover something up?

"From here it looks like he had on a clown nose. You telling me some guy committed suicide wearing a silly clown's nose on his face?"

"Look, lady, I don't explain 'em. I just call 'em. And just 'cause some nut-job climbs up on the Hollywood Sign and chooses to off himself while wearing some stupid clown nose on his face doesn't mean I understand it. Do us all a favor, will ya? This was a suicide. Plain and simple. Why don't you be a good little reporter and file your story and get out of here." Riley sounded as hot as I felt.

My cell buzzed before I could ask another question. It was Tyler, putting the heat on. He wanted a report for the seven a.m. news break.

Other stations were already reporting on police activity in the park, and I needed to *hurry it up*. News is always about being first and fast. As a result, accuracy sometimes falls through the cracks. But if this really was a suicide, as Riley wanted me to believe, I needed to be extra careful. Ordinarily, news organizations don't cover suicides. But, in a situation like this, with such a public death, KNST and others in the market would be forced to cover it. There's an unwritten rule among reporters never to sensationalize anything to do with the taking one's own life. And, in a case like this, brevity was best. With seconds to spare, I organized my thoughts, while in the background I could hear Tyler as he counted me down.

"Ten seconds to go, Carol."

"I'm ready."

Then, "Five...four...three...two...one."

"Thank you, Tyler. I'm here in Griffith Park, where a group of early morning hikers alerted police to a body on the Hollywood Sign. Police have identified the body to be that of a white male believed to be in his late twenties to mid-thirties. Investigators say there doesn't appear to have been a struggle and believe this may have been a suicide. This is Carol Childs live from the Hollywood Sign."

# CHAPTER 3

It was nearly eight a.m. by the time I got home. The police had blocked off my return route through the canyon, and traffic coming and going from the Hollywood Sign was rerouted onto the freeway. By the time I entered the front door, Charlie had already left for school. And at that point, all I wanted was a hot shower and to wash my hair. I had just started the water—my hair full of shampoo—when I heard the French doors in the kitchen downstairs slam shut. I froze, my hands on my head. I had left the doors partially open, with the screen latched, when I came in. At least I thought I had. I wanted to air the house out as much as I needed to wash my hair and clear my head of this morning's suicide. I stood for a moment, hearing nothing and thinking perhaps a breeze had jostled them. But then I heard something else. A loud scraping sound. Someone was in the house, downstairs, in the kitchen. It sounded like one of the barstools was being dragged across the kitchen floor. I turned off the water. Grabbed my robe, and with my hair sopping wet, tiptoed from the shower to the top of the stairs.

"Charlie?" I leaned over the banister and peaked down the stairway. One of the kitchen cabinet doors was standing wide open, and I could hear someone or something shuffling around. "That you?"

No response.

"Charlie, you home?"

I wasn't expecting Charlie home until tomorrow evening. He was spending the night with his dad while I prepped for tomorrow's party.

Still no reply. Quietly, I took two steps backward and reached inside Charlie's bedroom door for his baseball bat. For once I was thankful my son hadn't listened to me and put it away in his closet. Armed with the bat for self-defense, I approached the top of the stairs again. With one hand on the railing and the bat in the other, I slowly descended the staircase.

Suddenly, like a flash of light—quicker than I could have snapped my fingers—a cat raced up the steps. Its long hair brushing my bare legs sent chills up my spine as it disappeared into Charlie's bedroom. *Bossy Pants?* I hadn't seen the mixed Calico in months. He had vanished one day, and I thought we'd seen the last of him.

"Hello?" I yelled again, and continued slowly down the stairs, toward the kitchen.

The noise from the kitchen was getting louder. Whoever or whatever was in my kitchen was making no attempt to hide their presence. As I approached the bottom of the steps, I heard the refrigerator door open. I raised the bat to a slugger's position.

"Who's there?"

No answer.

I stepped forward, both hands gripped tightly around the bat, and stared into the kitchen like a slugger waiting for a fast pitch. There, bent over in the refrigerator with her backside to me, her long floral skirt not quite covering her dusty moccasins, was Misty Dawn.

"Misty?" I hadn't seen Misty Dawn since we'd parted ways after my next-door neighbor, Samantha Millhouse, had moved. Sam had been an invaluable source to me when I first started my job as a reporter. She was the niece of a big Hollywood agent who had been murdered. Misty had been her aunt's client—a kind of psychic to the stars—and over the course of the investigation, we had become friends, sort of. "What are *you* doing here?"

Misty turned and stared at me, her face frozen like a deer in headlights. Silence passed between us. I dropped the bat and steadied my shaking legs against the weight of it while I willed my heart to slow down. Misty appeared exactly like she had the last time I'd seen her. An aging hippie dressed in a long cotton skirt and a tie-dyed t-shirt. On her wrists and up and down her arms she wore enough beads and bangles, it was no wonder I'd heard her rustling in my kitchen. Her jewelry jangled with her every move like an early warning system. And in her long wavy gray hair, which I doubt she had ever cut, she wore synthetic feathers dyed pink and blue. But it was her blue eyes, the color of a spring sky with thin milky white clouds, now covered with cataracts, that stared back at me. I felt as though she could see my every thought.

"Oh, dear." She patted herself on her shoulders, then to her breasts to her waist, as though she was feeling for something that might help her to remember why she was in my house. "I suppose I should have called. I've been thinking about you. Didn't you know?" She paused, glanced back at the refrigerator, then said, "Anyway, I was listening to you on the air this morning, about that young man on the Hollywood Sign, and—"

"Misty." I snapped at her before she could ramble on any further. Misty could take forever to make a point. "Why are you here?" My next question was going to be, *In my house?* But she beat me to it. She answered like she had read my mind.

"I suppose you could say the cat let me in. I was out back, lounging on the patio. I was going to wait for you there. I must have fallen asleep, and when I woke, I saw the cat go in through the screen door. It wasn't latched, and, well, I—"

*The cat?* I took two steps to the door, and it slammed it shut. So much for airing the house out. *The spirits*—although I didn't believe Misty was one—had already invaded.

"That still doesn't explain why you're here, Misty."

"Well, I've been thinking, and it occurred to me you might need someone. Now that you're single again, what with Eric off with his Sea Mistress, and you with your new show."

I sighed and reached for the coffeepot, pressed the auto fill button and made myself a cup. I could never explain how Misty knew the things she did. She always made it sound far more *Twilight Zone* than the busybody I knew her to be. In truth, I suspected Misty had actually picked up a phone and called the FBI's Los Angeles' bureau and asked to speak with Agent Langdon. As a respected clairvoyant, her services had at times been useful to to the FBI. And I was sure Eric took her call and willingly shared the news about our mutual breakup. There was no reason he shouldn't.

"Anyway," she rattled on, "I thought I'd make myself available. As a housekeeper."

"A...housekeeper?" I nearly choked on my coffee.

I seriously doubted Misty possessed any domestic skills. Her clothes looked like ones she had dug out of the hamper, if she even owned such a thing, and the fringed bag she carried was stained with either red wine or dried blood. I preferred not to think about it. I spilled my coffee into the sink.

*Heaven help me.* My day had once again gone from the horrific to the absurd, but if Misty was here, there had to be a good reason. Then, remembering Misty's penchant for tea, I asked if she had any in her bag.

"You know I never travel without it." She reached into her bag and pulled out several small clear plastic baggies stuffed with tea leaves and herbs. "What would you like, dear? Perhaps jasmine, or maybe, ah, I know—I've just the thing. Blueberry. You look piqued. That'll put some color back in your cheeks."

I put on a pot of hot water and, once ready, watched as Misty carefully prepared two cups of tea. The act was more elaborate than a Japanese tea ceremony, with the inhaling of the herbs as they brewed in their own little hot baths of water. When they were ready, I suggested we retreat to the living room. With a tray full of store-bought cookies and an extra carafe of hot water, I followed her waddle into the living room.

Misty took a seat on the couch beneath Bossy Pants, who had returned from Charlie's room and was now curled up on his former perch beneath the window. It was as though the cat had never left.

I sat across from Misty in a wingback chair and reached for my tea. "How are things going?"

"Well, I 'spose one could say I've reached a bit of a dry spell. Probably nothing to worry about, but I haven't worked since...you know..." I knew Misty was referring to the death of her agent, Pepper Millhouse. After Pepper had died, my former neighbor, Sam, had taken over her aunt's agency and dropped Misty for *professional* reasons. None of which was ever explained to me.

Misty took a sip of her tea, then flailed one hand above her head, as though to clear the air of evil thoughts. "Not to speak ill of the dead, mind you, but I do find myself in an unusual situation and an opportunity at the same time."

I didn't have to read between the lines to know Misty's idea of an unusual situation and opportunity had something to do with me. Just looking at her, I could tell she was homeless, maybe hadn't had anything more than a spit-shower in days, and was possibly living in her mini-van. I was certain she had nowhere to go. I was her last resort, and she was too proud to ask. I poured more hot water into her tea cup.

"You know, it's funny you showing up right now. I could use some help. Tyler's changed some things around at the station, and as you already learned, he's offered me a late-night show on Sunday evenings. It's going to make things a little hectic around here. At least for a while." As I was saying it, I was thinking about how Tyler had promised to swing a little extra money my way in exchange for my working an additional evening shift. But with the format change and new management, the budget had been tightened, and a raise was definitely not happening. But with Misty's help, it could be a win-win situation. "If you'd like, I could use a housekeeper. At least temporarily."

"Absolutely." Misty grabbed Bossy Pants off the back of the couch and hugged him to her chest. I could almost hear the two of them purr in unison. "In fact, if you don't mind I could help with that garden of yours as well. I noticed it's overgrown and could use some tending."

"Help yourself."

"Good. My bags are out in my van." She pointed out the window toward the street. "It'll just take a minute to unpack. The guest room still at the top of the stairs?"

I nodded. *What had I done?* I couldn't say no. Lost dogs and kittens, I seemed to be a magnet for them.

Misty got as far as the back door then stopped. "You're going to be so happy I'm here. I promise. Oh, and Carol, you can put that baseball bat away. You're not going to need it. At least not for a while."

# CHAPTER 4

Saturday night, Tyler was on my doorstep. Charlie's party was in full swing and the front door was wide open to the courtyard where my best friend Sheri and I had hung colorful party lanterns. Tyler knocked on the doorsill, then spotted me in the kitchen and walked in, oblivious to the festivities. In one hand, he had several rolled up sheets of copy paper. Nervously, he slapped them like a baton against the palm of his other hand as he approached.

"Carol, I need to see you."

"Tyler?" I put my wine glass down on the counter. I hadn't expected my boss to show up at my son's birthday party. Despite the fact I had casually mentioned he'd be welcome, I never dreamed he'd actually come. In truth, I thought he would be uncomfortable. I seriously doubted the station's boy-wonder had ever had a birthday party of his own, much less would want to spend time at a chaperoned kids' party. "What are you doing here?"

"We need to talk. It's about the body they found up on the Hollywood Sign yesterday."

I put my finger to my lips, hopeful none of the kids had heard him, and grabbed Tyler by the hand and pulled him toward the French doors. "Tyler, this isn't the place or the time. There are kids here. Plus the police think it was a suicide, and we don't do news stories about suicides."

"Maybe not, Carol, but look at this." Tyler thrust the pages he was carrying into my hands. I glanced at a picture of the nude body hanging from the sign. Only the internet would have published such a gruesome photo. Not the kind of thing I wanted Charlie to see. Particularly not today.

"The police have confirmed his ID. His name's Bernard Sims, a.k.a. Bruno."

"Seriously? His name's Bruno?" I squinted at the pages in my hand.

"He's a former stuntman. Twenty-eight. You know how it is with industry folks. Bruno was probably a stage name. Used it so people would remember him. He was also employed as a bouncer for a nightclub on the strip."

I pushed the pages away. I didn't want to look at them anymore. I was still having trouble scrubbing the scene from my mind.

"Tyler, please, even if it's not a suicide, you promised me. You gave me the day off, remember? Look around. It's Charlie's birthday. I'm not working. Not tonight."

Tyler ignored my protests and started riffling through the pages, pointing to the headlines. *Bouncer Disappears after Wild Party. Former Doorman Found Hanging on Hollywood Sign.*

"And it's not just this, Carol. A private eye came to see me this afternoon. He thinks this case is related to several others he's working, and he wants to talk to you."

"Me? Why?"

"He thinks you might have seen something. And that Bruno's murder, if it was murder, isn't just a one-off."

I took the pages back from Tyler. If Bruno's death hadn't been a suicide and turned out to be part of something more nefarious, like a serial killing, the least I could do was look into it. *But not tonight.*

"Fine, Tyler, but please, give me tonight." I stuffed the papers in my bag beneath the kitchen table, where no one, particularly Charlie, would find them. "I'll read these later, and if it makes you happy, I'll call this PI—whoever he is—first thing in the morning. In the meantime, this is a birthday party, why don't you stay and have a piece of cake? Enjoy yourself."

# CHAPTER 5

I had mixed feelings as I dialed the PI's number Tyler had given me. I knew he would want to meet with me, and I hated the thought of leaving Charlie on a Sunday morning. Particularly the day after his birthday. I felt like I'd barely seen my son for his own party. His father had picked him up after school on Friday, and by the time he brought him home on Saturday, Charlie's friends had already started to arrive for the celebration. Plus, I didn't see the point in talking with some PI I didn't even know about a case the police had already ruled a suicide. I wasn't at all sure the articles Tyler shared with me about the other dead men were related to the body I'd seen. They read more like exposés. Fake news. Written by bloggers with questionable facts I felt sure hadn't been substantiated.

Trouble was I had one big nagging doubt that wouldn't go away. I wasn't convinced Bernard "Bruno" Sims had committed suicide either. It didn't make sense. Particularly if Bruno had been the same man I'd seen in the grocery store just days before trying to pick up Running-girl. Judging from her overly enthusiastic reaction, Bruno had a lot to look forward to, and suicide wasn't one of them. So when Private Investigator Gerhardt Chasen told me he had evidence—real hard evidence—that would prove Bruno hadn't killed himself, and that the police were covering something up, I agreed to meet with him, begrudgingly.

"Bring along a good pair of hiking shoes," he said. "We're going to take a walk."

We decided to meet at noon in the grassy field, the same spot where I had filed my report two days earlier. He said I'd recognize him. He'd be the dude in the cargo shorts, nursin' a sucker.

"A sucker?" I asked.

"Yeah. New Year's resolutions stuff. You know how it goes. Trying to kick some bad habits."

Gerhardt Chasen wasn't kidding about the shorts or the sucker, for that matter. As I parked my Jeep, I spotted him staring directly up at the Hollywood Sign. He was wearing a pair of khaki-colored cargo shorts, a camouflage vest, work boots, and a cowboy hat. It wasn't until he turned and looked at me that I noticed it. A bulbous object on the side of his bearded cheek with a thin white stick protruding from his mouth. A lollipop. He rolled it around like chewing tobacco, and as I approached, he smiled, taking the candy from his mouth.

Aside from the sucker, Gerhardt Chasen looked like a modern day Indiana Jones, about six-two, athletic, and on the youngish side. I pegged him to be in his mid-thirties.

"Gerhardt?" I asked.

"You don't look much like a radio reporter." He stuck his hand out expecting I'd shake it. "Bet you get that all the time. Friends call me Chase. Don't much care for Gerhardt, and Mr. Chasen is too formal."

I shook his hand, large and rough in my own. Then without waiting for a further introduction, he turned around, told me to follow him, and headed up a narrow footpath into the park.

After several minutes, I hollered after him. "Excuse me. I take it we're hiking up to the sign? Don't you think we should talk first?"

He stopped momentarily, his eyes on the forty-five-foot-tall letters that loomed over us like monolithic giants. "Not unless you're some Barbie doll who can't walk and talk at the same time." Then turning back to me, he added, "What's the matter, Blondie, can't keep up?"

He had to be joking? But if he wanted to test my mettle, I was more than capable. I hated being shown up.

I quickened my pace and passed him on the trail. "Not only can this *Barbie doll* walk and talk, she can even chew gum at the same time. Can you?" I was competitive by nature, and whoever this PI was, I wasn't about to lose this endurance race to the sign. "And my name's not Blondie or Barbie," I snapped. "It's Carol Childs."

I could hear him close behind me, his breathing heavy. The grade was getting steep, and the dry incline was slippery with small rocks, making it difficult to navigate. Several times, despite my surefootedness, I nearly stumbled but didn't.

Finally, after twenty rigorous minutes on the mountain, and with my heart beating like a threshing machine, I stopped. No need in one of us having a heart attack. I steadied myself on the loose rock and turned around.

"You need a break?" I hollered.

Ten feet behind me, Chase stood, nearly doubled over, with his hat in hand and one foot mounted on a rock. He was panting. Then catching his breath, he wiped his brow and squinted at me. "So, Ms. Childs, you notice anything unusual when you were here Friday morning?"

"You mean other than a nude body hanging on the sign?"

He laughed, then reached for a water bottle attached to his belt and took a long swig.

"You want a drink?"

"No." My heart was pounding, and I was sweating, but I'd be damned if I'd share a water bottle. "Thank you. I won't be needing your water. But as long as we're taking this little breather, why don't you tell me what it is you want to show me before you have a heart attack and I have to call the EMTs to come rescue you."

"What, you're not up to performing a little CPR?"

I smiled disingenuously. "Sorry, I have to draw the line at scruffy beards, they're not my thing."

Chase sat down on the rock, exhaled deeply, and took another long swig from his bottle.

I retreated down the hill and stood several feet in front of him.

He offered me the bottle again. "You sure? Don't wanna get dehydrated."

I was thirsty, and if he was willing to stop long enough to explain his mission, I was willing to risk a few germs. I grabbed the bottle, wiped it clean with the tail of my shirt then poured the water into my mouth. My lips never touching the mouth piece.

"I assume your boss, that skinny kid who calls himself a news director, filled you in on the other two deaths I'm investigating?"

"That's why I'm here. That and you insisted we meet in person. So here I am." I sat down on a rock a few feet away.

"Well don't go getting all big-headed about it. You're not the only reporter in town I've talked to. I finished up with everyone else yesterday. But you're the last. Tyler said you had some party to go to and couldn't be disturbed."

I wasn't about to dignify his dig into my personal life with a response. My balancing act between the kids, my private affairs, and work was none of his business.

"Just what is it you need to know?"

"Like I said, I'm asking what people saw when they were here."

I explained what he already knew, that the press had been kept at a distance from the actual crime scene, and that I had spoken to the detective in charge who had ruled Bruno's death a suicide.

"Detective Riley, right?"

He half-laughed as he said the name then chugged at the water bottle, nearly emptying it.

"You know him?"

"We've crossed paths before." Chase stood up, wiped his hands on his shorts, then clapped his palms clean. The gesture a clear indication that whatever had happened between the two hadn't been good. "What I don't know is what else you might have seen. Something the police may not have included in their report?"

I glanced back down at the grassy area where I had stood with the group of early morning hikers staring up at the sign.

"I was one of the first to arrive. A couple of hikers in the park and the cops. Nobody else, at least that I saw." I explained how the police had just begun to cordon off the area and pointed to a dusty knoll beneath the sign, leading into the park where I had been standing. "I thought I saw something on the man's face."

"What?" Chase's eyes narrowed like he knew there was something more the police hadn't included in their report.

"This is going to sound crazy. The police said it was nothing, but I can't stop thinking about it. There was a red clown nose on the guy's face. I asked Riley about it, but he dismissed it. Said it wasn't his job to determine why the vic did what he did, only that he did it. "

"A clown nose, huh? You're sure?"

"Yeah. And I'm not the only one who saw it. A couple of the hikers I was standing with saw it too."

"Really?" Chase took another sucker from his pocket, put it in his mouth, and stared back down at the spot where I'd been standing with the women. "And Riley never went up the hill? To check things out himself?"

"No." I shook my head. "Far as I could tell, he'd already sent a team up to investigate. He and a couple of other detectives stayed back in the field, checking out what I assumed was the vic's car."

"Anything else?"

"Not that I remember. Next thing I saw was a fire truck and a black coroner's van. They pulled up on the utility road behind the Hollywood Sign. Then some medic types, or rescue workers, climbed down from the road and took the body. I didn't see much else, and I wasn't about to climb up for a closer look. Particularly with it being a suicide. At that point, it just wasn't a story we'd cover."

"Follow me." Chase took the sucker from his mouth and pointed it at the sign. "I need to show you something."

I looked up at the top of the hill. It was still a good climb, most of it straight up, and despite the cooler January temperatures, it was getting warm. Before we went any further, I wanted more information. "You sure you can't just tell me?"

"Trust me. You'll see when we get there."

Chase started up the hill ahead of me. I followed, the both of us panting. Neither of us in much of a mood to talk as we pushed toward the top. It wasn't until we finally got to a chain-link security fence surrounding the sign that we stopped and I caught my breath.

"Just what is it you wanted me to see?" I asked.

"You're standing right next to it. You notice anything?"

"You mean the fence?"

"Yeah. After that artist prankster defaced the sign couple weeks back, changing it to read Hollyweed, the city put up a brand new security fence. You see where it's been patched?" Chase pointed to a section of the fence that had been rewired. "The police are saying Bruno cut through the fence from this side. They put a temporary patch on it. Thing is, I don't think that's what happened."

"Why not?"

"Because the fencing's been pulled forward, towards us, not like someone trying to get in might do. Check out the bend in the wire and the scraping on the rocks beneath it. They're scratched. And you can't get to the sign easily from this side. The only way to get beyond this barrier is from the utility road above us, where you said you saw the fire truck and the coroner's van."

"Hard to imagine the cops didn't notice that."

"Riley sent rookies up this hill to do a job he was too lazy to do himself. He might as well have sent boy scouts. They weren't about to question him. But I'll tell you this, Bruno didn't park his car down there in that grassy field and hike up here and hang himself on the sign. Not like Riley wanted you to think." Chase nodded to a bolted gate behind the sign. "My opinion, someone drove up to the sign from the back, cut through the lock on that gate over there with bolt cutters, then replaced the lock. You see that trail closest to the gate behind the sign?"

I could barely make out a trail. The area surrounding the sign all looked the same. Dry biscuit-colored hills with low scrub brush and cactus. Ideal for coyotes and rattlesnakes.

"Notice the branches of that scrub oak over there." Chase leaned down and broke off a twig from a decaying sagebrush, using it as a pointer to direct my attention to a tree just beyond a gated entrance to the sign. "They've been cut. The centers of the bark are still fresh, not dried and cracked like they would be if they'd been here for a spell. I think someone, or maybe a group of someones—a gang, drug cartel maybe—brought Bruno up the back way, murdered him, and then tried to hide their tracks in the dirt using the branches to sweep away any prints."

"What are you? Tonto?" I stared at the downed branches. A few broken tree limbs didn't necessarily mean anything. Much less a police conspiracy to cover up some gangland-style killing. "They might have just as easily been cut when the rescue workers took the body."

Chase threw the twig on the ground. "I've had training in this type of thing. And I can tell you, this was shoddy police work. You talked to Riley. The man barely got out of his car before he had the body cut down and declared it a suicide."

Chase was right about one thing, I wasn't comfortable with Bruno's death being a suicide. But my instincts as a reporter demanded I play devil's advocate.

"Okay, suppose you're right. What about security cameras or guards? Aren't they around twenty-four seven in the park? Didn't they back up what Riley reported?"

"You see that?" Chase nodded to a camera mounted on the top of one of the chain link fence posts. It looked like it had been used for target practice. The camera hung limply from its mounting. "The police are saying Bruno shot them out. They found a shotgun along with a bolt cutter with his things when they retrieved the body."

"And the guard? Where was security during all this?"

"The park has a rent-a-cop up here every couple hours. It's his job to make rounds. He claims he fell asleep. Says he's been pulling extra shifts and got tired. The police think Bruno waited until the guard made his last inspection, then shot out the cameras and used a pair of bolt cutters to cut through the lock on the gate."

I glanced up at the sign. I could still see Bruno's body hanging from the W.

"And then what? He stripped down, climbed up on the sign, and hung himself?"

"Forensics confirmed Bruno's prints on the shotgun and the bolt cutters. Reports came back faster than a game of blackjack. But hey, the police are claiming what Bruno did wouldn't have been hard. There's workman's scaffolding behind the letters. Easy enough, even you could climb up. A big guy like Bruno wouldn't have needed any help. All he had to do was attach ropes from his wrist to the outside of the W, put a rope around his neck and climb over."

"Only you don't think so."

"And neither does his family. They hired me right away to do the investigation. Didn't believe the police from the get-go. Said their son wasn't suicidal. And the more I dig into it, the more it feels like a cover-up. All the way down to the park's security guard-for-hire falling asleep. Little too convenient if you ask me."

Now would have been a good time to tell Chase how I had my own doubts about the investigation. How I felt certain I'd seen Bruno in the grocery store just days before with Running-girl, and that I didn't think he looked particularly depressed or about to commit suicide. But I wasn't convinced Chase's suspicions were any more valid than my own. Instead, I said, "And you're convinced Bruno's death is somehow related to those news stories you shared with Tyler? That they might all be connected?"

"I know a cover-up when I see it. And I suspect, with what you told me about Riley not getting his ass up the hill to check this scene out for himself, there's a reason nobody's talking. It's why I wanted to meet with you today. You were there." Chase put his fingers through the fence and fixed his eyes on mine. "You know how this investigation went down, and I think you can help."

"How?"

"There's something I'd like you to do for me. A favor."

# CHAPTER 6

What Chase wanted was to use my new Sunday night show as a forum to discuss his theory concerning Bruno's death, and the two other men whose deaths he was also investigating. He was convinced that under the cloak of late-night radio, in the pitch of darkness when the airwaves were full of what he believed to be conspiracy theories and talk of supernatural occurrences, that somebody—*out in radioland*—knew something, and might be listening.

"Think about it, Carol. All you've got to do is talk about the case. About how quickly the cops ruled Bruno's death a suicide. Suggest that maybe it's a cover-up, and that, as a reporter, you're having trouble accepting it."

"Oh, no." I put my hands up and shook my head. "You're not serious. I'm not comfortable making accusations about what the cops did or didn't do. Not without more of an investigation. Absolutely not."

"Trust me. If there's one thing I know, it's that somebody out there knows somebody who saw something. All you have to do is open the phone lines and let the calls come in. It's a gold mine. It'd be perfect."

"No," I said adamantly. "Not tonight. Besides the topic is already set. Tyler chose it himself."

I couldn't believe Chase had the audacity to ask. I explained to him this was not only my show, but my very first show. And, while I had to admit his theory concerning Bruno's murder was plausible, going on air and accusing the police of a cover-up wasn't how I wanted to kick things off. Plus, the articles Tyler had shared with me involving the other two cases Chase was investigating didn't seem believable, much less related to that of Bruno's murder. I wasn't convinced there was a connection at all. The news stories bordered on the bizarre. Cheap sensational reads like one might find inside some Hollywood rag while waiting in the checkout line at the grocery store.

One man's death was blamed on his abduction by aliens. His body believed to have been tossed from their space ship and later found beside an oil rig in an area of the city known for its forest of oil derricks. The other story was even creepier. The victim was believed to have been eaten by wild wolves or some mythical blood-sucking creature called a Chupacabra. His body was found half-buried in Griffith Park about six months ago. I remembered the story. The police, however, hadn't issued any such bizarre findings of wolves or blood-sucking creatures. More than likely, the victim had met with the park's sole mountain lion, P-22, tagged and tracked regularly by park rangers. But to date, the case was one of many LAPD was still investigating. With a city the size of LA, that wasn't unusual, and I wasn't about to turn a show Tyler had given me on a provisionary basis into a circus of conspiracy theories.

I would have thought my explanation would have been sufficient. That Chase might have thanked me for my time and consideration and moved on. At least, my experience had taught me that was what a normal person would do.

When I got home, I found Misty sitting on the couch with Charlie and the cat. The three of them were watching a Lakers game. Charlie glanced in my direction, waved a long, skinny arm over his head, then stared back at the TV. So much for my concern about being missed.

Misty smiled then hollered over the back of the sofa, "How's the investigation going?"

"Who said anything about an investigation? How did you—"

"Tyler called." Misty got up off the sofa, waddled into the kitchen, and turned on the coffeemaker. "I didn't want the phone to wake Charlie, so I answered. Didn't think you'd mind. He wanted to make sure you hadn't forgotten about meeting with that private investigator.

What's his name? Chance? Chase? Or something like that?" The light on the coffeemaker indicated ready, and she pressed the button. "Black, right? No cream. No sugar." She handed me the cup. "Nothing wrong with a gal who likes her whiskey straight, her men wild, and her coffee black. Enjoy."

I sighed. I was going to have to get used to Misty's puttering, at least for a while. I took the cup, opened the refrigerator and added cream. I refused to be that predictable.

"His name's Chase, Misty, and as far the investigation goes, it's not. He had a few questions for me about what I'd seen. That's it. Nothing more. Right now, the police are calling it a suicide, and for the time being, until I learn differently, that's as far as it goes."

I didn't think it was necessary to add that I thought the investigator was odd. Or that I had as many doubts about him as I did the police report on Bruno's death. But Misty seemed to have picked up on that. She took a step in my direction and shook a finger at me.

"But that's not what you think, is it? I know when you're not sure about something. You get that faraway look in your eye. And right now, your mind's back with that body on the Hollywood Sign and that investigator. Admit it."

I grabbed her finger, squeezed it gently, and stared into her cloudy eyes. I didn't want to get into anything concerning the case or Chase and certainly not in front of Charlie. Not now. I had barely five hours before I had to be back to the station for my new show, and I wanted to enjoy what free time I had left.

"You're wrong, Misty. The only thing I'm thinking about right now is spending the afternoon with my son." I let go of her hand and, taking my coffee, headed towards the couch. "But, if you like, you can make some popcorn and come sit down with us."

From the kitchen, I heard Misty. "Say what you will, Carol, but I've got a feeling about this. That man's going to call again. And when he does, you best be prepared."

# CHAPTER 7

Misty was right. Chase did call. He called in the middle of my new show, LA's Soapbox, exactly like he said he wanted to do. But the fact of the matter was, by the time he called I wasn't so sure it was all that bad. I needed something. My show was dying, generating about as much interest as an LA weather report in the middle of August, and for that, I blamed Tyler. Tyler was convinced Sunday nights needed to be a chatty wrap-up of LA City Council's news and views, and being as this was my first time as a solo anchor, he took it upon himself to assign a topic. A capsule summary of LA's new river project, its growth and development in relation to the California State Water Conservation Corp. No matter how much research or life I tried to bring to the subject, it was a dud. And judging from the lack of callers, it was generating zero interest. Even my producer, Matt, looked as though he was about to fall asleep.

Finally, when a single white light on the switchboard lit up, I lunged for it. I took the call myself, not waiting for Matt to set it up.

"Welcome to LA's Soapbox, your chance to sound off. This is Carol Childs, and with whom am I speaking?"

"Gerhardt Chasen."

"Gerhardt Chasen?" I nearly choked on his name, but I was live on-air, and there wasn't time for surprise. I collected myself and said, "Mr. Chasen, how may I help you tonight?"

Much as I disliked the thought of putting Chase on the air, I didn't feel I had much choice. What was I going to do? He was my first and only caller, and I was twenty minutes into a monolog about a river project that was drier than the LA riverbed itself.

"I've been listening to your show, and while I'd like to be calling in offering my two cents about this river project, I've got another issue I'd like to discuss. Something far more pressing. I hope you don't mind giving me a few minutes. I'm sure your listeners would find what I have to say interesting."

I swallowed hard and hoped for the best, vowing to myself I'd do everything I could to control the conversation.

"All right, and what is it you would like to talk about?"

"Murder, Ms. Childs. Or more specifically, I'd like to talk about that body that was found on the Hollywood Sign last Friday morning."

I was about to say the police had ruled that death a suicide and politely dismiss him, but Chase didn't give me the opportunity.

"And add to that a series of grisly, gangland-style murders I've been investigating that I believe LAPD doesn't want you or me to know about."

At the mention of grisly, gangland-style murders and the LAPD, the phone lines lit up like a landing strip at LAX. And Matt, who had been only half awake, nearly fell off his stool. His head jerked back so suddenly he had to grab the control desk to steady himself. I had no doubt Chase had stacked the calls. There was no reason for the phone lines to be jammed. Not that quickly. The only possible cause was that Chase had alerted his social media contacts he planned to be on the air and wanted them to call in. Matt shot me a thumbs-up.

Chase carefully laid out his theory. How he believed Bruno had been brutally murdered by a drug cartel trying to make headway into the Hollywood club scene, where Bruno had worked as a bouncer. With the calls stacked, I felt I had no choice but to keep Chase on the air. The first rule of radio was to keep your listeners engaged, and he had definitely done that. I figured the best thing to do was to join forces with him on the line and together we could field calls. The first seemed relatively tame. No doubt a staged call. The next claimed to be a close friend of Bruno's who said there was no way Bruno would have committed suicide. Two other calls followed saying much the same. Then Chase segued into the cases of the two other men whose deaths he was following up on. How both men appeared to have died under peculiar circumstances. But when he referenced the bizarre tabloid reports of their deaths, that's when things started to turn into a free-for-all.

Listeners began calling in with even more bizarre tales. Stories about friends and relatives who had also disappeared. Those kidnapped by aliens, eaten by wolves, or extraterrestrials suspected to be living amongst us as shapeshifters. My worst fear that my program would become a late-night horror show with tales of alien abductions and conspiracy theories was becoming a reality. I had to put a stop to it. I was just about to say good night to Chase and suggest we return to our original topic concerning the LA River when Matt interrupted.

"Carol, I'm sorry to break in, but we have a caller on line two. She wants to talk about the body on the Hollywood sign. She says she was there, and she knows who murdered Bruno Sims and why."

I glanced at the clock. It was 11:52. I had less than eight minutes to go before I had to sign off, and since the woman hadn't mentioned anything about aliens, I took the call.

"Welcome to the Soapbox. This is Carol Childs. May I ask your name and where you're calling from?"

There was a pause, followed by a heavy coughing like the caller was trying to clear their throat.

"Honey, I'm from everywhere and nowhere, but most people don't see me, not anymore. I'm at that age where women like me simply disappear into the background."

Her voice was unusually deep. Gravelly, like rocks in a cement mixer, churning. From the sound of it, I figured her to be a heavy smoker. Probably one of those two-pack-a-day types and somewhere in her late sixties or maybe older.

"I'm sure that's not true," I said. "Per—"

"It happens." She snapped back. Her voice like an ax hitting a block of wood. Harsh. Sudden and hard.

"You're too young to know, but a couple years from now you'll understand. Those heads that used to turn when you walked in a room, those smiles you'd get? They don't come so often. Sometimes not at all."

I paused and glanced over at Matt. Did he have a caller ID on the phone? He shook his head no.

"Okay, if you won't tell me where you're from, can you at least give me a name?"

"If it'll make you feel better, you can call me Mustang Sally."

"Mustang Sally? That's unusual. I take it that's not your real name?"

"It's a name. In my line of work, I can't afford to use my real one. None of us do. But I didn't call in to play name games."

"No, you didn't. And we don't have a lot of time. So, Sally, do you mind if I call you Sally for short?"

"Whatever you like."

"My screener tells me you know why Bruno was killed and who did it. Suppose you tell us what you think."

"I don't just think, Ms. Childs. I know. And I can tell you Bruno Sims deserved exactly what he got. And so do a lot of other men like him. Men like that don't know how to treat a woman. And he was just an example."

From within my headset, I could hear Chase. He whispered, "Ask her to tell you something about the scene, Carol. Something to prove she was really there and that this isn't just some prank call."

"What do you mean by an example, Sally? Why would Bruno have been an example?"

"'Cause of what that man did. It's why he had that silly clown's nose on his face. We marked him a fool, and he died one."

There had been no mention of the red clown's nose in the paper. The *LA Times* hadn't run the photo of his body on the sign, and the story about Bruno's death had run in the back of the city section, below the fold. It included very few details. Simply that the former Hollywood stunt man and bodybuilder had died. News organizations rarely listed suicide as a cause of death for private individuals. Respect for their privacy and the fear of copycat killings, particularly with something like a body hanging on the Hollywood Sign, was always an issue. The only pictures of Bruno that had surfaced had run on the internet—by less scrupulous organizations—and in those, his face was hidden by the angle of his arm. Unless Mustang Sally really had been there, as she claimed, there was no way she would have known about the clown's nose.

"Who...wha—Excuse me?" I leaned forward to the mic, my hands to my headset. "Are you saying *you* killed Bruno Sims?"

"Bruno Sims was a Neanderthal. A macho pig. A waste of mankind. He didn't deserve to inhabit the planet any longer. I simply did us all a favor and settled the score."

I pressed my headphones closer to my ears. This was insane. It wouldn't be the first time a late-night caller had called in, using the anonymity of radio to confess to a crime, but I couldn't believe what I was hearing. My first thought was that the caller was high, drugged, or calling from inside a mental health center and reaching out to a world she no longer had access to. Matt was usually better at screening the calls. But this one had slipped through, and with a steady stream of blinking lights in front of me, I asked another question.

"Sally, why would killing Bruno be doing us a favor?"

"Because he was an ass—"

I hit the delay button, deleting any attempt she might make to describe Bruno using any of the FCC's seven forbidden words. Asshole wasn't one of them, but she was treading close.

"I'm sorry, Sally, I understand you're angry, but I need you to be careful with the words you use. If you continue, I'll have to cut you off, and I really don't want to do that."

"Well, you asked. And since you won't let me tell you what he was really like, let me say this, men like Bruno need to watch out. We're mad as hell. Can I say that? And we're not going to take it anymore."

Sally's impersonation of Howard Beale's crazed speech from the movie *Network* echoed out over the airwaves like the deafening sound of a tsunami. I paused. The idea of what I was about to ask was so outlandish, I could scarcely believe it.

"Sally, Mr. Chasen has already said he believes Bruno's death was the result of some gangland slaying. Are you telling me the gang involved is a group of angry women? That Bruno's death was some revenge slaying by women who had a score to settle?"

"Surprised?" She responded with a slight lilt to her voice, a sense of sarcasm.

"You know the police believe Mr. Sims' death was suicide."

"Well, we wouldn't be very good at what we do if they didn't, would we?"

"We?" I could hear heavy breathing through the line and then nothing. The line had gone dead. "Sally?"

Matt tapped on the glass between the studio and the control room. We'd lost the call and time was running short. His fist was in the air, ready for the countdown. I had five seconds to go. *Five...four...three...*I had to think fast.

"Sally, we must have been disconnected, but if you can hear me, I hope you'll call me back. You sound distressed, and I'd like to talk to you before you have any other ideas about doing the world another favor."

# CHAPTER 8

I was surprised when I closed out the show that Chase wasn't still on the line. I expected once Mustang Sally had hung up, he'd be there. Anxious to talk. But he wasn't. And when he didn't try to call back, I was convinced he had set me up. Used me to hype the story for his own purposes. How perfect. A well-placed call, shortly before midnight, by a mystery caller who went by Mustang Sally and had a voice like that of a cement mixer. It had to be a hoax. Chase had either set it up or some random caller, the friend of a friend he'd tipped off about being on the show, had caught Chase's report about Bruno's death and called in, putting their own spin on the story. As for Sally, she was probably either an out-of-work actress, a crazy woman, or maybe just some prankster. Tyler had warned me, late-night callers lived in a world of their own.

I must have sat in the studio and waited for something to happen for a good twenty minutes, and when nothing did, I decided I had had enough for the evening. My head ached, and I promised myself I wasn't going to think about Chase or Mustang Sally again until I'd had a good night's sleep.

In fact, it was almost noon the next day before I thought about much of anything at all. I couldn't believe the time when I rolled over and checked the clock on my bedside table. I had overslept. Someone had turned off my alarm.

"Misty?" I grabbed my robe and headed for the stairs. The only possible culprit was my new housekeeper. Clearly, I needed to establish some boundaries. Much as I enjoy sleeping in, a school day was not one of them, and I had missed breakfast with my son. We needed to talk.

From downstairs, I could hear Misty in the kitchen, chairs moving, water running. She must have heard me too.

She hollered back, "Carol, dear, you up? Come on down. We have company."

I tugged on my robe's tie, pushed my hair out of my face, and in a sleepy stupor started down the stairs toward the kitchen, still blurry-eyed. As I approached, I could hear Misty prattling on, something about unplugging my phone, making breakfast for Charlie, and not wanting to wake me.

Still only semi-alert, I noticed Sheri sitting at the kitchen table with Misty, a cup of hot coffee in front of her. On the table, her cake plate was filled with several slices of birthday cake left over from Charlie's party. Seeing me, Sheri raised her cup, a morning greeting I wasn't ready for.

"I came by to pick up my cake plate, and Misty invited me in." She smiled sheepishly as though to say none of this was her idea, then nodded at the French doors standing slightly ajar. "And I'm not the only one."

My eyes followed Sheri's to the base of the door. Outside, I recognized a familiar looking pair of work boots, covered with dirt.

"Chase?" I adjusted the collar of my robe up around my neck and, crossing my arms, leaned back against the banister.

Chase entered the room. He still hadn't shaved and was dressed exactly as he had been yesterday, in a pair of dusty cargo shorts.

"Morning, Carol." He rolled what I was beginning to think of as his trademark sucker, from one side of his cheek to another, then removed it and smiled. From the dimpled grin on his face, I could tell he clearly enjoyed catching me so ill prepared.

Crossing my arms tighter, I fired back, "What are you doing here? How did you even know where I lived?"

"I'm a private investigator." He took a step toward the table and put his hands on the back of the chair. "It's my job to know things like that. And after what happened on the air last night, I thought it was important we talk. So I stopped by—thinking you might be up by now—had no idea you'd sleep so late. Misty invited me in." He glanced at the cake in the center of the table, as though it were nothing out of the ordinary for him to be in my kitchen, then nodded to Misty, and asked, "May I?"

I glared at Misty. She turned her back to me and focused her attention on Chase like an honored guest. Then she took a piece of cake, put it on a plate, and handed it to him.

"Would you like a cup of my special tea to go with it?" she asked.

"Thank you," he said. "That's very hospitable of you."

*Humph.* I gave my robe another firm tug, walked into the kitchen, and poured myself a cup of coffee. I'd be damned if I was going to join this group. All I could think of was how uncomfortable I was standing in the middle of the kitchen barefoot and in my bathrobe with nothing but my shorty pajamas on and how quickly I could get my coffee and retreat upstairs.

But before I could escape, Chase spoke. "Carol, I realize this is awkward, and I apologize for interrupting your morning. I know this isn't the best timing, but I need to speak with you."

"You could have called," I said.

"I did. Several times. Both the house phone and your cell. The calls went to voicemail, that's when I decided I'd best come by." He sat down at the table.

Misty smiled back at me broadly, her jaws clenched, her hands in the air. Guilty as charged. No wonder I didn't get the calls. I was fast asleep. Misty had unplugged both my alarm and the house phone. And my cell was in my bag beneath the kitchen table where I always left it. How could I have known?

"Seems to me," Chase said, "this Mustang Sally woman who called the station last night might just be the real thing."

"Oh, really?" I let the sarcasm sneak into my voice and tucked several loose hairs behind my ear. "Because when you didn't call back last night, I figured maybe she was one of your setups, and that the two of you were out celebrating about how you'd hijacked my show."

"Okay, I confess. I did set up a few callers. Bruno's mother for one, just to make certain we'd get something on the air. If I didn't, Bruno's murder would be over and done with exactly as the police want. Suicide. End of story."

"Are you trying to tell me Mustang Sally wasn't one of your pre-arranged calls?" I decided it was best I confronted this situation now and took a seat at the table. Misty shoved a piece of cake in front of me. I pushed it away.

"Not at all. I didn't know anything about her. I was as surprised as you were when she called."

"Then how did she know about the clown's nose? It wasn't in the papers. Nobody knew. You had to have told her."

"But I didn't." Chase shook his head and put his tea down.

"I don't believe you. You told her I'd been there that morning covering the story, and then you told her about the clown's nose. It was all a setup. Admit it. There was no other way she would have known."

"I swear to you, Carol. I didn't."

Misty and Sheri sat silent, their eyes sliding back and forth between Chase and me like a tennis match. It was my serve.

"Then tell me, Chase, how is it, do you suppose, Mustang Sally was listening? Happenstance maybe? I don't think so."

"I may have publicized it, you know, tweeted it a bit. Put the word out I'd be on the show and to listen in. Like I told you before, I knew if I could get on the air and talk about Bruno's murder, somebody out there was bound to hear. And, hey—it happened."

"So Mustang Sally is part of your social network. You do know her."

"No. I don't. And it's not that easy. Mustang Sally may have seen one of my tweets or a retweet for that matter. But she called in on her own. I promise you, I didn't set her up to call. And I don't know who she is."

I paused. My patience was wearing thin. Sheri nudged me, a slight elbow to my side. The ball was in my court.

"Let me get this straight. Yesterday you thought Bruno's death and the deaths of the other two men you're investigating were the result of some gangland murder the cops are trying to cover up. Maybe some drug cartel was trying to send a message. And now, after last night, you believe it's some revenge slaying by a group of angry women? And Mustang Sally is the matriarch of that gang?"

"Like I said, I don't know Sally or what she's all about, but I think she's involved."

"Okay, suppose you're right. Why would she call in and confess to a crime like this?"

"Strange as it may seem to you, perps have been known to shadow an investigation. I think that's what we've got here. She wants to know what we know."

I was skeptical. I wasn't one hundred percent certain about Chase, but a female assassin, a serial female assassin, calling in to confess was an even bigger stretch.

"I'll agree I've heard stories about such things; arsonists hanging around a fire, murderers calling an investigator with some excuse so they can learn what it is the police know. But far as I'm concerned, it's more likely Sally's just some crazy person. The station gets a lot of oddball calls late at night. People who can't sleep. Drunks. Prank calls. She may very well just be one of them."

"I don't think so. After you went off the air, I went back to my notes. That's why I didn't call you back. I wanted to go through the information I had regarding the murders of the two other men, and that's when I found it."

"Found what?"

"The other two men whose murders I've been investigating. They'd each been in a relationship." He paused and waited for me to get it. Like this was a big deal and he expected my applause or something.

"So?" I shrugged.

"Each of them had just broken up."

"And your point is?" I couldn't believe he thought that odd.

"Maybe these breakups didn't go down so well. Maybe the ex-girlfriends weren't happy about the circumstances and wanted to...you know—"

"What? Settle the score? I don't think so. Couples break up all the time, and in my experience, most women, jilted or otherwise, don't suddenly pick up with a pack of serial murderers."

"I know. Crazy, right? But then Sally—I mean, you heard her— what she said on the air. 'Bruno Sims deserved exactly what he got. And so do a lot of other men like him.' What type of woman wants to do that?"

Sheri nudged my leg beneath the table. She must have been reading my thoughts. After last night, I felt like I could have killed Chase. Despite his saying differently, I still believe he had set Mustang Sally up to call, overstepped his bounds, and hijacked my first radio show. And, as far as I was concerned, he had no real proof Bruno had been murdered, much less was part of a police cover-up connected to the two other deaths he was investigating.

"So you're convinced, just because these men had recent breakups, that there's a connection between them? That their exes all killed them or arranged to have them killed by this Mustang Sally and her posse. And that the cops are in cahoots, trying to cover it all up?" I shook my head and held my hands up in a surrender position. "Why?"

"I don't know that yet. But my gut tells me there's something more about her claim to settling the score than we know."

I glanced back at Sheri and Misty, the expression on their faces mum.

"I'd prefer to think the cops are covering up a drug deal and not just looking the other way because some woman's been dissed by her boyfriend and knocked him off." I stood up. I was convinced Chase was delusional.

"I think you need to be going. I need to take a shower and—"

"I'm not playing with you, Carol. Sally's for real. I can't prove it, but I can feel it, and I need you and your show to help do that."

"My help? Again? After last night, you expect me to let you on the show next week and do more of the same?"

"Work with me. Go back on the air next Sunday night. Ask Sally to call back. I don't care what you do. Tell your listeners you're doing some heartbreak show. Ask women to call in with their worst stories about the men in their lives and what they've done to them."

"You've got to be kidding. I'm not about to do that, and Tyler would never agree to such a thing."

Chase put his elbows on the table and clasped his hands, rubbing them together. "He's already approved it, Carol."

"What?"

"I was at the station earlier this morning. I shared with him about Sally and my theory, and he's onboard. He checked the call logs and said as long as you're generating listeners he doesn't care."

I was furious. Chase had gone too far. I pointed to the door. "Go. And don't call me again. Ever."

Chase got up from the table, thanked Misty for the tea, and grabbed another piece of cake.

"Look, Carol, I know you're mad, but trust me. You're going to see I'm right. This Mustang Sally's for real."

# CHAPTER 9

Chase closed the door behind him. But just to make sure, I got up from the table and gave it a strong shove. Then leaned against it and vowed silently to talk to Tyler as soon as possible. He needed to know Chase wasn't going to dictate the content of my new show no matter how much he wanted to brag about his ability to deliver an audience. I wouldn't have it.

Sheri interrupted my momentary respite as I leaned against the door with a remark I hadn't expected.

"I like him."

"What?"

"You heard me." Sheri began clearing the table and putting the dishes in the sink.

I crossed the room and put my coffee cup on the counter. "You've got to be kidding."

"No, not at all," she said. "There's something about him. Rough around edges, maybe, but kinda sexy in a rebel sort of way." Sheri rinsed a dish under the water and handed it to me. "And he appeals to you too. I can tell."

"Appeals to me?" I grabbed a dish, took a dishtowel off the rack, and began drying. "You're not serious. The guy's got a beard like a mountain man, and he's...well, he's obnoxious, that's what he is. And his theory about this murder, if you can even call it that, is beyond crazy. Plus he's interfering with my work and my personal life, and you know how I feel about that."

"Maybe you don't," Misty said. She ambled over to the sink and placed the cake plate on the counter. "From what I could see, there's no denying there's chemistry between the two of you. 'Less that was some hot flash bringing color to your cheeks, I'd say the auras between the two of you were glowing like a heat wave off the Sonora Desert."

"I don't believe in auras, Misty."

"Well you, my dear, can believe whatever you like." Misty untied her apron strings and returned to the table, "But, for what it's worth, I think he's right."

"About Sally?" I asked.

"All of it. Sally. The revenge slayings. I'd say he's on to something."

"You're not serious?" I pulled a chair up to the table and sat down. I could discount Chase's suspicions. I didn't have a lot of confidence in him. And I had my doubts about the police and the cause of Bruno's death, but nothing even close to what Mustang Sally had hinted. "You don't honestly believe there's really a Sally and some team of female assassins out there, do you?"

"Hell hath no fury like a woman scorned," Misty said. "I've seen it firsthand. In my practice, before I retired anyway, I heard from more than a few women who would have done anything to settle the score. And believe me, I wouldn't have wanted to be on the receiving end of what they wanted to do to the men who crossed them."

For years, Misty had worked as a Hollywood medium, a Psychic to the Stars, and her talents had been legendary. She had done a lot of late-night shows and even gone on tour, and on more than one occasion, she had been helpful to the police in locating victims and helping solve crimes. I had never much believed in psychics, but I did credit Misty with being highly intuitive.

"Yes, but you can't really believe she's behind Bruno's murder or that she has a team of female assassins out there to do her dirty work? Murderesses for hire? That's extreme. And even if Bruno's murder turns out to be part of a series of horrific deaths, the likelihood of a female serial killer is extremely low. Serial killers are usually men, not women."

Sheri joined us at the table. "Maybe, but I think Misty has a point. While most men are good guys, there are a few players out there who think of a woman as no more than a trophy, and once they've taken that trophy off the shelf, they want the next. Thing like that can drive a woman to do all kinds of terrible things."

I wondered if Sheri was talking about herself. While she had never openly admitted it, I felt certain Sheri's ex, the father of her son, had been a first class jerk.

Misty validated Sheri's statement. "More than once I've heard from women who felt it was their right to punish their ex."

"Lorena Bobbit might have agreed with you," Sheri said.

"You mean the woman who bobbed—" I pantomimed a swift knife blade across my lower regions.

"Her husband's private parts," Sheri said. "And when the news broke about what she'd done, the tabloids were full of stories about women who didn't think she was so wrong."

Misty leaned forward in the chair and patted my hand. "Carol, I think Chase has a point. The idea of murder by proxy isn't new. In fact, women are much more likely to hire someone to do their dirty work for them than do it themselves. And if you do the show as Chase suggested, I wouldn't be at all surprised if Sally called back."

"I don't think Tyler would seriously go for something like that. I can't believe Chase spoke to him. I think he was just testing the waters."

"I don't know," Sheri said, "I was listening to the show last night. The LA River Project? Not so interesting. But women complaining anonymously about bad men and bad dates...you got my interest."

# CHAPTER 10

My cell phone buzzed with a text as I left the house Tuesday morning. *C Me. ASAP.*

The message was from Tyler. I wasn't surprised. Tyler never sent a message that didn't end in an acronym requesting immediate action. And, because I wanted to see him too, I did exactly as asked. I bypassed my cubicle and walked directly into the newsroom where I found Tyler in a surprisingly good mood. He was standing by the desk, his arms reached up over his head in a full-body stretch that made his slim body appear rail thin. With his red hair and a goofy smile on his face, he looked more like Alfred E. Neuman, the cartoon character from the cover of *Mad Magazine*, than the news and programming director for a talk radio station. I bit back my smile and walked in the office.

"You're in a good mood," I said.

"I am. Our new GM appears to be happy with the station's format change." Tyler finished stretching and rubbed his hands together then sat down. "However, there are a few things I need to discuss with you."

Tyler nodded to the hot seat in front of his desk. I took a seat.

"Okay, I'm listening."

"Presley didn't like your show Sunday night. She admitted she didn't listen to the entire broadcast, but...she doesn't believe you fit the format. She thinks an older, more statesman-like reporter might be better suited, and so do I."

I could see where this was going. Stations changed formats all the time and with it frequently swept house. I mentally crossed my fingers this wasn't why Tyler had asked me to sit down.

"And..." I asked.

"And...with the station's recent format change, we think it might be best if we fine-tuned some things and made a few changes internally." Tyler's eyes left his computer screen and met mine. Silence followed for what seemed like an eternity. I could hear the clock on Tyler's desk slowly ticking. If he was going to fire me, I wondered just how long he'd give me before he let me go. Mentally I started balancing my checkbook. I had maybe two months in reserve.

"It's not all bad news, Carol. I managed to save your spot on Sunday nights. We're going to have you do a late-night call-in show for women. I think you might be better suited for something with a more female angle."

I knew where Tyler was going with this. I could feel my throat tighten before I spoke. "Chase got to you, didn't he?"

"And you should be glad he did. The GM doesn't think you're ready for a show of your own and was about to suggest you go back to doing rip-and-reads, top of the hour news reports, and your favorite—traffic updates." Tyler paused, smiled like I should be thankful, then went on. "It was just luck Chase called right before Presley asked to see me. If I hadn't spoken to him, I doubt I'd have come up with a better alternative for you."

My cell phone buzzed as I was trying to think of a response. I glanced at the caller ID. Chase. I sent the call to voicemail and turned my phone off.

"It's just that—"

"Carol, stop. Before you go any further, let me say, between you and me, I don't care if this guy Chase is on the level or not. For all I know, he's a loose cannon with crazy conspiracy ideas. But until he called into the show last night, you had nothing. Nada. Not a single listener calling in to talk, and this morning we've got women emailing and calling about it. Asking when it's going to be on again. Hey, they liked it. You were a hit. As long as you do a show that delivers an audience, I'm happy. And so is Presley. So you can take it or leave it. Your call."

"Yes, but Chase—"

Before I could finish my reply, Tyler's office phone rang. He raised his hand to silence me, picked up the receiver and smiled. "Yes, yes, she's here right now." Cupping the mouthpiece, he leaned across the desk. "The walls must have ears, Carol. It's your friend Chase. Shall I tell him it's a go?"

I got up from the hot seat, my hands above my head. "It doesn't appear I have much of a choice."

# CHAPTER 11

I wasn't about to call Chase back, certainly not right away. If I was so valuable to him that he had already called twice, he could wait while I sorted through my thoughts about what I wanted to do. Misty may have believed Sally was real, but I was still on the fence. And Chase's cozying up to Tyler wasn't helping him win any points with me. Either way, I decided before I sat down and outlined exactly what this new show would be, I needed to do a little detective work. I wanted more information about Bruno's death and a certain private investigator named Gerhardt Chasen.

I started by calling LAPD's Hollywood division. I had a few more questions for Detective Riley and wanted to see what I could get from him about his relationship with Chase.

The desk sergeant answered, and before I could finish asking for him, Sergeant Browne explained Riley was off at his retirement party.

"Big deal, twenty-five years today. Nobody here's gonna blame him for leaving early. Can I help you, ma'am?"

I paused while I processed the idea of Riley's retirement, wondering if it might all be related to Bruno's death. "Actually, that's why I was calling. My name's Carol Childs, I'm a reporter. We've worked together on a couple of cases. He's been a big help to me, and I'm afraid I've forgotten where the party was." I wasn't one-hundred percent honest. I hadn't met Riley before the day of Bruno's murder, but if I said anything else, it would be at least until tomorrow before anyone called me back, if at all. And I wasn't feeling particularly patient. "I was hoping you'd be able to tell me? I promised I'd stop by."

"I'm surprised you don't remember. It's his favorite."

"Ha! Detective Riley has more than one, sergeant, believe me, I know. We've eaten at several."

I heard a muffled laugh. "Yeah, the man does like to eat."

"So, Chinese or Italian?" It wasn't much of a guess. All reporters knew where cops went to eat. The restaurants they chose were usually good, inexpensive, and easy to spot with their unmarked squad cars parked up and down the street. "There's the Chinese in the valley, Mr. Chow's, I think, or the Italian place, maybe in Hollywood?"

"Chinese," he said.

"Mr. Chow's then."

"You got it. Seven p.m."

I was familiar with the restaurant. Sheri and I had dined there numerous times with the boys. The food was good and the price even better. I remember a large banquet room in the back. It wouldn't be the first time I'd seen a group of cops dining there.

I entered Riley's retirement dinner on my calendar and checked my assignment sheet. It was a slow news day, and even with my daily activities plus updates for the top of the hour news reports and rewrites from the wire, I could easily squeeze in a background check on Chase without anyone noticing.

The more I thought about Chase, the more curious I became. Who was this PI who knew where I lived and had managed to get through to my boss in such a way that Tyler was now entertaining his ideas for my show?

My online search revealed the typical biographical information. Gerhardt Chasen, a.k.a. Chase, was thirty-six years old, couple years younger than me, and born in LA. He had attended South Pasadena High, graduated in the top ten percent of his class and played football. And from the stories I found online, he was pretty good. He'd made all-state and was awarded a football scholarship to UCLA. Then 9-11 happened, and he bailed. Left school, joined the Army, and became a member of the 75th Ranger Regiment, assigned to Afghanistan. That's when things took an unfortunate twist. Sergeant Chasen had been injured in a roadside bombing and was shipped home, the recipient of a Purple Heart. Further research showed after being medically discharged from the service, he returned to LA, married briefly, divorced six months later, then returned to the university only to drop out mid-semester. The record showed he was arrested for drunk driving and assaulting an officer. But for reasons not listed in the court docs, the charge of assaulting an officer was dropped and the drunk driving charge reduced to a lesser misdemeanor of wet and reckless. Shortly after that, Chase got his PI license and hung out his shingle.

It was almost eight p.m. when I arrived at the restaurant where Riley and his cronies were hosting his retirement party. The restaurant was crowded with diners, but even above the normal din of families and friends sitting together, I could make out the sounds of their boisterous voices coming from the banquet room in the back of the restaurant. Next to the party room was a small empty booth. It was obvious the waitress had chosen not to seat anyone there due to the noise. But, as far as I was concerned, it was the perfect place for me to sit and accidently-on-purpose run into Riley without appearing too obvious. He would have to file right past me on his way out. I told the waitress I'd take the table and asked for a pot of tea.

When the party ended, a parade of plainclothes LAPD detectives and off-duty officers walked past me down a long narrow hallway to the back exit. I'd never seen so many heavily armed people in one group. When Riley approached, I stood up.

"Detective Riley?" I extended my hand in a friendly gesture. "Carol Childs."

He stopped. I could see his mind working behind his eyes, trying to place me, then he took my hand, and said, "The reporter...from the radio station. Right?"

"Yes, I was hoping I might get a few words with you."

He glanced at the table where I'd been sitting. "You alone?"

"I am."

"Buy me a drink, little lady, and I'm yours for the evening." Riley looked back over his shoulder to a couple of plainclothes detectives who appeared to be waiting. He nodded for them to go on ahead. I caught one wink as they waved goodbye. "Got nowhere to go and no one waiting for me at home. Unless you plan on invitin' me back to your place?"

"I think we both know that's not going to happen."

Riley was drunk, not falling-down drunk, but the alcohol had loosened his tongue. He put his hands like giant paws on the table while he adjusted his heavy frame onto the chair. "Well, you never know. I sit and hang with you for a bit, you just might change your mind." Riley signaled the waiter to bring him a scotch on the rocks, then asked if I wanted anything.

"No, thanks, I'm not drinking. But this is on me." I put my credit card on the table and told the waiter to start a tab.

"What's on your mind?"

"The suicide last Friday morning."

Riley shifted his big bulky frame uncomfortably in the chair before answering.

"Reporters don't usually follow up on suicides. Not unless it's some superstar, and Bruno Sims certainly wasn't that. He was a nobody. What's the deal?"

I waited for the waiter to return with his drink.

"Mr. Sims' family hired a PI to investigate the case."

"It happens." Riley took a swig of his drink.

"They're disputing the LAPD's findings. They think he was murdered."

Riley downed the last of his scotch and waved to the waiter for another. "Sometimes families have trouble accepting the truth. Waste of money. The man killed himself. You should move on."

"It's just...there was no suicide note."

"Doesn't mean the family won't find one. Had a case once where this guy attached a suicide note to a homing pigeon. Wife didn't find the note for nearly a week. Not until a friend called and said the bird arrived with a message attached to it. Fact is, a lot of suicides never leave a note. People don't always come right out and tell ya what they're gonna do. They just do it. Trust me, my job's not to explain why. I just call 'em as I see 'em. And this, Ms. Childs, was a suicide. I've seen enough to know."

"But this PI, he's pretty convinced someone else, maybe even a group of people, was there with him. That he wasn't alone."

Riley swirled the scotch in his glass, his eyes heavy.

"And then I've got this woman named Mustang Sally who called my show the other night and confessed to the murder."

"Really?" Riley guffawed. He sat back in his seat and gripped his drink with both hands. His fat fingers, like sausages, turned white with the pressure. Clearly, the man wasn't well. "You look like a smart woman, Ms. Childs. I really hate to see you wastin' your time on some crackpot caller named Sally Mustang—"

"Mustang Sally."

"—confessing on the air of all places. If I were you, I'd be more concerned about getting a reputation for entertaining conspiracy theories. You don't want to end up like Geraldo Rivera."

"I'm just checking things out."

"With the wrong people, obviously. Who is this hawkshaw you been talkin' to?"

"His name's Gerhardt—"

"Gerhardt Chasen." Riley slammed his drink down on the table, spilling some, and glared at me, his eyes red and puffy. "Goes by Chase? Big guy? Built like a former football player?"

I nodded. "You know him?"

"He's a drunk, Ms. Childs. Nothing but trouble. The man bends the truth like a pretzel. If you're smart, you'll stay away from him."

The waiter arrived with another drink. Riley stood up, swigged it down, then wiped his mouth with the back of his hand. "Unless you have anything else for me, I think we're done here. I know I am. Twenty-five years worth of done and sick and tired. Now if you'll excuse me, I need to get my car."

The man was drunk. I had just watched him down three scotches, and I had no idea how much he had before. He started to stumble down the hallway, one hand on the wall to steady himself, towards the rear exit of the restaurant. No way he belonged behind the wheel.

"Detective. You're not planning on driving, are you?"

"I'm a cop, Carol." He leaned back against the wall, took a cigarette from his pocket and lit it. "What do you think?"

"I think you're drunk." I put my hand on his chest and pushed back against the wall. "And maybe I should call you a cab."

"You going to try and stop me?" He shoved my hand away, pushing me back against the wall, and started again towards the exit.

I followed.

Outside Riley grabbed a set of keys off the valet's keyboard and tossed the man a couple bucks. Told him not to worry about bringing his car around. He could get it. I was no match for Riley. The man easily had better than a hundred pounds on me and trying to restrain him was hopeless. I watched as he got into a vintage gray Porsche convertible, cherry as the day it had come off the showroom floor. The match was totally inappropriate. His beefy body sandwiched with his big belly pinned against the wheel.

"Nice car," I hollered at him as he backed out of the small parking area and pulled up to a stop in front of me. "Really, why don't you let me call you a cab."

"You worry too much, Ms. Childs. You really should leave things that don't concern you alone. 'Sides, this here's my baby. Tuned her up and took her off the blocks for just this occasion." He gunned the engine, and like a caged lion, the car roared. "Sure you don't wanna come home with me now?"

"Riley, please, don't." I gripped my hands to the passenger door. Dammit, where was the valet? His chair was empty, and the alley deserted. "You shouldn't be driving."

"I shouldn't be doing a lot of things. But you...you should stay clear of Chase, you understand? He's trouble. Just leave this whole thing with Chase and that body on the Hollywood Sign alone." He ran his pudgy hand across the driver's wheel like he was caressing a woman's backside and smiled. "Trust me, Ms. Childs, you don't want to know what I know."

Revving the engine one more time, Riley swept my hands from the door and took his foot off the brake, then slammed the accelerator to the floor. I fell back as the car broke like a filly on the track. The sudden explosion of speed and the rear wheel steering sending a cloud of smoke up behind it.

"Stop! Riley, no!"

Directly ahead of him, about one hundred feet down the alley was a large concrete pylon, used to keep traffic from using the alleyway as a thoroughfare. He was aiming for it. I watched, helpless as he plowed directly into it. Head on into a concrete wall.

Within seconds the valet came running from within the restaurant, followed by patrons who had heard the crash.

"Call 911!"

I ran toward the wreck. But I knew before I got there it was useless. The Porsche's body had crumpled like a tin can with Riley's body pinned behind the wheel. His head hung limply off to the left side of his shoulder, his mouth and eyes open. Blood began a slow trickle from the corner of his mouth. I turned away.

While I waited for the ambulance, I walked back to the restaurant's exit and surveyed the scene. There were no skid marks. Riley had never applied the brakes. He hadn't tried to steer clear of the pylon. It was his target. Riley wasn't just drunk, he was suicidal.

It wasn't until I went back inside to pay the bill and get my bag that it hit me. *Suicides don't all leave notes.* It was exactly like Riley had said. *Sometimes they just do it.*

# CHAPTER 12

I called Tyler from my car as I headed home from the scene of the accident. Not to report Riley's suicide for the news, but because I needed to hear another human voice. Something to help settle my shaking hands and drown out the vision of him trapped behind the wheel of the car. I kept replaying bits and pieces of our conversation and wondering if there was something I could have done.

But, if it was support I wanted, Tyler was the wrong person to ask.

"Sorry, Carol, but you can't be too surprised about this kind of thing. Cops are high risk when it comes to suicide. More likely to die by their own hand than in the line of duty. And if what you're telling me about Riley's true, twenty-five years on the force, single, and in poor health, I wouldn't be surprised if he'd been planning the whole thing. Not your problem."

*Right. Not my problem.* Why didn't I think before I picked up the phone? I could have predicted Tyler's unemotional response. It wasn't within his nature to nurture. As a result, I didn't share with Tyler what Riley had told me about Chase. Instead, I hung up the phone and, eyes burning, holding back the tears, I drove home in silence. I couldn't even listen to the radio. It just felt wrong.


It was almost eleven o'clock by the time I got home. I had stopped to pick up groceries, Charlie was in bed and hopefully asleep. Misty, however, was sitting on the front porch. As I approached, I could see she wasn't alone. Sitting with her in the dark, illuminated by a thin trail of smoke, was Chase.

"Smoking?" I stood with a bag of groceries balanced on my hip. "I thought you quit." I hadn't expected to see Chase on my porch, and I wasn't about to greet him with any civility. I wasn't in the mood. Not after what I had witnessed at the restaurant.

Chase stood up. An attempt to block my passing. "This isn't a cigarette, Carol, it's—"

"I know what it is." I reeled out of his way, using the groceries as a shield between us. "I could smell it coming up the steps. And Misty, you can't bring that stuff into my house. Not around Charlie. I won't have it."

I was to about leave them both on the patio and lock the door behind me. If smoking weed was something Misty planned to do, she could leave right now. Misty knew how I felt about drugs. Nothing in the house. And absolutely nothing around my son. I was very firm about that.

Misty grabbed my hand as I passed. "It's not recreational, Carol. It's—"

"Medical," Chase said. "I have a prescription. But if it bothers you, I can stop. Right now, if it'll make you feel better."

"A prescription, huh?" I shook Misty's hand from my own and looked at Chase skeptically. If the story about his injuries in Afghanistan were correct, he might be telling the truth. But after talking to Riley, I didn't know what to believe, and I really didn't want to stand there and listen.

Chase snuffed out the joint and put the butt in a pocket of his jacket.

"I came by to talk to you. You haven't returned any of my calls. Misty suggested I wait outside."

"This isn't a good time, Chase." I put my hand on the handle to the front door but paused before opening it. I wanted to see what Chase's reaction would be if I told him where I'd been. "I went to see Detective Riley tonight after work, and you know what he told me? He told me you were a drunk and that I shouldn't trust you. That you were nothing but trouble. And then you know what he did? He killed himself. Right in front of me. Drove his car head-on into a concrete pylon. Crushed himself behind the wheel. Do you have any idea what that was like?" I shook my head and gave the door a shove. "So if you'll excuse me, I'm not in the mood to sit out on the patio and listen to any more of your theories."

Chase stood up. "Did he tell you he was the officer who arrested me for drunk driving? And that he was the same cop I was accused of assaulting and went to jail for?"

I stopped in the doorway. Misty was on her feet, standing directly behind Chase, the moonlight on her face, begging me to stay.

"I'm sorry you had to see that, Carol. And I do know what that looks like. I spent a year in Afghanistan. Saw lots of things I'd like to un-see. But the truth is, Riley wasn't the most stable of detectives. And I don't have a lot of good things to say about him. He should never have done that in front of you."

Misty walked out from behind Chase and took the groceries from my arms. "Why don't you sit down and listen to what Chase has to say? You know you won't sleep until you do, and I can put these groceries away. I've got an early morning. I want to get started on that garden in the back, and you two don't need me."

I waited for Misty to close the door, then crossed my arms and stared at Chase. "What's so important you had to drive all the way over here to talk to me in person, tonight of all nights?"

"Couldn't it just be I missed seeing your pretty face?"

"Flattery's not going to work, Chase. Not tonight."

"I didn't think so. And to be honest, much as I might like it to be, that's not why I'm here." Chase nodded to the table. "Please, there's some things you need to know. And if after I've told you, you don't like what you hear, I'll leave you alone. But I'm hoping you'll at least hear me out."

I sat down at the table and listened as Chase told me his story. Much of it I already knew based on my research. What I didn't know was how Chase's life and Riley's had intersected.

Chase explained how he had gotten himself into trouble after he returned from Afghanistan. His reentry, he said, had been anything but smooth. A brain injury had required an operation and follow-up treatments. He married, hoping the woman might help him get his life back on track, and then went back to school. But things went south, and both the marriage and his attempt to finish school ended unsuccessfully.

"I started drinking, and that's when I got myself arrested. I was pulling out of a bar where Detective Riley and a bunch of buddies had been doing some after-hours partying. They saw me leave and pulled me over. Seems the cops can get away with things we civilians can't, and unfortunately, I told him so."

"I'm sure that didn't go over well," I said.

"No, it didn't. In fact, I took a swing at him and ended up in jail. If it weren't for the fact one of my college professors was a lawyer and also a former Army Ranger, I probably would have gone down for a DUI and assaulting a police officer. After that, I started to get my life together. I got my PI's license, and a couple months ago, I started back to night school. The medical marijuana's the only drug I allow myself. It helps with the headaches and concentration."

"So this thing between you and Riley, it's personal?"

"It was. He thought I had it in for him. I showed up on a case he'd been working a couple years back. Victim's family hired me to do some digging around, and I found evidence Riley and his detectives had missed. Riley accused me of planting evidence, which was a joke. Far as our relationship went, I'd say it was pretty much downhill from there. He considered me a drunk, and I thought he was a lazy cop who didn't give a damn anymore."

"Did Riley know you were investigating Bruno's death, as well?"

"I doubt you were the first person to tell him so, Carol. And I'm certain it didn't have anything to do with his taking his own life. He made that decision a long time ago. The guy had a string of ex-wives, kids who wouldn't talk him, alimony payments he couldn't make, and he was being forced into retirement. The man wasn't happy, Carol. It had nothing to do with you."

I looked up at the stars. From the sound of things, both Riley and Chase had a rough past.

"But, I'm not here to talk about me. I needed you to see this."

Chase sat back and reached into his pocket, then handed me a small red ball. "It's a clown's rubber nose. And if I'm not wrong, it's exactly like the one Bruno was wearing the day he was murdered."

"Where did you get this?" I stared down at the ball and rolled it around in my hand.

"From the family of one of the vic's whose death I've been investigating. I'm sure the cases are tied now that I have this."

"Tell me this isn't connected to one of those bizarre deaths in the tabloids."

"If you're referring to the story about the UFO sighting. Yes, it is. Aaron Morris. The man the tabloids reported was abducted by a UFO. And who the cops said died from a hit-and-run. But I don't believe any of it, and neither does his family."

"And just what is it you think did happen to Mr. Morris?"

"He was returning from a UFO Convention in Vegas. He'd left his car at LAX, and when he flew back, he disappeared. Vanished. The tabloids had a heyday with it. Started publishing stories that he'd been abducted by aliens. Type of stuff that made all the conventioneers happy. That was until his body showed up. The coroner said Morris' clothes reeked of alcohol. It was as though he'd gone on a bender. Thing is, Morris didn't drink. He was in AA. Family said he hadn't touched alcohol in years. Yet when the cops found his car, they also found a half dozen little airline whiskey bottles open on the front seat. Detectives figured he took a wrong turn out of LAX, ended up in the Inglewood Oil Fields, then decided to go for a walk. Big mistake. Morris ended up getting himself hit by a car. The remote site where the cops found his body may explain why he wasn't found for several days."

"That explains Morris, but not how you found the nose."

"After you mentioned seeing a red nose on Bruno, I began to wonder if maybe the nose might be some type of sign. I went back to the family. Looking for some kind of connection. I asked if they had gone through Morris' personal effects and found anything out of the ordinary. At first, they weren't certain what I meant. Morris' briefcase was full of trinkets from the UFO show. But then they found the nose, along with his wallet, in a brown paper bag the coroner provided after he released the body."

"So, according to you, somebody, maybe Mustang Sally and her buddies, met Morris at the airport, got him liquored up, drove him out to the oil fields, and then, for reasons I can't begin to understand, put a clown's nose on his face and ran him over? And the police are covering it up?"

I handed the red nose back to Chase. With everything Chase had just told me about his injury in Afghanistan, I wasn't sure if maybe he was having trouble deciphering the truth. I wasn't about to chase down a lot of rabbit holes.

"What if I told you the lead detective on that case and the other case I've been investigating was Riley's ex-partner?"

I paused. There were a couple hundred LAPD detectives on the force, all of them juggling too many cases. The idea that Riley's ex-partner had investigated a death Chase thought was related didn't sound all that usual.

"I'm sorry, Chase, but I'm going to need more than a rubber ball you could have bought in some toy store and a story about Riley's ex-partner working a homicide case, you and you alone seem to think is related. For all I know you could have killed Bruno."

Chase exhaled and leaned forward with his elbows in his lap and dropped his head. For a moment, he appeared almost defeated. Then he looked up at me, his hands clasped and shaking like he was praying.

"I'm not that man, Carol. Like I told you, I saw enough murder and mayhem in Afghanistan for a lifetime. I'm one of the lucky ones. I came home. I got better. And I vowed I'd make a difference. There's enough pain in the world, I'm not about to be adding to it."

Maybe it was the moonlight, the soft tenor of Chase's voice, his cologne, or the fact I hadn't sat alone in the dark with a man in so long, but my mind started to wander. Misty would say it was the blending of our auras. Like a teenage girl, I caught myself daydreaming, then swept the thought from my mind and stood up.

Chase grabbed my wrist and held it gently. "Carol, wait. You know Detective Riley was covering something up. Something he couldn't live with any longer. And maybe you can walk away from this, but the families of these men can't. They want answers. And right now, you're the only one I know who can help me find them. Promise me you'll think about it."

How could I not think about it? With everything that had happened today—Riley's suicide, Chase's confession—and sitting here alone with him in the dark, what else could I think about? I shook my wrist loose from his hand and walked to the door. I wasn't ready to give him an answer.

"Goodnight, Chase."

# CHAPTER 13

Wednesday was a nightmare. It started with a yellow sticky note on my computer screen. I didn't have to read it to know who it was from. Tyler had already called me twice on my cell and texted me as I was on the way in. My office phone had a flashing red light on it. No doubt another important message from Tyler.

I dumped my things on my desk, grabbed the note, and headed down the hall to Tyler's office. In my rush, I nearly bumped into an LAPD officer and a plainclothes detective in the hallway. I nodded as I passed. It was early for them to be at the station, but not unusual, particularly if there was a breaking story. Trouble was I hadn't heard anything on the news, and the fact they appeared to have just left Tyler's office signaled trouble.

Tyler was standing behind his desk when I came in the door.

"Sit down."

I crunched the yellow sticky note in my hand and sat.

"What's wrong?" Tyler was pale. His red hair was spiked and chunky from running his fingers through it. "You look awful."

"We have a situation, and we need to get ahead of it."

I pointed my thumb over my shoulder in the direction of the doorway. "This have anything to do with the LAPD cop and detective in the hallway?"

Tyler raised his eyes to the ceiling, exhaled, then sat down. "Silva's wife had an accident last night. I need you to include something in the next update before anyone else in town gets hold of the news and reports it."

Ben Silva, a.k.a. Saint Silva, was the station's host for The Righteous Way. On his evenings, he engaged his audience in talk about everything from the Bible to politics and was never shy about including his own moral interpretation of things.

"What kind of accident?" I asked. "Is she okay?"

"She is, but he may not be."

"What do you mean?"

"He called me last night, right before he went on air. Said his wife was driving him to work in his car about nine o'clock and he thinks she may have hit something."

"Like what?"

"A girl on a bike. But he wasn't sure."

"Not sure? Was there a girl? Is she okay?"

"She's dead. But that's not the worst of it." Tyler took out a roll of antacids from his desk and popped one in his mouth, chewing it as he spoke. "Ben said he panicked. He said he couldn't see anything in the dark, and when he realized he'd be late for work, he told his wife to drive him home. He then took her car and drove himself to work." Tyler took a swig from a water bottle on the desk.

"He left the scene?"

"Worse. He told his wife to go back to the scene and meet with the police by herself."

"And he never mentioned anything?"

"Other than to me, no. Not a word. And when he didn't call me back, I assumed it was nothing. Which is why the police were here. They arrested her, and she's out on bail. But they wanted to know what I knew and when."

It was no wonder Tyler was stressed. The story sounded kind of fishy. But if Tyler knew Silva had been involved in an accident and didn't report it, it wasn't going to be good news for the station.

"And where's his wife now?" I asked.

"Home. The police have spoken to her, but they were here because they're not buying her story, and they wanted to talk to me. They think maybe Silva was driving, and she's covering for him."

I had met Silva's wife, Martha, a couple of times when I filled in during the week for one of the other staff reporters on the night shift. I didn't know much about her. She was a small woman, dark hair, middle-aged, and the few times I'd seen her at the station she kept to herself. Usually sitting quietly in the corner of the studio while her husband did his show. I didn't think I'd ever heard the woman utter much more than a hello, and I doubted she would do well in any kind of interrogation.

"You think he'd do that? Get her to take the blame?"

"I don't know. What I do know is that we need to get something on the air and fast."

I bit my tongue. With both Silva's reputation, and possibly Tyler's, on the line, I knew better than to ask questions or risk a showdown.

"Ben's family. What happens to Ben reflects on the station. For the time being, we're going with the story he's told us. I need you to put together a report that mirrors exactly what Ben shared with me last night. Keep it simple. You know the drill. Martha Silva, wife of KNST personality Ben Silva, was involved in a tragic accident last night that resulted in the death of a young woman. Add the entire staff at KNST is deeply disturbed over the circumstances, and that we offer our condolences to the woman's family and friends. Nothing more. Meanwhile, I'll issue a statement to the staff. No one is to talk with anyone concerning the events of last night. If they do, it will result in their immediate dismissal. You got that?" Tyler turned his head back to his computer screen.

"Yeah, I got it." I nodded. I felt numb. I didn't believe a word of what I had just heard, but I wasn't about to say anything. Tyler had made it very clear what the company policy was going to be, and without any facts, there was no point in arguing. I started to get up.

"Oh, and Carol, I'm afraid that's not all."

"There's more?"

"Unfortunately, this next story couldn't come at a worse time, but it's news, and we're going to need to include it in the morning report."

"What's that?"

"That young college coed, the victim of the hit-and-run in Westwood two weeks ago."

"Caty Beardsley?" I remembered the name because she reminded me of Cate, my own college-aged daughter who was away at school. Caty had been hit by a car at night as she crossed the street on the way to class.

Nobody remembered anything about the car or the driver. Witnesses said it seemed to come out of nowhere and disappear. The police suspected a drunk driver. A lot of good it did. Caty had been rushed to Cedar Sinai Hospital in critical condition and had spent the last couple of weeks in a coma. The accident had created a flurry of calls about unmarked crosswalks and the city's need to do more to protect pedestrians.

"She died this morning. You're going to have to include the story with our own news about Ben. I'm not asking you to bury it, but in light of the circumstances, you might also include something about the City Council investigating the increasing number of hit-and-run accidents. How LA's becoming one of the leading cities for the pedestrian accidents...something like that."

I felt like I'd just been hit in the gut. But this time, I did get up. I wanted to get out of the office before Tyler thought of anything else he wanted to add to the morning report.

I made it as far as the door when he said, "Carol, one last thing. Your show Sunday night? I'm going to need a synopsis before you leave today. Plus, I want a dozen promos as well. They have to be on the air first thing tomorrow morning. Got that?"

"Yeah, I got it."


Ordinarily, when I worked the morning show, Kit and Carson, our morning team, found a way to include me in their program. It was usually just a couple words, a casual remark about what I was wearing or if I looked like I hadn't gotten enough sleep lately. There was little sanctity when it came to the on-air staff. Political correctness went out the door. They'd even been known to make remarks about my being a single woman of a certain age, which was usually followed by the sound effects of roaring cougar. Radio was not for the faint of heart. If

I were thin-skinned, I would have a problem, but the banter made us all sound like family, and for whatever reason, it worked.

The news about Martha Silva's arrest and the accident was especially difficult. Not just because I knew Ben, but because I didn't believe a word of it and suspected most of KNST's news staff didn't either. Many show hosts were egomaniacs, and Ben was no different. He enjoyed the limelight—thought he was always right—and seldom allowed anyone else to get a word in edgewise. I was certain he had bullied his wife into taking the rap, and Martha had rolled over and agreed to do whatever Silva told her. The woman didn't strike me as much of a fighter.

But after I delivered the news about Ben's wife, there were no casual remarks between the morning team and myself. Instead, their producer cut me off and went straight to a station break. Not that Kit or Carson had anything to do with it. But Tyler's strict warning that any mention of the accident, on air or otherwise, would result in the immediate termination of the employee had everybody on edge. And sensing I had falsely reported on the accident had me feeling like a Judas. I had betrayed my own sense of justice. Not to mention Martha, who I felt was the ultimate victim. I left the news booth feeling like the messenger everyone wanted to kill.

My cell phone buzzed as I headed back to the office. I glanced down at the caller ID. Chase. I answered it, annoyed by the interruption. "What's up?"

"Well, good morning to you too, Sunshine."

"I'm not in the mood, Chase. This isn't the time—"

"Hey, I called to apologize. I know I surprised you last night. You didn't expect to see me, and then there I was on your porch with Misty. Smoking a joint. I wanted you to know I appreciate your listening to me, and I respect your need to keep your personal life separate from your work. I get it. I just want you to know, it won't happen again. I'm sorry."

I sat down at my desk. I was still undecided about Chase, but after listening to his story last night, the least I could do was recognize his apology.

"I appreciate your understanding," I said.

"And I'm sorry about what you went through yesterday. Riley wasn't a well man, and it's too bad you had to see that. It couldn't have been easy."

"It wasn't." I exhaled. The pressures of Riley's suicide and Silva's accident were straining my patience.

"We're good then?"

"Yeah. We're good."

"'Cause I was thinking about your show again and I—"

"Don't push it, Chase." In an instant, Chase's apology went from sincere to opportunistic, and I found myself on the defense. "Look, I'm sorry. This isn't a good time. I told you, I'll let you know."

I hung up the phone. I knew Chase hoped his apology would lead into a longer conversation concerning my show and how we might work together. That wasn't going to happen. Instead, I opened up a file on my computer marked Sunday Night Show and started working on a series of promos for Tyler sans anything Chase could possibly be involved in.

*Women, when it comes to your views on news and sports, do you feel discounted by the men in your life? When it's game time, does your boyfriend or your husband sit in front of the TV and ignore you? Is your opinion dwarfed by those of the men in your house? Tune in this Sunday night for The Soap Box and a little girl talk. Join me, Carol Childs, from eleven to midnight, as we sound off on sports, news, the men in our lives, and offer the female perspective on what's happening in the world.*

I typed out six variations of the same promo along with a detailed program synopsis for *The Soap Box* and felt like I had found a safe middle ground. *The Soap Box* sounded like it fit the station's news and sports talk format. It targeted women, which should please Tyler's need to attract more female listeners at that hour, and it was one I could live with. I wasn't about to promote a show that focused solely on women complaining about the men in their lives. I didn't care how much Chase had convinced Tyler it would be a good idea. I knew better. A show with a bunch of women whining about the men in their lives would be here today and gone tomorrow, and so would I. And since management hadn't been pleased with my first attempt to host a late-night show, I had to find a way to make this new opportunity work. I figured my best option was to take the high road and find some common ground that made sense for the format. I crossed my fingers and hit send.

# CHAPTER 14

Every other Friday night, when Charlie goes to his dad's and Sheri's son Clint visits his uncle, we have dinner together. It's become a tradition, two single moms and a night out without the kids. Tonight she had made reservations at Shutters in Santa Monica. I opened the Jeep's window for the drive over and let the cool sea breeze blow my hair while I ignored the buzzing of my cell. I knew from the different ringtones one of the callers was Chase and the other Charlie's dad. I didn't want to talk to either of them. Not until I had a glass of wine, dinner, and had vented my frustrations with Sheri about work and the men in my life.

I knew Chase wanted an update on the show, and for the time being, I wanted as much distance between the two of us as possible. As for Charlie's dad, he had promised Charlie a car for his birthday, and I was totally opposed to the idea. It was a discussion I had been avoiding, and I wasn't prepared to have it now. But judging by the number of missed calls registered on my phone, it was probably going to be sooner than I liked.

I met Sheri on the hotel's terrace, an elegant outdoor dining area with small candlelit tables and space heaters that zapped the chill in the air. At this hour, the inky black ocean waters blended seamlessly into the night sky, making the sound of the crashing waves on the shore all the more powerful. As I approached the table, Sheri put the menu down and glanced up at me.

"You look awful."

"That good, huh?" I pushed the hair away from my face and took a seat. Ordinarily, the cool night air and the sound of the waves would have relieved my stress, but not tonight.

"I'm surprised," I said. "After Riley's suicide this week, Tyler nearly pulling me off the Sunday Night Show, and Silva's accident, or more correctly his wife's accident—which I'm not supposed to talk about—awful would be a big step up."

Sheri bit her bottom lip as I explained how the station's GM had told Tyler she wanted me off the Sunday night show. But that Tyler, after talking with Chase, believed Chase had come up with an idea that saved my job.

"Go Chase." Sheri gave a small fist pump, her hand no higher than her shoulder.

"I wish you didn't like him so much."

"He's perfect, Carol. Not for me, but for you, and why not? You could use a little dalliance in your life. I'm surprised you don't see it."

I put my hands up. "Don't. Much as both you and Misty think he's so great, I'm not sure he's on the level. Before Riley died, he said Chase was a drunk. That he'd had run-ins with him and he couldn't be trusted. Not that I'm so willing to take the word of a dead man, but right now I'm on the fence." I crossed my arms and sat forward, hugging myself, my voice barely above a whisper. "You know he came by the other night?"

"Misty mentioned it. She said she left the two of you to talk."

"He wanted to talk about the case. Thing is, I don't know what to believe. I checked his background out online, and he's got a medical discharge from the Army. And despite Chase's saying differently, I'm not so certain he's any saner than this Mustang Sally who's been calling the station. Nor am I convinced Riley was right about Bruno's death being a suicide. Cops hold things back during an investigation. Could be he knew something and was doing just that. In fact, right now I've got more questions than I've got answers."

"Well, my vote's with Misty on this one, Carol. I like him. And I think you're being too quick to judge."

"Yes, well, that is my prerogative. But I can tell you this, Chase is definitely not happening. The man's not my type. I'm not into beards, and if anything he's too scrappy for me." I shook my head and grabbed the menu. I was starving.

"You'll excuse me if I say 'methinks the lady doth protest too much.'" Sheri put her elbows on the table, clasped her hands together, and shaking her head smartly from side to side, smiled widely at me.

"Very funny." I looked up over the top of the menu, my eyes challenging hers. "I'm not into one-nighters."

"Who said anything about a one-nighter? Go out with him. Have a good time. He's a nice guy, Carol, and right now you're wound about as tight as I've ever seen you. Think of it as therapy."

"Let's change the subject."

"Okay. How about we talk about Silva? I heard the report. What's up with that?"

"I'm not supposed to say. Station's orders."

Sheri glanced at the waiter. "That's too bad. There's a bottle of red on the way, and I'd love to share it."

The waiter arrived with the bottle of wine, opened it and poured a small amount of the rich red Bordeaux into Sheri's glass. Then, like a good sommelier, he stood back with the bottle in hand and waited while she sampled it.

Swirling the wine in the bottom of the glass, Sheri took a whiff then tasted it. She gently smacked her lips together, declaring it a truth serum.

"I'd offer you a glass, but it'll cost you."

"Fine," I said. "Pour me a glass. You know I was going to tell you anyway, but you're sworn to secrecy."

"Like this should be any different than any other time?"

Sheri was right. I didn't have many secrets I hadn't shared with her. I trusted her implicitly. We were as close as sisters, maybe even closer. And, if I'd asked, I knew she would swear an oath on her son's life without thinking twice.

I began by repeating the news story about Ben's wife's accident. The same story I had used in my news update that morning, then stopped and put my elbows on the table and clasped my hands together.

"But you don't believe it's true. Do you?" Sheri asked.

I shook my head. "No. I don't. The car that hit the girl was his car, a yellow Corvette, not his wife's. I think he was racing into work, probably running late as usual, when he hit the girl and panicked. Then he went home and told his wife what had happened. Took his wife's car to work and told her to take his car back to the scene of the accident and call it in."

"Can you prove it?"

"I can't even talk about it. Right now the police are investigating, but Tyler's put out a gag order on the staff. Threatening to fire anyone who talks about it."

"And I know that doesn't rest well with you."

"Not at all. And I'm convinced Silva's wife is too afraid to say anything."

"You could ask Chase to check it out."

I rolled my eyes.

"After all, he is an investigator. It'd be easy enough for him to keep you out of it. You know he'd do it in a heartbeat."

I glanced back at my menu. Sheri did have a point. I mulled the idea over, weighing how I might mention it to Chase when Sheri kicked me under the table. I eyeballed her over the top of my menu, uncertain what the urgent signal might be. Perhaps some Hollywood star or political big shot. The restaurant was famous for star sightings. Sheri's eyes met mine, then swept to the table next to us. *Look.*

Seated less than three feet away was an attractive couple in the middle of a very uncomfortable situation. The woman, about thirty-five, was dressed conservatively, her long dark hair about her shoulders. The expression on her face was as though her world were about to fall apart. Tears were forming in her eyes, and one rolled delicately down her cheek. Opposite her was a man about the same age, his dark hair mussed as though he had been running his hands through it. Whatever the altercation, he appeared to be trying to comfort her and had leaned across the table to put his hand on her forearm. She pulled away and harbored her left hand in her right against her chest, as though trying to keep something from him.

My eyes snapped back to Sheri. She pointed silently to her ring finger and mouthed, *He wants the ring back.*

Suddenly the woman shrieked at the man. "I can't believe you would do this. How could you? Here of all places. I thought you wanted to take me out for a nice dinner and talk about the wedding. You jerk!"

Sheri and I stared at each other. Too close to the impending disaster to ignore it and with nowhere else to turn, we both stared down at our menus.

"I knew I never should have trusted you. You lied. You never intended to go through with it!"

The man mumbled something, and out of the corner of my eye, I watched as he reached once again for her hand. She shrieked like injured animal.

Finally, the man stood up.

"I can't deal with you. I can't deal with any of this."

Throwing his napkin down, he brushed past our table, leaving his dinner jacket on the chair behind him and nearly knocking over our wine glasses. An awkward silence followed. I bit my lip while Sheri's eyes went from me to the empty seat across from the woman. I think we both hoped the man would come back. But when he didn't, and the waiter came instead to fetch his jacket, we both knew we couldn't ignore the situation.

Sheri's eyes met mine. *What do we do?*

I shrugged and glanced over at the woman. She sat crumpled in her seat, her elbows on the table, hands folded with her head bowed against them, staring straight ahead. I reached over and gently put my hand on her shoulder.

"Miss, are you okay? Is there something we can do for you? Maybe someone we could call?"

The woman sniffed and shook her head. I dug for a tissue in my bag and handed it to her.

"I don't believe it," she said. Her voice cracked. "He's left me. I've given up everything for him, and he just walked out."

"Would you like to join us?" Sheri signaled the waiter to set another place at our table.

It wasn't the evening we'd had planned, but at that moment we felt an unspoken sisterhood. We ordered ravioli for the three of us. Sheri said it was comfort food and poured her a large glass of red wine while we listened to her story. Her name was Jennifer, and she'd given up her job when her fiancé had asked her to move to Southern California in hopes of creating a life together. Once here, he appeared to have cooled to the idea of a wedding, insisting she get her own apartment while he finished preparing his place for the two of them. The first of many excuses, she said, and now he had dumped her. Left her without so much as taxi fare home.

When we'd finished dinner, Sheri scribbled her number on a napkin and tucked it inside Jennifer's purse. If she needed to talk, Sheri said, all she had to do was call, night or day. She'd be there for her. Then with Jennifer between us, we escorted her back out through the lobby, helped her to dry her tears, and waited until a taxi arrived to take her home.

"You still think there's not an audience for women to vent about how some men have treated them?" Sheri asked.

"Maybe," I said.

# CHAPTER 15

I wasn't sure if it was the music coming through my bedroom window at six forty-five on a Saturday morning or the sound of metal chairs scraping across the cement patio outside—like fingernails on a chalkboard—but either way, I was awake.

With Charlie at his dad's for the weekend, I figured it had to be Misty. I grabbed my robe, my eyes feeling like they were filled with sand and only partially open, and followed the sounds of "California Dreamin'" downstairs to the kitchen. The French doors leading to the terrace were ajar.

Misty stood in the middle of the patio. She was dressed in a long gingham skirt that had seen better days and a red gardening apron with matching red gloves. I hollered to her, but with her back to me, she appeared to be in a state of confusion, looking around as though she heard my voice but didn't know from where it was coming.

"Misty?" I hollered again. I stepped over to the patio table where she had placed an old boombox and turned the sound down. "What are you doing?"

Misty turned around and, with a look of surprise on her face, raised her gloved hands to her chest and patted her heart, like the slow beating of a butterfly's wings.

"Oh, there you are. Beautiful morning, isn't it?"

I repeated the question.

Misty pointed to a bag of potting soil and several small cartons of plants. "Exactly as I told you I planned to do. Planting a garden. Did you forget?"

I sighed, grabbed one of the small nursery cartons off the table, and took a whiff. "Herbs, I hope."

Misty turned her back to me and adjusted her work gloves. "I was thinking of an herb garden, and then when Chase called yesterday, I had another idea. Maybe an arbor. Something decorative, where we might grow—"

"Chase called? Here?"

"He wants to talk to you, Carol. I got the feeling it wasn't just the case you're working on." Misty looked over her shoulder at me and winked.

"Misty, Chase and I aren't working on a case."

"Whatever. He said it was important. But if you ask me, it was only an excuse." She turned her head back toward the planters. "So I asked if he'd do us a favor."

"A favor?" I put the small nursery carton back on the table. "Just what kind of favor, Misty?"

"Like I said, I was thinking about a...a...what do you call it...a—"

"An arbor?" I reminded her.

"Yes. If we're going to be growing grapes, we'll need one."

"Grapes?" I quickly inventoried the table. I didn't see any evidence of grapevines. "Where are you planning on planting grapes, Misty?"

"Over there." She pointed to a corner area of the patio. "The light's good, and I think it'd be an ideal place to put one of those small romantic patio tables with a couple of chairs." She winked knowingly, then turned her back to me and picked up one of the small herb containers.

"And I suppose Chase agreed and volunteered to come by and help?"

"He did. Said he'd be more than happy to. In fact, I suspect a man like that is quite good with his hands." She raised a brow knowingly.

I let the innuendo slide.

"And did he happen to mention exactly *when* he planned to come by?"

"This afternoon sometime. I forget exactly, but you might want to get yourself gussied up a bit."

Trying to keep my cool, I said, "Misty, when Chase was here the other day, do you remember me saying I wasn't wild about the idea of his coming by the house? That I like to keep my work and my personal life separate?"

"Did you say that? I must have forgotten. I've had so much to do. Charlie and I have been busy going back and forth to the nursery picking up plants and pots. You know how it is. And when he wasn't here to drive me after school yesterday, I went by myself and—"

"Excuse me, Misty." I stepped forward and took the plant from her hand. "Did you say Charlie's been driving your van? Strange how neither of you mentioned it to me."

"Didn't I?" Misty pursed her lips. "Well, I must have forgotten. You know how forgetful I can be. But yesterday, I couldn't wait, so I drove myself."

I glanced down at the street where Misty had parked her van. My condo was built on top of the parking garage, and from the patio, I had a good view of the street below. Painted with peace symbols and psychedelic flowers, it was like a traveling billboard for the sixties. That and the fact she'd taken up two spaces with one bald tire resting on the curb was a ticket waiting to happen.

"You know, Misty, the cops won't like you parked like that, even if you do live here. They'll give you a ticket. And with your poor memory and cataracts, we really should talk about your not driving."

Misty exhaled sharply. "Well, just what do you expect me to do? Fly?"

"Uber, perhaps?" I placed my hand gently on her shoulder.

"Humph." Misty turned back to her seedlings.

"We should think about it, Misty." Misty's state of confusion and memory were becoming a concern. Recently I had found dishtowels in the trash and the newspaper in the laundry basket. I pulled my robe tight around me and turned to go back inside. "Were there any other calls?"

"Your bag was ringing when I got up. It's on the table."

"Thanks."

"And Charlie called last night on the house phone. I assume it's okay for me to answer it?" Misty's voice sounded brittle.

"You don't need to ask, Misty. You can use the house phone anytime you like."

"He said he left a message on your cell. He's all excited. His dad wants to buy him a car."

# CHAPTER 16

I checked my cell phone for messages. Tyler had called. One of the station's weekend reporters was down with a bad case of laryngitis and Tyler needed me to fill in.

"I'd do it myself, Carol, but I have a dinner scheduled. See you at four."

With an eye on the clock, I spent the morning working with Misty on her new herb garden. Doing my best to smooth over any ill feelings she had about my comments concerning her driving. Like a sous chef, I followed along, handing Misty the small herbs while she tucked them neatly into the ground.

Finally, around one o'clock, relieved that Chase hadn't shown up, I excused myself to get ready for work. I had some prep work I wanted to do for tomorrow's show, and I had no intention of making myself available if he did show up. As far as Misty's arbor went, I planned to discourage that idea. Maybe not right now, particularly after she had reacted so sensitively to my concern about her driving. But later I planned to tell her, I'd cooled to the idea. That I thought Chase might be using her to get to me so that he could pitch himself or any of his ideas for my show. I didn't need his input, and I definitely didn't want him seeding my audience with the likes of Mustang Sally or anyone else like her. Tomorrow night's show was going to be on my terms.

Trouble was, I needed something gritty. Something that hadn't already been talked to death and that my listeners could get their teeth into. I had several ideas, but nothing that really grabbed me. I was still mentally sorting through them as I pulled out of the garage and nosed into the street. Just as I was about to put my foot on the accelerator, a late model candy red Corvette pulled up directly in front of me. I stomped on the brake. My notebook, bag, and phone flying onto the floor beneath my feet. Directly in front of my Jeep, just inches from my front bumper, was my ex's car. And behind the wheel was my son. Putting the Jeep in park, I got out, slammed the door behind me, and screamed at my ex.

"What are you doing here?" I glared at him, glanced back at Charlie behind the wheel, then with as much control as I could muster, asked, "And why is Charlie driving your car?"

Robert put his hands up and grinned. Then shook his head like he had just been caught trying to sneak one by the goalie.

"We just came by to pick up a few things Charlie forgot for school. You weren't supposed to see."

"Not supposed to see? Did you see how close he was to the curb? Any closer and I would have broadsided you. Were you even watching?"

Robert and I squared off in front of his car, my hands on my hips while Charlie sank down behind the wheel like a prairie dog diving for cover. When it came to the kids, I was like a mother lion, protecting her brood. If I didn't like something, my reactions were more visceral than rational. Legally there was no reason Robert couldn't let Charlie drive. He had his driver's permit. The truth was, I just didn't like it. I had reported on too many teenage accidents to be comfortable with the idea of my son behind the wheel of my ex's high-performance sports car, particularly on California's freeways. It frightened me, and Robert knew how I felt. And, as far as I was concerned, my ex only wanted Charlie to get his license so he could avoid the back and forth commute between my home in Sherman Oaks and his place twenty miles north of me in Santa Clarita.

I was about to lash out with a second round of what I thought about the situation when a large black SUV pulled up in front of Misty's van and parked. With a coffee cup in one hand and a sucker in his mouth, Chase got out and nodded to me, then reached back into the car to retrieve a tool box.

"You expecting company?" Robert asked.

I shook my head. Aside from the toolbox, Chase looked like he was here for a social visit. He was dressed in jeans and a freshly pressed, blue chambray shirt, and it looked like he had even trimmed his beard. How could I explain? "He's a friend of Misty's."

Robert's eyes shifted from the SUV to Misty's van. With its macramé curtains, peace symbols, and multi-colored flowers painted on its sides, it was like a neon sign. Hard to miss.

"Charlie tells me she's living here now. She's in the guest bedroom."

Robert was never wild about Misty. He didn't care for the whole Psychic to the Stars, clairvoyant thing, and I knew he was suspicious of her so-called magic potions. If he had any idea I had spent the afternoon helping her plant an herb garden, I would never hear the end of it.

"She's retired," I said, "and she was in need of a roof over her head. I offered to let her stay here until she found something suitable."

"Always the rescuer, aren't you, Carol?"

I bit my lip and smiled disingenuously. It was best we ended our conversation on a respectful note before things got any more heated. I suggested Charlie run inside and get whatever it was he had forgotten.

"I'm sure your dad wants to get home in time for dinner." Then to Robert, I said, "I know how Stephie worries."

Robert's much younger wife, Stephie, kept tabs on him. I suspected she never quite trusted him, which was foolish on her part. When Rob and I married, we were kids, barely out of high school. I couldn't fault either of us for growing up or growing apart. It just happened.

After Charlie and his dad had left, I went back inside the house. I wanted to make certain Charlie hadn't forgotten anything he might need for school. Plus, I told myself I ought to at least see whatever plans Misty had Chase drawing up for my arbor. That was until I walked into the kitchen.

The French doors were open. Chase was leaning with his back against the counter, looking out onto the patio, his long legs extended before him. In his lap was a pad of paper. He appeared to be sketching something and stopped when he saw me.

"Carol, you have a minute?"

"If this is about the show, I—"

"Actually, it's about the arbor Misty wants, but I may have something with regard to the show as well. That is if you're interested."

I felt the muscles in my back stiffen. So this was about my show. Another excuse to pitch me an idea to secure time on the air. Worse yet, he was using Misty, exactly as I suspected. I wasn't going to give him a chance to say anything.

"Thing is, Chase, I really don't think now's the time. Misty's busy with the garden, and an arbor really isn't what I'm looking to do right now. Sorry," I said dismissively. "I just came back in to make sure Charlie got everything he needed for school and to get my phone."

Chase glanced down at my hand. "You mean that thing in your hand?"

I shook my head and pushed a loose strand of hair behind my ear as though I had misspoken. "Did I say phone? I meant my notepad. I was taking notes and left it on the counter." I reached for a blank notepad I kept by the phone and started to leave.

"Well, just in case. You remember that runaway mom last week? During the big bowl game? Her husband didn't report her missing until he was ready to go to bed and realized she was gone?"

I stopped, my hand on the door handle. He had my attention.

"She's back. No harm, no foul. I spent the morning with a bunch of detectives who'd been working the case. The woman said she just needed a break. Got tired of hubby sitting around in front of the TV all weekend, drinking beer and eating chips, and walked out. Said she didn't think he'd even notice."

I nearly laughed out loud. "Runaway Mom, huh? That's perfect."

I thanked Chase for the tip and opened the door.

"No problem. But just so you know, I'll be listening, just in case our Mustang Sally calls. But don't worry. I won't call. I promise."

# CHAPTER 17

Chase's lead concerning the runaway mom was a godsend. The press hadn't given Heidi Graham's disappearance a lot of coverage. The story had amounted to little more than two inches in the metro section of the *LA Times*. Not unusual for a city of eleven million people, particularly when there was no body, and the investigators didn't believe the circumstances suggested foul play. Added to the fact was Ms. Graham's vanishing act had coincided with an unusually busy news day, and her story was lost in the mix. Bad news for the Graham family, good news for me. Ms. Graham's disappearance, and now her sudden reappearance, was exactly the type of story I needed for my show.

Women, whether they could relate to the young mother's frustration or not, were flooding the call lines. Some had a thing or two to say about Heidi. How could she leave her husband? Her home? Or her kids? Others wanted to vent their own frustrations with their own inattentive husbands.

The show was going great. I could feel the listeners with me and started to relax. At the commercial break, I told my producer I was going to grab a coffee. As I headed for the employee's lounge my cell phone buzzed. Caller ID flashed Chase's name on the screen.

"I thought you weren't going to call—"

"Marcus Reddings is dead."

"What?" I pressed the phone close to my ear and sprinted towards the newsroom. If Marcus Reddings was dead, this was big. Reddings was the former owner of the LA Stars, one of Los Angeles' premier basketball franchises, and a successful real estate mogul. At nearly seventy-six years old, he was rumored to be one of LA's wealthiest businessmen.

I checked the newswire. My fingers were shaking so badly, I could barely strike the right keys. There was nothing. Across the room, the police scanner sat silent. "How do you know?"

"His wife called. I've done surveillance work for her. Most of it on him."

I knew the Reddings were in the midst of a messy divorce. Pictures of Marcus Reddings with a scantily clad young woman were splashed on the covers of every tabloid in town, some with a smaller inset of his wife sitting alone in their Bel Air mansion. The photos had all been retouched to make her appear old and haggard.

"She's afraid, because of the divorce and all his public philanderings, the police will think she did it."

"What happened?"

"He took a header off the top of the Wilshire Oceana. His girlfriend has an apartment in the building. Supposedly, she's out of town, and the cops are saying it looks like a suicide. But I don't think so."

"You think she did it?"

"The girlfriend? Can't say. However, that's not the reason I called. Ms. Reddings wants to talk. She wants to tell the world what's really been going on inside their marriage. She was about to pick up the phone and call one of your competitors when I suggested a better idea."

"You told her about my show?"

"I did."

"And she'd be willing to talk about her husband? Tonight? After all that's just happened?"

"Andrea Reddings has got a lot to say. Particularly about her husband's lover, Ava Yablonski. She thinks she killed him."

"I thought you said his girlfriend wasn't in town."

"That's the point, Carol. Andrea's convinced Ava set it up. And if she's right, wouldn't hurt if you pursued that line of questioning with her. Could work in our favor."

"*Our* favor?"

"Think about it. Contract killings? Bruno's death. Mustang Sally. Not that it's tied together, but if Sally's listening, it might get her to call."

I felt like someone had just thrown a bucket of ice water on me. I should have known Chase had an ulterior motive.

"I can't even tell you on how many levels that would be wrong. Ava Yablonski's not a public figure. I can't allow Andrea Reddings to call her out on charges of murder without getting us all in trouble. We'd be sued, and—"

"And if Sally's listening, it's exactly the type of story she'd call in about."

"That's why you told her to talk to me, isn't it?"

"It is. But if you're not interested—"

"No. I am. Absolutely." I answered without thinking twice about it. Regardless of Chase's motive, the prospect of interviewing Andrea Reddings was worth any misgivings I had about Mustang Sally. The Reddings had been in the news for years: their contentious divorce, his philandering, the recent sale of the LA Stars, her charitable donations, all of them big stories on their own. But despite their fame and notoriety, nobody had been able to get them to do a sit-down interview about their personal lives. If I could get Andrea Reddings to talk, this could be a big win for the station and me as a reporter. The fact that I had Ms. Reddings on the air, that she was calling me and no other reporter in town, was pure gold and worth the risk.

"I'll do it."

# CHAPTER 18

I couldn't remember a time when felt so nervous about an interview. I could feel myself sweating. I was glad Tyler had decided to never go with cameras in the studio. A lot of radio stations had, but Tyler felt cameras were a distraction, making the studio look like nothing more than a poorly directed TV show with talking heads. I glanced up at the studio's digital clock: 11:37:22. The second timer was flashing slower than the beating of my heart. What if Andrea Reddings didn't call? What if Chase wasn't right? What if this was just another of his crazy conspiracy theories? I must have entertained a dozen worrisome thoughts before I heard the phone ring. Matt picked up the line.

"Carol, it's Andrea Reddings. Want me to transfer it to you on the inside line?"

I nodded and picked up the small black receiver beneath the console. A line reserved for private calls, not those intended to be broadcast. I had never met Andrea Reddings in person. Except for the recent tabloid photos, every other picture I'd seen of her was the same. Her perfectly coiffed silver-gray hair, her stately attire, and rigidly straight posture were like royalty. I felt as though I had an image of her sitting in the studio with me.

"Ms. Reddings, thank you for calling. I'm sorry for your—"

"Please, Ms. Childs, spare me. If you're about to say you're sorry for my loss, I think we both know I'm hardly prepared to play the role of the bereaved widow."

Her voice was flat and void of any feeling, as though she was already bored by her own commentary. I wondered if this was her way of masking emotion.

"All the same," I said. "I'm sure this has come as quite a shock."

"The shock, Ms. Childs, is not that my husband is dead, but that he was pushed to his death from the balcony of Ava Yablonski's apartment less than two hours ago."

"Pushed? Ms. Reddings, I'm sure you're aware LAPD hasn't released any—"

"Hold your tongue, child. I'm well aware of what LAPD is prepared to say or not say. And if you're about to caution me on what I can and can't speak about, let me tell you, this isn't my first rodeo."

"It's just I need to warn you about making any kind of statement in a moment of grief that might be libelous."

"Sweetheart, I've been around the block a time or two. I know exactly what I'm doing. Like I told Chase, I want to get out in front of this story before everyone in LA thinks it was me who killed my husband. There're a lot of people in town who are going to assume such."

Matt signaled me. I had thirty seconds. I asked Ms. Reddings to hold while Matt transferred the call to a abroadcast line.

"Welcome back to *The Soap Box*. This is Carol Childs, but before we begin, I want to say we've just received some shocking news. A few moments ago, I received a call here in the studio that Marcus Reddings, the former owner of the LA Stars, has died. His body was found earlier this evening outside the Wilshire Oceana, an apartment building he owned on the Wilshire corridor. Police have yet to release any information regarding the cause of Mr. Reddings' death, but his wife, Andrea, has asked to be with us tonight. I have her on the phone with me now. Andrea."

In a slow, modulated voice, as though she was reading from a prepared script, Ms. Reddings began.

"Thank you, Carol. I realize my call may sound unusual to those listening, particularly considering the circumstances, but then what about my life with Marcus hasn't been?" Andrea paused, took a beat then continued. "Around nine o'clock this evening, I received a call from LAPD informing me that Marcus appeared to have fallen from the balcony apartment of the Oceana where he had gone to visit a friend. I'd like to go on record right now saying I don't believe Marcus' death was accidental or that this was a suicide. I believe my husband was pushed and that investigators will find he was murdered. And I want the person who killed him to know I intend to prove it."

"However, at this moment, Ms. Reddings, the police have said nothing to indicate there was any foul play or—"

"The foul play, Ms. Childs, was my husband's flagrant womanizing. It's been going on throughout my marriage. I would have had to be blind not to notice. But the idea that he would take his own life is preposterous. He'd no more kill himself than empty our bank accounts. The man loved life. He was full of it. He wasn't about to commit suicide. I'm not saying the young woman whose apartment he *allegedly* jumped from is personally involved. The police tell me she wasn't there. But we all know Marcus had enemies, and contract killings don't just happen in the movies."

"Are you saying you think someone was hired to—"

"I'm saying, Carol, that Marcus didn't kill himself."

I paused. On the computer screen in front of me, I had pulled up a string of stories about Marcus Reddings and the sale of the LA Stars. It had been a contentious sale that dragged out for months.

"There have been several stories in the paper quoting that you were frustrated with the recent sale of the team, and the two of you were separated and had filed for divorce. Perhaps—"

"There was nothing, Ms. Childs, I didn't know about Marcus. And in answer to your statement that we were separated, let me update you. We'd reconciled. Privately. We didn't broadcast news of it, but Marcus had moved back home."

I glanced down at the bio I'd pulled up on Marcus. "In fact, if my math is correct, you would have been married sixty years this April."

"There're not many couples in this town who can say that. But let's be real, Carol, marriage is hardly the happy ending Hollywood would have us believe. At the end of the day, marriage is a business relationship as much as it is a social contract."

"Is that how you'd describe what you and Mr. Reddings had? A social contract."

"We had our ups and downs. I think any gal who enters into marriage believing it's going to be some endless romantic spiral of happily-ever-after is in for a surprise. If a gal wants romance, she best check into a motel."

Matt signaled me we needed to go to a station break. Andrea's last statement had ignited a wildfire of callers. All of them waiting to speak with a woman who was one of LA's great mysteries. I asked Andrea if she would stay on the line and take a few calls, but she declined. She felt she had said enough for the night, and, sensing she was about to hang up, I signaled Matt to get her number. If I needed her later, I wanted to make sure I had a way of contacting her.

I opened the second half of the show recapping Marcus Reddings' death and referencing Andrea's statement regarding romance and marriage.

"So let's talk. Is Andrea Reddings right? Is marriage more of a business arrangement? And what about our Runaway Mom? Should she have expected less romance and demanded more of a shared role when it came to the distribution of work and play? What about you, what do you expect?"

I was thrilled with the response. Not only were the phone lines lit, but each time a caller hung up, another took their place. The callers and their comments were lively and for the most part fun. I couldn't have planned a better show. If Tyler were listening, he had to be smiling. Judging from the number of callers, both male and female, my numbers had to be off the charts.

Twenty minutes later, I was in the middle of a debate with a young woman. She thought the institution of marriage was passé and couldn't imagine herself in such a situation. I was about to open the lines for further discussion when Matt smacked an erasable white board against the glass of his small controller's booth. Scribbled in red letters was the very name I had told him to alert me to. *Mustang Sally! Line 3.*

I felt my stomach drop. With less than five minutes to go, I had almost forgotten about Sally. I considered not taking the call but felt I owed it to Chase. After all, he had given me the heads up on the

Runaway Mom and convinced Andrea Reddings to call. If Mustang Sally wanted to talk and knew something about Bruno's death and the death of the other two men Chase was investigating, I needed to allow her the airtime to reveal herself.

I braced myself for the unexpected and gripped the mic. "Welcome to *The Soap Box*. This is Carol Childs, may I ask—"

"This is Sally. Mustang Sally. We spoke last week." Her voice was even coarser than I remembered. "And I called to say Andrea Reddings is right."

"Right? You mean about marriage being a contract?"

"Hardly a contract." She chortled a deep dry throaty laugh. A chill ran down my back. "At least not the kind of contract I'm referring to."

I should have disconnected the call right then and wrapped the show. Ignored her invitation to open what I felt for sure would be a Pandora's box, but I didn't. I knew Chase would be listening, and I thought, okay, just this once because I owe you, but after tonight, we're through.

"Certainly, you're not talking about contract killings?"

"She's right about them. They're a necessary evil. It would be nice if we didn't need them, but for some women, we have our own special court of appeals."

"Court of Appeals? I'm not sure I understand."

"But Ms. Reddings does."

"You're not saying you think Ms. Reddings—"

"You know the song Frankie and Johnny were sweethearts?" Mustang Sally started singing. "Oh Lordy." She slurring her speech, then suddenly stopped. "He done her so wrong. Surely your listeners know the story." Sally wailed a few more lines, her voice like a washboard, echoing into my headphones and out across the airwaves, and then stopped. "When a man does a woman wrong, Carol, it's up to us to take care of him."

"How, Sally? How do you take care of him?"

# CHAPTER 19

Just like the first time Mustang Sally called, the line went dead before I could get her to tell me anything more about herself. Where she was or how I might reach her again. I closed the show, made a brief mention about how sometimes, late at night, the station got unusual calls, pranks and that kind of thing, and moved on. I thanked my listeners and Ms. Reddings for sharing her story. And then I waited alone in the studio as Matt turned out the lights and uploaded the programming for the overnight—old-time radio plays.

With nothing but the lights coming from the computer screen, an eerie shadow cast itself across the studio. I stared at the phone line, willing it to ring, but it sat silent while voices from the radio play echoed throughout the empty station like ghosts. Finally, I picked up the phone and called Chase. I didn't wait for him to say hello.

"You did it again. You promised you wouldn't, but you did. You got Mustang Sally to call, didn't you?"

"Carol, I swear. I had nothing to do with that."

"Then how did she know about Andrea?"

"I don't know how she knew about Andrea. I haven't got a clue. But whoever Sally is, she obviously knew about your show. Think about it, Carol. It wouldn't be hard. The station's been running promo spots all week. I caught one this afternoon. If Sally's listening to the station, she probably did too."

I paused. Chase had a point. Tyler had doubled up on the promos. Sally might have heard one and tuned in to listen.

"Face it, Carol. You have a fan, and she's hooked on your show like a fish on the line. Now all you have to do is keep playing with her while we reel her in."

"What do you mean *we* reel her in? We, you and I, aren't going to do anything. From here on out, if Sally calls the station, I'm telling my screener not to put her calls through. I'm not turning my broadcast into some late-night freak show. Look, I appreciate the tip you gave me about the runaway mom and what you did with Andrea Reddings. Getting her to call. I really do. And, much as I think Bruno Sims didn't commit suicide, I don't share your conspiracy theories that there's some wild group of women out there going around killing men because they were rude or pissed them off or jilted by the men in their lives. That's not enough reason to kill someone."

"But—"

"Chase, I'm sorry. Even if you didn't set this Mustang Sally up to call, whoever she is, she's nuts, and—"

"And you're not convinced I'm not either."

"I didn't say that."

Chase's reference to his brain injury caused me to pause. I didn't want to sound totally unsympathetic to what I suspected had been a long hard struggle.

"I'm not crazy, Carol. Something's going on."

"Maybe. But I'm not risking my career or this show on some hunch you have she might be out there knocking off men. It's too far-fetched. So you're on your own here. Good night."

I hung up the phone, left the station, and drove home in silence. I wasn't going to allow Chase to interfere with my show or my personal life. He was probably as crazy as the tabloid stories he was trying to convince Tyler were connected to Bruno's murder. And even though my concerns as to the cause of Bruno's death continued to fester, I wasn't about to jeopardize my reputation and that of my show or waste my time chasing crazies with the likes of Chase.


It was almost one a.m. by the time I got home. When I closed the front door, I noticed a light coming in from the kitchen. Despite my constant reminders to both Charlie and Misty, neither of them ever remembered to turn off the lights when they left a room. I was about to shut it off when I realized Misty was sitting at the kitchen table staring at a steaming pot of tea as though she were in some kind of trance.

Quietly I tiptoed into the kitchen and placed my bag on the table.

"You okay?"

Misty tilted her head in my direction. Her pale gray eyes so clouded with cataracts that in the low light I doubted she could see much more than my shadow.

"Couldn't sleep. I'm afraid I have a lot of that lately. Made me a special pot of my tea, though. That should help."

In front of Misty was a silver warming plate, the heat provided by a small candle cast a shadow from its decorative base. On top of it was a clear glass tea kettle and inside was a bouquet of flowering herbs, the type of which I couldn't identify.

"You're sure you should be self-medicating like this?" I knew Misty wasn't big on western medicines, but some of the weeds I'd seen her pull from the garden and mix together in lieu of any over-the-counter medications concerned me.

"Relax, my Sleeping Beauty tea won't kill me. Just knock me out for a couple of hours. Give these old arthritic fingers a break from the pain and settle my mind. Sure you wouldn't like some?"

I shook my head.

"I'll stick to my own medication, thank you." I reached for a wine glass from above the bar and poured myself a glass of red wine. "You hear the show tonight?"

"If you mean did I hear Mustang Sally, yes, I did." Misty raised a glass of tea to her lips and blew across the top. "I've been sitting here thinking about her."

"You mean meditating." I said it with as much of a question in my voice as I did a statement.

"Call it what you will, but I agree with Chase. Sally's for real."

I took a slow sip of my wine.

"It's a stretch, Misty. And even if it were true, serial killers are seldom women. They're usually young, white males. And based on the way she sounds, Mustang Sally, if she is for real, must be somewhere in her late sixties. She hardly fits the profile."

"Don't underestimate the fury of a scorned woman, Carol."

"It's just the only reason we know anything at all about this is because of Chase, and I'm not sure about him."

"Don't you ever listen to anything on the radio besides news? Music, maybe?" I could see Misty was growing irritated with me. "That's where the passion is, Carol. Women have been singing about revenge for years. They aren't any less likely to seek revenge than men. It's just how they go about it. They're sneakier."

I sat down at the table and kicked off my shoes. "You really do believe Chase then, don't you? That there's some female assassin out there who's the head of an organized group of vigilantes, and they're calling for the murder of certain men?"

"There have always been black widows, Carol. Women who murder men because they feel they've been mistreated and justified in their slayings." Misty put her teacup down and focused her cloudy eyes in my direction. "You ever hear of the Betty Lou Beets? She was accused of killing five of her husbands before she was finally tried and executed. And then there was Mrs. Christy. The newspapers described her as a modern-day Bluebeard. She poisoned her seventh and eighth husbands. Numbers one through six died suspiciously, but nobody ever knew for sure how. And the Killer Grannies. Surely you remember them. It was a few years ago, right here in Los Angeles. Like something out of *Arsenic and Old Lace*, only this was for real. Two little old ladies who took in old men and killed them for the insurance." Misty yawned. The tea was starting to have an effect.

I put my glass down and ran my fingers along the stem while I spoke.

"Assuming you're right and Mustang Sally is behind Bruno's death and the deaths of the two other men Chase is investigating, how'd she do it?"

"She may have had help."

"All right, I'll play along. Sally did mention a Court of Appeals. So let's just say this court of appeals is a group of women, and they're responsible for carrying out these horrendous deeds. Do you really think they could have lifted Bruno's body up on the Hollywood Sign?"

"Several of them could."

"Maybe. But Bruno was a pretty big guy, and carrying a body up a fifty-foot scaffolding would be no easy task."

"They may have had help. Like the old ladies in *Arsenic and Old Lace*."

"Ha. Now you really sound crazy, Misty."

"The ladies had their nephew Teddy, who used to help bury the bodies in the basement. Who's to say Mustang Sally doesn't have a Teddy or someone like him?"

"Tell me, is this the musing of an old lady or some psychic prediction?"

"If it makes you feel better, think of it as just the experience of an old lady talking."

"Good to know," I said.

"But if it's a reading you'd like, I have had a pestering about you lately."

"A pestering?" I took another sip of my wine, expecting Misty to tell me something about Chase. About how right she thought he was for me. "And just exactly what is it you've been feeling, Misty?"

"You've recently met someone. It appears to have been an accidental encounter you considered to be of no consequence. But she's coming back into your life. And she'll have information about something you think is out of your reach."

"Now that does sound like a prediction."

"I don't have a name. But the name Jay or the letter J keeps coming to mind. Sound familiar?"

"No, Misty. I don't know anyone named Jay who has anything to do with anything I'm working on. But thanks."

"It feels to me like she's angry. That she's been spurned. But she's not like the others, Carol. She's different."

# CHAPTER 20

Tyler called me first thing in the morning. It didn't matter that Mondays were my day off. If he needed me, he called. And today it was because the new general manager wanted to see me in her office. Immediately.

"I hope you haven't let anything slip about Silva's accident, Carol. You know the policy. But whatever it is, Presley wants you in her office right away. She said it was urgent."

I had half expected Tyler's call. Not so much because I feared someone knew I'd shared my thoughts about Silva with Sheri, but because of last night's interview with Andrea Reddings. I figured, at the very least, Tyler would ring me to say good work. But not before seven a.m. After all, nobody else in town had spoken to Andrea, and far as I knew, I had an exclusive. As for the rogue call from Sally, I wasn't at all certain what Tyler would have to say about that. But the fact the general manager wanted to see me was worrisome. GM's didn't waste time with low ranking talent. Not unless there was a problem.

Uncertain what I was about to face, and with my insides starting to tie themselves in knots, I got out of bed and went to the closet. I'd never been called on the carpet like this before, and what I needed was a little confidence. If I were going to go see the new GM, the least I could do was appear as though I had it all together. I pulled on a pair of my favorite slim jeans—this was my day off, after all—a cashmere sweater, heels, and a cool-looking tweed blazer. Whoever said fashion made the woman certainly knew the right outfit could cover a world of insecurities, and right now I felt like I needed all the help I could get.

I stopped by the newsroom before I headed down to the GM's office. I was hoping Tyler might give me a heads-up about what it was

Presley wanted. But typical Tyler, his eyes remained fixed on his computer, ignoring me as I stood in the doorway.

"Just wanted to tell you I was here. Anything I should know before I head into the lion's den?" I tried to sound confident and nonchalant.

Tyler's eyes clicked to mine then back to his computer. "Nope. 'Fraid you're on your own on this one, Childs. Haven't a clue."

Tyler dismissed me with a wave of his hand. He was obviously too preoccupied to bother with me. I would have appreciated a *good luck*, or at least an invitation to see him afterward. Something to indicate I wasn't totally done for. Instead, all I got was a shake of his head.

Taking a deep breath, I headed down the hall. What if Tyler's indifference was because he knew I was finished? That I'd slipped up about Silva and shared what I knew with Sheri and was about to be fired. What if I lost my job? What would I do? I was deep into my litany of what-ifs when Molly McCray, Presley's assistant, caught me in the hallway.

"Oh, good, Carol, you're here. DJ's been expecting you. I told her I saw your car in the lot. I was just coming to see if you were in the newsroom. Go on in."

I quickened my pace and hurried down the hall. Now not only was I expected in the GM's office, but I'd kept the general manager waiting, and she knew it. I prepared for the worst.

I had seen DJ Presley in person exactly twice. Each time had been as I passed her in the hallway en route to a meeting. Most of the time she was either buried in her office behind closed doors or traveling between Los Angeles and New York on business. The woman was constantly busy, and if her picture hadn't hung on the wall outside her office, I might not recognize her at all. Like most of the staff, we jokingly referred to her as Oz, pulling strings behind a green curtain to which few of us were privy. All I knew about DJ was that she had red hair and drove a late model Jaguar she parked cattywampus in the employee's lot, taking up both the FM and AM general managers' parking spaces. To which she was entitled. DJ Presley was lord and master of both.

I approached DJ's paneled office, passing Molly's desk with an ornate flower arrangement in the corner. I knocked softly on the door frame.

"DJ? Tyler said you wanted to see me."

"Carol." DJ stood up from behind a large mahogany desk, her petite figure nearly dwarfed by its gigantic size. "You're here. Please, come in. And shut the door behind you. I've something to say I'd prefer not leave this room."

I wanted to blurt out that if this was about Silva that it was a mistake. That I hadn't meant to say anything to anyone. Instead, I kept my mouth shut and took another deep breath while I grabbed the gold knob on the door and gently shut it behind me.

DJ remained standing until I took a seat in front of her desk. In my nervous state, she appeared extremely well-polished and poised. I pegged her to be somewhere in her early fifties, but like most professional women, with the proper makeup and clothes, it was difficult to tell. She was dressed in an expensive, custom-tailored leopard jacket and slim black pencil skirt. I immediately felt underdressed and regretted my choice of jeans. I crossed my legs several times before finding a semi-comfortable position, locking one leg behind the other like a pretzel.

"Thank you for coming in, Carol. I know it's your day off, but I felt it was important we talk. Privately."

She paused for what felt like an eternity. If she was going to fire me, I wished she'd hurry up and get it over with. The palms of my hands were beginning to sweat. Slowly I started to massage them on my thighs, hoping she'd not notice how nervous I was.

"I heard your show last night. I liked it."

I readjusted myself in the chair. Maybe this wasn't going to be so bad after all.

"I think you've hit on something, Carol. I don't know how you've done it, but you have." She smiled and leaned back in her chair, head cocked slightly to one side, studying me. "But I have a problem, and I thought maybe you and I should have a little talk."

"I'm not sure I understand." Silently, I breathed a sigh of relief. I felt like I had dodged a bullet and vowed I'd never whisper another word about Silva and his accident. I uncrossed my legs and sat forward in the chair. "I thought maybe you called me in here because you didn't like the show."

"On the contrary, Carol. I think you have a lot of talent. But there's something you need to know. It concerns the show you did last night. I don't want anyone, Tyler included, to know what I'm about to tell you."

"Okay." I couldn't imagine where she was going with this, but as long as she wasn't going to fire me, I didn't care. "Is there something you'd like me to be doing differently?"

"No. Not at all," she said abruptly. Placing her elbows on her desk, she steepled her hands and leaned forward. "I want you to continue to do exactly what you've been doing. And I want you to do something that will cause Mustang Sally to call back."

"Mustang Sally?" I jerked my head back. "I'm sorry, I thought maybe you liked that Andrea—"

"Forget Andrea Reddings. Your interview with her was just fine, and I compliment you on getting it. But it's not Andrea I'm worried about."

DJ leaned down and opened a desk drawer. She brought out a crystal decanter and placed it on the desk between us.

"What I have to say to you is between you and me. It doesn't leave this room. It can't. Lives, mine included, depend on your secrecy."

"Okay." I shifted in the chair again, crossing and re-crossing my legs.

DJ poured us each a small glass of what I assumed was scotch and handed it to me.

"To secrets," she said.

I leaned forward, we clicked glasses, and I took the smallest of sips. Just the taste gave me an immediate buzz.

Then DJ said, "I think I know Sally."

I coughed. The hot liquor caught in my throat, burning as I forced myself to swallow.

"What?"

"Years ago, I was in a very abusive relationship. The man I was with was crazy, and when I tried to end the relationship the first time, he killed my dog. I say the first time, because back then I wasn't a well woman. I thought the arguments and his escalating violence was my fault and that I could fix him. So I didn't leave. I thought I could make it better. Abusive men can do that to you." She took a second sip of whiskey, then continued. "The second time I did leave, but he found me and burnt my house down. As you can imagine, I did what any sane woman would do. I went to the police. But I had no proof. Then my dog was hit by a car, but I had no evidence it was even him. And the house, the fire marshalls said, was the result of an electrical short. So I got a restraining order and an attorney."

"That must have been awful. I can't imagine—"

"There's more. When I got the restraining order, the police warned me, if I really thought he was abusive, not to go near him. They couldn't guarantee my safety, but if he showed up again, I should call them. Which I did. But the problem was, by the time they showed up, he was gone. So I moved. And the next time I saw him, I was living in a high-rise where he managed to pass himself off as a repairman. He was waiting for me when I got home. Hiding on my balcony, seventeen floors up. He threatened to push me off if I didn't come home with him. Fortunately, a neighbor saw me struggling with him and called the cops. He got scared and ran. When I tried to file charges, the police said I had no physical proof it was him. My word against his. And the neighbor, who had tried to be so helpful, said she couldn't identify him. Didn't get a good enough look. Plus, he was wearing gloves and a jacket, so I had no finger prints, no DNA beneath my nails, nothing. And when I insisted it had to be him, he claimed he had an alibi, he was with his new girlfriend, and I was crazy. As expected, she backed up his story. So I moved again. Only this time, I changed my name, dyed my hair, got a different job, and I was careful about who I contacted and where I went."

"I'm so sorry. I had no idea."

"No one here does. What saved me was a self-help group I found online. It was for women recovering from abusive relationships, a kind of ten-step program. A support group for those in need of getting away from their abuser and starting over. It was also a way to pass notes back and forth to loved ones without our abusers ever knowing."

I looked at the wall of photos behind DJ. Pictures with stars and politicians. I never would have guessed her life had been anything but perfect.

"Only I wasn't so lucky. I don't know how, but he found me again. I was at my wit's end. By then I'd moved three times, I was constantly looking over my shoulder, and I didn't think my life would ever be my own again. You've no idea how awful that can be. That's when one of the women in the group approached me online and invited me to another kind of meeting. She said it was a secretive offsite kind of thing. I had to agree that anything I heard or saw would remain between the women I was about to meet and no one else."

"Where was it?"

"It wouldn't make any difference if I told you. The location was never the same. All I was told was that she'd be my handler and that I couldn't bring any ID, my cell phone, or anything that might track my whereabouts. She told me she was taking me to meet with her high court, a group of women who would hear my story. She said it was this tribunal's job to make certain justice was administered properly. I never asked their names. The only thing I knew about these women was that they seemed to understand what I'd been through. I suspect they were all survivors themselves."

"So there really is such a thing? Mustang Sally didn't make it up?"

"I'm telling you I was given money, a car, and a job at a small radio station out in Palm Springs. The kind of place where nobody checks a person's background, and it was easy enough to fit in. I changed my name to Doris Jean, after a favorite aunt of mine. My handler added the last name Presley because she thought it fit. After a while, I shorted it to DJ. Seemed to fit since I was working at a radio station, and I guess it did. Nobody ever questioned it. I had a new job, new life, and a fresh start. Whatever the tribunal did, it worked. I never heard from my abuser again. He simply disappeared, and one day my handler told me I didn't need to worry about him anymore."

I put my glass down on her desk and closed my mouth. "And your handler? What was her name?"

"Sally." DJ took a drink, finished the glass and put it back down on the desk next to mine. "Which is why I wanted to talk to you. All this happened ten years ago, Carol, but last night, when I heard your show, I realized Mustang Sally was the woman who helped me. I recognized her voice."

"That deep, gravely voice?"

"Even then it was like she had rocks in her throat and had to strain to speak. I remember one time when she picked me up there was an old Patsy Cline song playing on the radio. I got the feeling she'd wanted to sing along with it but couldn't. Instead she just kind of mumbled the words. Odd isn't it, how certain voices stick with you?"

"It's distinct all right. Any idea what happened to make it so?"

"She never said, but I didn't have any doubts she'd been abused. I suspect someone tried to strangle her, probably damaged her vocal chords and ruined her voice forever."

Just thinking about it made the muscles in my neck strain. My hand went to my neck and massaged it lightly. "Talk about motivation," I said.

DJ continued. "I can tell you we were never asked to do anything in return. But when I heard her talking to you, I realized something was wrong. Mustang Sally would never speak out like she is. She could barely talk as it was. And we were all sworn to secrecy. I think she's in trouble. Something's happened to her. She's lost it and gone off the deep end."

"Do you have any idea what?"

"Maybe. There was a man in the car with her the first time she picked me up. I think he must have been in his late twenties, and he might have been her son. He was wearing headphones, and he didn't speak. At the time, I thought there was something wrong with him. I don't know what it was that made me think that, other than she was very maternal towards him. Making sure he kept his jacket on, and his seatbelt buckled. That kind of thing. She was more than a bit overprotective. If I had to guess, I'd say something might have happened to him. I've no idea. But what I do know is I need you to find her. Listening to her last night, I can tell from the way she was talking, she's not going to stop calling this station or any other for that matter. You've got to stop her. If you don't and she's found out, her life—and the lives of several other innocent women living free of fear for the first time in a long time—is going to change for the worse. Drastically. You understand?"

I nodded. "You're afraid she'll talk, and if she does, your name and the names of the others will be attached to that of a serial killer—"

"And we'll all be charged as accessories to murder. I'm not asking you to break the law, Carol. All I need you to do is find her. And when you do, I need you to tell me where she is. I'll take care of the rest."

# CHAPTER 21

I texted Chase as I left DJ's office. *We need to talk.*

After my meeting with DJ, I knew if I was going to find Sally, I'd need his skills as an investigator. And, despite my doubts about him, he was closer to the case than anyone I knew.

He buzzed back almost immediately. *Meet me. Griddle Café. Ten.*

The minute I read Chase's text I knew he suspected my invitation to talk implied a change of heart on my part, that I had somehow come to my senses after hanging up on him last night and wanted to apologize. It was clear he viewed this as a social invitation. When I got to the Griddle Café, I spotted him nursing a cup of hot coffee at the counter. He looked like he had just gotten out of the shower, his dark hair damp and slicked back from his face, almost touching the collar of his work shirt. As I approached, he stood up, and I thought I caught a gleam in his eye like he knew what I looked liked without my clothes on. I squelched a nervous smile and ignored the thought.

"Hope you like pancakes, Carol."

"I've only time for coffee, Chase. There's something important we need to discuss."

He ignored the urgency in my voice. Taking his cup, he turned and made his way through a maze of closely grouped tables like a linebacker. I followed, catching the faint scent of his cologne as he continued to talk about the pancakes.

Between the cologne, an empty stomach, and the pancakes, I felt momentarily lightheaded.

"They're the size of dinner plates. Best in the city. You really ought to try them." Then coming to a small table marked reserved, he nodded for me to take a seat. "'Course, I'm gonna have to cut back some if we're going to be hanging together." He stood behind the chair opposite me and patted his mid-section.

I waited for him to sit down. I needed to put a stop to his idle flirtation. I put my elbows on the table, leaned closer to him, and whispered, "Chase, this isn't a social invitation. We're not hanging together. Not now. Not ever. It's not happening."

He sat back in the chair, took his napkin, and spread it neatly on his lap, as though my words had no effect. "And I thought you asked me to breakfast as a thank you for helping you with Ms. Reddings."

"I already said thank you. Last night. And while I do appreciate it, that's not why I needed to see you. Right now I've got a job to do, and difficult as it is for me to ask for your help, I need to. More than anything, I'm going to need you to focus on the job and not me."

Chase put both hands on his legs and stared at me from across the table. "And you don't think I can do that?"

I rolled my eyes. "Do I really need to answer that?"

"Okay, look, I know you've had your doubts about me. You're not sure about my theories concerning the recent deaths I'm investigating. But I'm not delusional. I didn't lose my mind in Afghanistan, and I haven't smoked so much weed I can't think straight. The docs tell me everything's fine. Now that, and the fact I find you attractive should be proof enough for you to know I'm a healthy, red-blooded American male. But, hey, if you're not into me," he held hands up as though to surrender, "I'm fine with it."

"Good." I poured myself a cup of coffee from the French press in front of me. "I mean, it's not that I don't find you attractive. I do. It's just complicated, that's all. I try to keep my work life separate from my personal. And I'm not about to get involved with any cops or—"

"I'm not a cop, Carol. I'm a private investigator. But, like I said, I'm not pushing this. I respect your boundaries. Besides, right now, if it's between you and these red velvet pancakes, I'm afraid you'd lose." Chase signaled the waiter and ordered a tall stack. "Wanna split?"

I nodded yes. By now I was ravenous, and while we waited for our food, I checked out the tables closely bunched on either side of us. I didn't dare speak too loudly.

I leaned forward and whispered. "I think I know more about who Mustang Sally might be."

Chase raised a brow, his coffee cup inches from his mouth. "What happened between last night and this morning to make you say that?"

"I'm not at liberty to say." I certainly wasn't about to tell him what DJ had revealed to me. I'd have to find a way to tap dance around her secret without revealing my source. "Only that someone contacted me, someone whose identity I agreed not to share, and who claims they know her or knew her. But even more importantly, I may have some idea as to why the police are calling Bruno's death a suicide."

"Go on." Chase put his coffee down, clasped his large hands together like fists and, with his elbows on the table, stared at me.

"Bruno wasn't a victim. Not at all." I waited for that to sink in. "You were right about his being killed by a gang of women, but it wasn't because they were jilted or seeking revenge on a philandering ex-boyfriend. It's the other way around. The women were the victims. They were abused. And Bruno, and maybe the other two men whose deaths you're investigating, were stalking them. They were abusers, Chase. And this group Mustang Sally belongs to, they were contracted to take care of the situation."

"And the police knew it and looked the other way?"

"I think it was easier to do that than to try to get a conviction. It's the only reason someone like Riley didn't pursue the investigation. I suspect in his mind, he believed justice had been served."

"No." Chase jerked his head back like I'd just slapped him across the face. "There would have been a record. Restraining orders or something."

"Women don't always file restraining orders. They're not exactly a Teflon shield against a predator. Remember Nicole Simpson? She had the police on speed dial. The cops all knew Nicole was in trouble, but there wasn't much they could do beyond suggesting OJ take some time to cool down and maybe file a report. Things have changed some today but not enough. Abuse is a social stigma. A lot of women are too embarrassed to tell their friends and family the truth about what's happening. Most end up living in fear."

"You're saying none of the women reported it?"

"Maybe, maybe not. But if the cops are in on it, I doubt you'd find any records. It's likely any reports made have since been destroyed."

"But somebody must know something. Their friends? Family?"

"If you're talking about the men's friends and family, I don't think they'd tell you much of anything. My experience with the cases I've reported on is when something like this happens, friends and family will swear the abuser was a squared away guy. That the girl was throwing false accusations. That she was a loose cannon, always going off the deep end, and he couldn't deal with her."

"That might explain why I haven't been able to talk to any ex-girlfriends."

"And I can't guarantee you'll be able to find any either. If Sally's been telling the truth and she's involved in the deaths you're investigating, these women don't want to be found. Not ever."

The waiter returned with a large stack of pancakes, piled nearly ten inches high. Chase cut the stack in half and placed some of them on an empty plate in front of me, then slathered the remaining cakes with melted butter and drenched them in syrup.

"This source of yours, what is it she wants?"

"She wants me to find Sally."

"It's a woman then?"

"She was a former victim who recognized Sally's voice."

"Anything else?"

"She thinks Mustang Sally may also have been abused. That she's in trouble. That something's gone terribly wrong, and that's why she's speaking out."

"And does this source of yours have any idea who this Mustang Sally is? How old? Where she might be living?" Chase cut into the stack of cakes and took a bite.

"No, but Misty might."

"Misty?" Chase swallowed hard, then put his knife and fork down. I nodded.

"Is this some psychic prediction or just her opinion?"

"Believe me, I'm as blown away by what I'm about to tell you as you are. But this person who thinks she recognized the voice thinks Sally may have a son."

"A son?"

"And if she's right, then something Misty said to me last night is starting to make some sense to me."

"Like what?"

"Are you familiar with the play *Arsenic and Old Lace*?"

"About the old ladies who murdered a bunch of lonely old men." Chase laughed and wiped his mouth with his napkin. "You think this is that?"

"Not exactly. But Misty does. She thinks the women had help like in the play. They buried the bodies with the help of their adult nephew."

"It might explain how an old lady or even a group of women were able to hoist Bruno's body up on the scaffolding of the Hollywood Sign. They had to have a little muscle."

I pushed my plate away. The thought of Bruno's body on the Hollywood Sign had killed my appetite.

"And I suppose since you believe I planted your audience with callers the first time Mustang Sally called that the only reason you're talking to me now is because you think I have some way of finding her?"

"I was thinking you could check back through your social media contacts, see who you tweeted and who retweeted. Maybe somebody who knows somebody has a couple of old lady aunts in their friend files?"

"Even if I could do that, Carol, there's no way of tracking word of mouth. Someone saw something online, told a friend, who told another friend. Or maybe heard a promotional spot for your show. The station ran enough. There's no way of knowing."

I was growing exasperated. I didn't want to hear excuses.

"Yeah, well, there's got to be a way to find her, Chase. Someone must know something. Go through your sources. Because other than hoping she'll call back, it's all we've got."

# CHAPTER 22

I left Chase in the restaurant and arrived home to find Sheri and Misty in the kitchen. On the counter between them was a clear plastic bag full of freshly cut herbs along with a few other store-bought items— onions, garlic, and a small jar of honey Misty had asked Sheri to bring by. An herbal remedy, she said.

Sheri explained Clint was home with a low-grade fever and upset stomach and that she was worried. Despite the fact she'd rushed him to the doctor and been assured it was nothing more than a cold, Sheri was convinced it was something serious.

I wasn't surprised. Sheri was a bit of a hypochondriac, and recently there had been an outbreak of West Nile Virus. It was all over the news. I had covered the story for the station, and because of the concern of an outbreak, I had included a short update in each of my top of the hour news reports. While the Center for Disease Control had confirmed two deaths, they believed the likelihood of a serious outbreak was low. But Sheri was convinced Clint had been exposed. After leaving the doctor, she had called to talk to me, thinking I was privy to more inside information. When Misty answered in my absence, Sheri shared her fear, and Misty being Misty suggested she come by for a home remedy and some chamomile tea.

To calm Sheri's nerves, I repeated everything I knew about West Nile Virus. The disease was carried by mosquitos, and the risk was highest for those working outside, particularly those working around horses after dark or around standing pools of water. Both fatalities had been older people, and according to the CDC, the most susceptible were those in poor health. None of which applied to Clint.

Finally, after my reassurance and a pot of Misty's chamomile tea, the issue appeared to be settled. Sheri changed the subject and asked where I'd been.

"I had a breakfast meeting," I said. I paused and, feeling as though Misty might be reading my mind and about to broadcast news of my meeting like a tabloid headline, blurted out, "With Chase."

"Breakfast?" Sheri raised a brow. "I thought you didn't like him."

"I don't. I needed to discuss last night's show." I paused and glanced quickly between Misty and Sheri. "Mustang Sally called the show last night."

"I heard. And evidently, so did Jennifer Lamb."

"Who?" I couldn't place the name.

"The woman who sat next to us at Shutters the night we went to dinner. The one whose fiancé dumped her? We rescued her." Sheri filled Misty in on the breakup we'd witnessed a week ago, and how we had consoled Jennifer while we waited with her for a cab. "She called to say she recognized Sally's voice."

I put my teacup down. No amount of chamomile tea could stop my heart from racing.

"She's serious? She knows who Mustang Sally is?"

"I've no idea. I was in a rush to get Clint to the doctor, but I told her I'd give you her number. I knew you'd want to call her back."

Misty put her teacup down. "Jennifer. That's the name I couldn't remember the other night. And I was right, Carol, she is connected. I knew it."


That afternoon, I met Jennifer at her apartment in Santa Monica, a dingy second-story walk-up with bars on the windows, just blocks from the beach. She answered the door dressed in sweats, her hair in a ponytail, and looking like she hadn't glanced in the mirror or been outdoors in better than a week. Through the bars on the screen door, I could see stacks of boxes behind her, things I assumed she'd shipped to LA in anticipation of a new life with her fiancé.

"You okay?"

"'Bout as good as can be expected."

Jennifer invited me in, and I took a seat on a worn sofa facing a small studio kitchen. The place reminded me of a cheap motel, colorless and furnished with aging mid-century modern furniture. I wondered just how long she'd been there. On the counter was an open box of Oreos.

"You want coffee?" Jennifer went to the kitchen, moved some boxes around, and finding the coffeemaker, began making a pot.

"No," I said.

She proceeded as though she hadn't heard me.

"I apologize for not calling the station last night. I probably should have. But it didn't hit me until this morning that that caller on your show last night was Mustang Sally. I recognized her voice."

Clearing a space on the coffee table in front of me, Jennifer put the cup down and joined me on the sofa.

"Do you know her?"

"Not personally. But her voice, very definitely. She left a message for me on my voicemail."

"You've spoken to her?" I wrapped both my hands around the coffee cup and held on tight.

"No, not exactly. But like I told Sheri, after hearing her voice on your show last night, and listening to what she said, I know it's her. It's got to be. I don't think I'll ever forget that voice."

"But how? I mean if you don't know her, how'd she get your number?"

Jennifer explained that after her fiancé had left her, she had taken my advice and got herself into a women's self-help group.

"I found it online the night we broke up. They call themselves the Butterflies. I don't know what I was expecting from an online group, but they were there when I needed them, and they made me feel better. Not so alone. Here, you can see for yourself."

Jennifer reached for a small notebook computer on the table in front of us and opened it. A chat room full of odd names like Dead2me, NoseyNan, CupidsGottaPistol, and MerryWidow filled the screen, followed by their short missives.

"None of us use our real names. But the stories, they could fill a book. There's NeverAgain. Her boyfriend got her pregnant, then left with her best friend and now wants the baby. And Pennywise&Wiser, her husband was a con artist. He was married to two other people at the same time." Jennifer signified air quotes with the tips of fingers at the use of the term people then bit her lips tight.

"People?" I furrowed my brow.

"One was a man, the other was a woman. Pennywise found out when she was waiting in line at the post office behind a woman and realized the woman in front of her wasn't a woman at all. But her husband in drag!"

I shook my head and stared back at the screen and tried not to let the shock on my face register. New comments and replies were populating the page every couple of seconds.

"And Mustang Sally, the woman you heard on my show last night, is part of this group?"

"Judge for yourself." Jennifer pulled the computer back into her lap and scrolled back through the conversation until she came to her own. "Here. I'm DumpedAndDepressed."

Jennifer's entry was all about the breakup. How her fiancé had publicly humiliated her, breaking up with her in a classy restaurant, leaving her totally devastated. Several responses from other women, appearing to reach out to offer support, claimed similar experiences. It wasn't until Jennifer entered something about how abusive she felt Jason's treatment of her had been that Mustang Sally's name appeared on the screen.

The message read: *You're never alone. You've come to the right place. If he's hurt you, you have resources. We're here with everything from advice to relocation.*

"I had no idea what she was talking about or how crazy she was. I just wanted someone to listen to me and tell me everything was going to be okay. But reading back through all this now, I realize how it must have sounded. I think she mistook Jason for being physically abusive."

"And he's not?" I pulled the computer towards me and scanned back through the postings. "He's never hit you or anything like that?"

"Hit me? No. What's wrong with Jason is that he's got a bad case of cold feet. And it's killing me. I thought for sure once he and I got engaged everything would be okay. I moved here expecting to set up a house and be done with our crazy on-again, off-again relationship. Only instead of moving in together when I got here, he got me this crummy little apartment. Said he wanted to fix his place up all nice before I moved in. Then next thing I know he's right back to his old self. Acting all nervous about our engagement. Starts saying he's not so sure we're right for each other. Can you believe that? I give up everything. Leave my home. My friends. My family. My job. And for what? A broken heart?" Jennifer took a tissue from inside the sleeve of her sweatshirt and wiped her eyes.

I scrolled through the rest of the conversations between Mustang Sally and Jennifer. It was clear Mustang Sally had fixated on her once the word "abuse" came into play. In one entry, Sally suggested they meet for coffee.

*Why not join us for a meeting? I'll text you an address.*

I didn't see a response and asked Jennifer what happened next?

"She sent me a private message. Said when I was ready all I needed to do was go back online and type in the words, *I'm sick and tired of it all, and I'm not going to take it anymore.* After that, I would receive a phone call telling me where to go to meet her. From there she said we'd go to a meeting. But I didn't want anything to do with it. She sounded strange, and I wasn't feeling particularly trusting. I'm angry and heartbroken, yes. But Jason's not a totally bad guy. He even texted me yesterday. Told me how much better he felt about us now that we'd broken up. Can you believe that?"

I shook my head. For all the heartbreak Jason had caused her, I had the feeling they were far from done.

I glanced back at the screen. "But Sally called you anyway. Even though you didn't reply."

"She did. And that's why I called you. I was required to give an emergency contact number when I signed up for the chat room. And when I didn't respond to Sally's online suggestion that we meet, she called me. Only I didn't answer. I thought it might be Jason. I forgot

I'd used the number on the cell phone he gave me, and I didn't want to talk."

"And you said, she left a message."

"That's why I recognized her voice. You have to admit, it's not like a normal human voice. All gravely like that. And what she said. It was creepy. She told me I could arrange for a contract. Do you believe that? A contract. That I'd be doing women everywhere a favor if I did. And then she said something about some type of tribunal or high council who would hear my case. All of it was as she said on your show. I probably should have called you after you got off the air last night, but I've been living in such a fog. It really didn't click for me until this morning."

If I hadn't witnessed Jennifer's breakup firsthand and taken Mustang Sally's call on the air, I wouldn't have believed what I was hearing. It was beyond any crazy conspiracy theory. I could understand women spewing their anger, sharing their grief, but plotting murder? It was hard to think something like this could really happen.

"I'm hoping you saved the message."

"I did." Jennifer reached into her purse and took out a cell phone with a jewel tone aquamarine cover, lots of bling, and a screensaver with a picture of her and Jason together. "It's on here if you want to listen. In fact, you can have the phone if it helps. It was an engagement gift from Jason. I think he got a two-for-one special. His and hers. Charming, isn't it?"

She slapped the phone into my hand.

"I don't need to keep it. Just borrow it for a bit if I could."

"Take it. I still have my old phone. It's the number you called me on. I wanted to keep it. Just in case, you know, this happened." Jennifer glanced around the apartment. "I hadn't even downloaded my contacts onto the new phone. But who cares. I'm going home. I'm going to finish packing all this stuff up and leave soon as I can. If I'm lucky, maybe I can still get my old job back, and the fewer reminders I have of him, the better."

I turned on the phone. "Is there a passcode?"

"J J three two two. It was supposed to be our wedding day."

I typed in the combination and went immediately to voicemail. The last message posted read No Caller ID.

"I hope it helps, Carol. For whatever it's worth, I think the woman's nuts, but if I were really in a bad way—like some of the women on the Butterfly site—I'd want someone like Mustang Sally on my side."

I stared back at the computer screen. In the back of my mind, I was already starting to form a plan.

"Jennifer, these other women, the Butterflies, did you ever meet any of them? Do any of them know what you look like?"

"Never." She took a sip of her coffee and sat back on the couch. "I got so caught up in the online thing and thinking about Jason I didn't go anywhere. Couple times to the corner for coffee and whatever I could pick up at the market, but as far as meeting people goes, I haven't been anywhere or seen anyone since the breakup."

This could work. I held the phone out in my hand. "And other than Jason and Sally, does anyone else have this number?"

"No. Jason got us both new numbers. His ends in three-three-two-one, mine ends in three-three-two-two. Cute, huh?"

# CHAPTER 23

It was after three p.m. by the time I left Jennifer's apartment. Without thinking, I got onto the freeway and instantly melted into a sea of red lights. Traffic was stop and go, with more stop than go and speeds less than twenty-five miles an hour. Kicking myself, I tuned to the station for a traffic report. Instead, I got Dr. Sam, KNST's new health and fitness personality. He was talking about the recent outbreak of West Nile Virus, and chatting with him was a caller whose voice was becoming unmistakably familiar to me.

*Sally!*

With the unexpected excitement of hearing Sally's voice, I nearly slid into the car in front of me. Before my fender could kiss the expensive import, I slammed on the brakes and gripped the wheel. I turned up the volume on the radio and listened. The sound of Mustang Sally's rusty voice was unmistakable, and the purpose of her call even more disturbing. Sally was accusing the CDC of trying to downplay the dangers of West Nile Virus. Another death had been attributed to the virus this morning in the Antelope Valley, and she was convinced the outbreak was greater than reported. She sounded desperate, as though she were choking back emotion, her broken voice halting between accusations of a cover-up and denial.

Dr. Sam handled her like a pro. He was doing his best to calm her, repeating everything the CDC report had said, stressing that the virus could not be passed from an infected animal to a human. West Nile, he said, was not an airborne disease but a pathogen carried by mosquitos.

"Tell that to my dead son. He caught it from my neighbor's horse."

The line went still, and Dr. Sam was silent. There was an unusually long pause, and I could imagine the scene inside the studio. Matt scrambling to let Sam know the caller had hung up and that he needed to fill dead air. Quickly.

Finally, Dr. Sam came back on the air. After a brief and very sincere apology, he suggested a few things we all might do to help prevent the spread of the virus. "I think now would be a good time to say that while the chances of contracting the virus are low, there are things we should all be aware of to prevent another incident. Dead birds are a definite sign. If you see them, call the CDC. Also, if you've seen standing water or anything that might attract mosquitos, get rid of it. And if you go outside and see mosquitos, use an insect repellent. As for symptoms, watch for a low-grade fever, headache, body ache, vomiting, diarrhea, fatigue, and skin rash. The good news is that for those persons who do contract the virus, only about twenty percent would show any signs or symptoms of the disease at all."

I picked up the phone and dialed Sheri. "How's Clint?"

"Like a caged gerbil. Housebound and sick of being inside. Can you do me a favor? Have Charlie pick up his history book? He's got a test tomorrow. If you do, I'll make dinner."

The prospect of Sheri cooking was a no-brainer. Misty had told me not to expect her for dinner. She planned to do some meditating in her room in hopes of improving her talents. Whatever that meant. And given a choice between my cooking, which usually consisted of anything that came out of a box, versus Sheri's gourmet special, I opted for the latter and told Sheri to expect us by seven.

"There's something important I need to discuss with you. It concerns Jennifer."

Charlie and I arrived at Sheri's just after sunset. The view from her SoCal manse located at the top of Mulholland Drive overlooking the city was spectacular. During the day, she had a three-hundred-and-sixty-degree view of the valley below on one side and the city with the ocean wrapped behind it like a blue baby blanket on the other. At night, the sky was so black all the street lights and the stars blended together like diamonds on an inky black canvas. I buzzed the security gate. Sheri's voice came through the intercom just as the huge metal entry gate swung open.

"Back door's unlocked. Come in and make yourself at home. Clint's in the den, Charlie. I'll be down in a minute."

If it had been anyone else, I might have been intimidated by the size of the Billings' estate. But Sheri had grown up here and inherited the property upon her father's death. It was the family home, a seven-thousand-square-foot red-tiled Mediterranean mansion her father had built in the early seventies as a showcase to his illustrious career. Sheri was so used to her surroundings, I didn't think she even realized how opulent it all was. And since meeting her ten years ago, I had spent as much time at her home as I had my own. When you were both single moms with boys of the same age, you bonded.

I pulled up the drive, drove around to the back of the house, and parked my Jeep in front of the garage, an oversized complex that had once housed Sheri's father's collection of vintage cars. Charlie hopped out, and I followed, entering the house through the kitchen door as instructed.

Two feet inside, Charlie deserted me and followed the sounds of the television coming from the den while I trailed the warm smell of roasted garlic and tomatoes wafting from the oven. Dropping my bag on the kitchen's large center island, I was about to open the oven door and peer inside when Sheri walked in.

"Don't you dare." Grabbing an apron, Sheri pushed me aside. "Why don't you fetch us a glass of red while I check on the manicotti. Cross your fingers it's as good as it smells."

I nodded. Taking steps towards the bar, I peered over Sheri's shoulder as she opened the oven. For something Sheri had just thrown together, it looked as though it belonged on the cover of *Gourmet Magazine*, all hot and bubbly with cheese dripping from within the pasta.

"I thought we'd eat out on the patio. I set the boys a place in the den. Didn't want Clint to catch a cold, but we can always turn the portable heater on for us. That work for you?" Sheri took the manicotti out of the oven and put together two plates for the boys. "I can't wait to hear what Jennifer had to say."

"You won't believe," I said. "It's bigger than I thought. Much bigger."

"Good, then grab a plate and meet me outside."

I slung my reporter's bag over my shoulder and did as Sheri said, fixed myself a plate, then grabbed a bottle of wine and a wine glass and headed outside to the deck. Sheri had set up a small café table next to a space heater overlooking a koi pond and lap pool.

Moments later Sheri joined me. She held a plate of manicotti, a basket of garlic bread, and a bowl of Caesar Salad tucked beneath one arm. Without missing a beat, she settled herself and asked, "Okay, so tell me, just how does Jennifer know Mustang Sally? I can't wait to hear."

Sheri picked up her wine glass, poised to take a sip.

"First off, it's not just Jennifer who knows Sally. There's someone else as well."

"What?" Sheri put her glass down, spilling some of the wine on the table. "Who else?"

"If I tell you, you have to promise you won't say anything. Not to anyone."

"Again with the promises?" Sheri held her hands up. "Didn't we just go through this with Silva?"

"It's bigger. Only this time, it's not just my job at stake, but lives."

Sheri sat back and stared at me. In a slow, deliberate manner, she asked, "Who is it?"

"DJ," I said.

"The general manager of the radio station?" Sheri leaned forward, both hands on the table. "She's involved?"

I explained that before I had breakfast with Chase, Tyler had called to tell me the GM wanted to see me in her office, *immediately.*

"Turns out Jennifer wasn't the only one to recognize Sally's voice on the air last night. DJ did too. And the reason she recognized her voice was because—"

"They're friends?" Sheri interrupted.

"Not exactly. Mustang Sally rescued her. DJ was an abuse victim. Sally helped her escape."

"Does Chase know?"

"Not about DJ. And he can't. Not ever. She made it very clear, her name can't be associated with any of this. Meanwhile, I have asked Chase to go back through his social media contacts to see if he can find Sally. But if he finds her before I do and Sally confesses, he's going to want to turn her over to the police and then—"

"And then women who think their past is behind them may suddenly find themselves being hauled into court to answer a whole lot of questions they'd rather not talk about."

"You got it."

"Does DJ have any idea how to find Sally?"

"No, but I think Jennifer may have stumbled on to something. Here, let me show you."

I took my laptop out of my bag and then fired up my computer. While waiting for the online chat room to open, I explained to Sheri how I had come to learn about it.

"Jennifer described it as a self-help group for women whose relationships have blown up and are trying to get their lives back on track. She thinks that's where Mustang Sally found her."

Sheri pulled her chair around the table and stared at the screen, then started reading the various posts.

"Geez, if I had known about this back when I was with Clint's father, my dad wouldn't have had to do what he did."

"What?" I felt my jaw drop. It never occurred to me Sheri might have been involved in anything so sinister. "He didn't murder him, did he?"

"No. But he might as well have."

"Why?" I asked slowly and cautiously. This was a story I hadn't heard, and I wasn't so sure I wanted to.

"It's not something I like to discuss, and I wouldn't want it to get back to Clint. Ever."

"You know better than to ask. What happened?"

"What didn't? The man was an actor. Not a particularly good one. But handsome? Oh yeah. And what he lacked in talent he made up for in the romance department. Unfortunately, not just with me."

"I take it you kicked him out?"

"Not quite. At the time, I was pregnant with Clint, and he was working on a movie with my father. We were going to be the perfect little family. Everything I wanted and didn't have growing up. At least that's what he told me." Sheri sighed and took a sip of her wine. "To make a long story short, he was supposedly out filming a scene when I was home alone and went into labor early. When I tried to phone him, I couldn't reach him. So I called my dad, who was directing the film. Only thing was, they weren't shooting that night. I later found out they hadn't even begun. And when Dad found him, by the time he was finished *talking* with him, I doubt he was fit for the part anymore. I never knew what happened. Only that Dad didn't use him in the movie, and I suspect made him an offer he couldn't refuse."

"You mean like leave town or die? I thought that only happened in the movies."

"It was the movies, Carol. And like I said, I don't know what happened. All I know is my father told me he would never work in this town again."

"And you haven't heard from him since?"

"No. As far as Clint knows, his father deserted us before he was born and has never tried to make contact again. It's not something I like to talk about." Sheri stared back at the page and switched the subject. "I don't see any names I recognize."

"You won't," I said. "The women all use aliases to hide their identity. Jennifer's was DumpedAndDepressed. But that's not what I want to show you. I've been thinking about it ever since Jennifer shared this with me this afternoon. And I think I've found something."

I moved the mouse up the page, back through conversations that were at least a month old. "What do you see?"

"A bunch of crazy pen names and conversations. Why?"

"Look at the names. Dead2Me, NoseyNan, MerryWidow. They're all like Jennifer, women who were dumped or are angry at their ex-boyfriends. They call themselves Butterflies. Doesn't take long before you start to recognize them. But if you scroll up through the older entries, you'll start to see some other names. Only these don't appear to be women who are posting about their relationships but instead offering support. My guess is these are counselors. They're there almost every day."

Sheri scrolled back through the screen. "You mean like these. Greymare. GuardianAngel. Never2Late, and Mustang Sally."

"Exactly. And look at the date." I pointed to the computer screen. "Bruno's body was found on the Hollywood Sign the day before Charlie's birthday. I remember because I was planning his party. Then Mustang Sally called my show Sunday night, two days later, and suddenly the rest of the Butterfly handlers or counselors, whatever you want to call them, disappear."

"Except for Sally." Sheri scrolled back through the entries, noting Sally's response to several, and then stopped when she came to DumpedAndDepressed. "Look here, she's chatting with Jennifer, right after her fiancé dumped her."

Sheri took a bite of her manicotti, her eyes focused down at the table, then back at the screen. "But Jennifer claimed she recognized Sally's voice, how could she do that from this?"

"Because Sally called her." I explained when Jennifer had signed up for the site she had given an emergency number and that Sally had used it to reach out to her when Jennifer didn't respond to her online. "That's what nailed it for her. Jennifer said the woman's voice on the phone was the same one that she heard on my show. The woman told her she wanted her to meet with people who could help her."

"As in get rid of her boyfriend type help? Permanently?"

"That's what Jennifer thought she meant."

"And these other names, the ones you call handlers or counselors, you think they're part of Mustang Sally's tribunal, her team of assassins?"

"Probably. And I suspect the reason the other three names disappeared from the site is because Sally's been speaking out. I think they're worried they might be discovered."

"With what Sally's said on the air, I would be too. But what I don't understand is why. Why would Sally start rocking the boat? Isn't she afraid of being caught?"

"I think something happened after Bruno was murdered that upset Sally, and that's why she started calling the station. And not just my show." I explained how I had heard Sally on Dr. Sam's show, talking about the recent outbreak of West Nile Virus and that she sounded distraught. "She said her son had died. That alone would be enough to send a woman off the deep end. If she's had some type of emotional breakdown, and her team can't control her, my guess is they're all lying low, afraid of what she may do."

"Then why would Mustang Sally call and tell Jennifer she wanted her to meet someone?"

"I'm not sure how clear-headed Sally is right now. If she's calling the station and talking about murdering men and settling some phantom score, she's certainly not thinking straight. And if she lost her son, she may be delusional."

"Let me get this straight. DJ wants you to find Mustang Sally so you can rescue her. Chase, who only understands half of what's going on, wants to find Mustang Sally so he can turn her in for Bruno's murder. And if he does, he'll blow this case wide open. While Sally's posse, if there really is one, is pissed off and headed for the hills."

"That's how I see it."

"And meanwhile, you've no way of tracking her down or getting in touch with her?"

"I might. Sally sent Jennifer a private message via the website telling her when she was ready to set up a meeting to go online and type in the phrase, *I'm sick and tired of it all, and I'm not going to take it anymore.*"

"Exactly like she said that first time on the air."

"Right. And after that, Mustang Sally would call and give her instructions where to go. Which is why I have this."

I took Jennifer's aquamarine cell phone from my bag and slid it across the table. "This is the phone Jason gave Jennifer as an engagement present. It's also the number Jennifer used when she went online to register with the Butterflies. They required an emergency number. And it's the number Mustang Sally used when she called Jennifer."

Sheri picked up the phone and stared at it. "So why not just call her back?"

"Unfortunately, I can't. Sally's call to Jennifer was from a blocked number. But I do have another idea."

"Don't tell me." Sheri put the phone down and pushed it in my direction. "You want to assume Jennifer's identity and try to find Sally, don't you?"

"Why not? Mustang Sally doesn't know what Jennifer looks or sounds like. The phone's so new Jennifer hadn't even set up her voicemail yet. And they've never met in person. All she could possibly know about Jennifer is what she read in the chat room. And if I don't find Mustang Sally soon, someone else will."

I reached for the open bottle of wine between us and filled Sheri's glass. "But I'm going to need your help."

"What do you need?"

"Monitor the site. Type in the phrase Sally gave to Jennifer and cross your fingers. With any luck, Sally will take the bait."

# CHAPTER 24

*Marcus Reddings Murdered.* For the second day in a row, the story of Reddings' death was headlined above the fold in the *LA Times*. The coroner's report had found scratch marks and bruising on his body, and the police were now reporting signs of a struggle inside the apartment. The story was driving KNST's morning show. Listeners were calling in with all kinds of bizarre theories. Everything from why one of LA's richest men would never have voluntarily taken a nose dive off the top of Ava Yablonski's high-rise apartment building, to his being a victim of organized crime or perhaps a murder-for-hire by his wife.

My cell phone rang before I'd even reached the station. Tyler wanted to see me in his office. A copy of the newspaper was on his desk when I walked in.

Without looking up, Tyler barked at me, the incessant sound of his fingers hitting the keyboard in the background, like pigeons pecking for food.

"I need you to get Andrea Reddings on the phone again. Our morning team's got nothing. Just a bunch of blowhards calling in with conspiracy theories."

I leaned against the doorway. Despite the fact Andrea Reddings had given me her phone number, I didn't hold out much hope the woman would talk to me again. Sunday night had been Chase's doing. He had convinced her she needed to get the news out, to stay a step ahead of the gossip they both knew would follow. But now that the news was out, I doubted a woman as cold and calculating as Andrea would feel she needed me.

"I can try. But no guarantees."

"Make it happen, Childs." Tyler stopped typing long enough to grab the newspaper off his desk and shove it in my direction. "Get her to talk, and you've got yourself a seat in the studio with the morning team. At least for today."

I dialed the number Andrea had used to call into the station. I was surprised when by the fourth ring neither her butler nor any of her help had answered. My guess was that she'd instructed that nobody pick up the phone. I let it ring a few more times, and then, as I was about to hang up Andrea answered the phone herself. I recognized the firm, flat delivery of her voice.

"Whatever you want, I'm not interested in talking—"

"Ms. Reddings, please, this is Carol Childs with KNST. I was hoping I might talk with you."

"I'm sure you are. And I assume the purpose of your call this morning concerns the story in the paper?"

"It does." There was a long pause. I wondered if she was debating whether or not to hang up or if she had simply walked away from the phone and left me dangling. "Ms. Reddings?"

There was another pause, a heavy sigh, and then finally, "You realize,—other than that little chat we had on Sunday—I have not spoken with any reporter in town, including the *Times*. They didn't have so much as one quote from me. And I'm not about to give them one either. Not with all the photos they've run over the years of Marcus with his various female companions. If it weren't for the fact you're a friend of Chase's, there's no way I'd talk to you. But I do owe the man a favor."

"I'd be very grateful. And, like I said Sunday night, it might be good for people to hear your side. I can help you do that."

"Save it, Ms. Childs. You're overselling. I've been listening to your station. I've heard what your listeners are saying about Marcus and me. How they think I killed him in a jealous rage. Believe me, if they only knew what—" Andrea stopped herself short and exhaled, as though she'd been debating that very thought. Then said, "If I do agree to speak with you on the air, I've got a few conditions."

"What do you need?"

Andrea Reddings wasn't exactly a sympathetic figure. Her voice alone was off-putting, harsh, and menacing. But after hearing this morning's listeners rant on about her husband's underhanded business dealings and his numerous affairs, part of me pitied the woman. It had to be tough to live such a public life, where everything she did was subject to the public's scrutiny.

"I'd like you to remind your listeners that Marcus and I were very much together. The story in *The Times* this morning focused on Marcus' affair with Ms. Yablonski and referred to her apartment as their love nest. That's a lie. As I already told you, Marcus and I had mended our relationship, and the proceedings for our divorce had been withdrawn from the court."

"I can do that."

"And, I'd like to propose a few questions of my own. Things I think your listeners might find of interest. If you can promise me that, Ms. Childs, I'd be happy to answer a few questions. And if not—"

"Not a problem. You've got it." I answered quickly. I didn't want to give Andrea a chance to say anything else. I was afraid she would change her mind. I told her not to go anywhere. That I'd call her back in the next couple of minutes. Then I hung up the phone and ran down the hallway to the newsroom.

"Reddings is a go!" I yelled at Tyler as I entered his office, my heart beating like a mix-master. I leaned up against the door and tried to catch my breath. I couldn't believe the opportunity. Twice in forty-eight hours I'd spoken with Andrea Reddings, and now I was about to have her on the air again. Nobody in LA had had such luck.

Fifteen minutes later, I took a seat between Kit and Carson in the studio and immediately felt as though I had entered a man cave. Sports memorabilia was everywhere. Baseball caps, team towels, and a copy of KNST's billboard, with the words Fake Right/Fake Left, splashed across a tightly framed close-up of a couple Double-D's in a bikini top, hung on the wall behind the console. All of which was very fitting for two former college football jocks turned broadcasters. Fate had sidelined Kit, a once hopeful Raider linebacker, with a knee injury, and Carson had never been big enough or fast enough for the pros. But together they talked enough smack with listeners about news and sports that Tyler had given them a shot at the morning show.

Kit set up the interview, his voice hard and fast like he was calling a game.

"All right, fans. You've been listening to this morning's top story. And we've been listening to you. We've heard the accusations. The conspiracy theories. Marcus Reddings is dead. Possibly murdered. And now, coming up next, we've got the wife, Andrea Reddings, in an exclusive interview with KNST's late-night news host Carol Childs. Stay tuned."

Kit cut his mic and addressed Carson, ignoring me completely. The two were more interested in returning to a private conversation about the upcoming bowl game for Super Sunday. When we returned, Carson introduced me.

I leaned forward and welcomed Andrea to the show. I reminded those listening that I'd spoken with her on my show Sunday night.

"At that time, Ms. Reddings, you mentioned you and your husband had stopped divorce proceedings and—"

"And we were living together, as husband and wife. Which is why I take great exception to the article in the *Times* this morning describing Marcus' apartment with Ms. Yablonski as their love nest."

"I can imagine that was quite upsetting."

"The truth is, Ms. Yablonski is nothing but a money-hungry vixen. That apartment was only part of what she had her claws into. And while your listeners' recent comments concerning Marcus' death appear to have cast suspicion upon me, I'd like to introduce an item of my own I believe they'll find equally as compelling."

"That's fair. We're listening."

"My attorney informed me this morning that Ms. Yablonski had recently taken out a life insurance policy on my husband for seven million dollars, naming herself as the beneficiary."

I gagged. *Seven million?*

"How is that even possible? He was married to you."

"Anything's possible, Ms. Childs. The question is, is it legal? It's called an insurable interest, and my attorneys are checking into the matter now. Ms. Yablonski is a lot of things, but a dummy she's not. She claims Marcus was paying her mortgage and supporting her. I'm quite sure whatever papers Marcus signed, he had no idea what he was doing."

"And you're convinced this policy has something to do with your husband's murder?"

"I believe Ms. Yablonski was upset when she heard Marcus and I had reconciled. The girl thought Marcus would marry her. And she knew if Marcus died before that happened, she'd lose everything. The apartment. Her fancy cars. Not to mention her monthly income. I suspect the insurance policy was a last-ditch effort on her part to protect what gifts Marcus had given her."

"I don't understand. Were the gifts in question?"

"Everything Marcus and I own is in a trust. He couldn't have violated that trust without my consent. The attorneys will no doubt fight it out, but it's my understanding any monies he used to purchase anything—gifts or otherwise—is essentially mine."

"And you think this new insurance policy is evidence that Ms. Yablonski may have had something to do with your husband's death?"

"Carol, what I want your listeners to understand is that I didn't kill my husband. I was home when the police came by to inform me of his death. And my butler can verify I never left my home that night. And, frankly, I don't imagine Ms. Yablonski killed him either, at least not personally. I doubt she'd have the nerve for it, much less the strength to push him off the balcony of her apartment. Marcus was a big man. He might have been old, but he wasn't frail. But there are other ways in which she could've arranged for him to fall."

"Are you saying Ms. Yablonski may have hired someone?"

"I could certainly understand it. Marcus was a very powerful, attractive, and exasperating man. He had a way of driving a woman crazy. I'm not proud to say I once considered taking out a contract on him myself. I even went so far as to buy a gun. But a woman I had gone to for counseling, and who I thought might be persuaded to do such a thing, refused."

"You sound like you've been through a lot."

"Enough so I was going to do it myself. But thankfully, a close friend talked me out of it."

*A close friend?* I wanted to ask but didn't dare. Not on the air. Instead, I said, "And still you stuck with him all those years."

"It wasn't exactly a bed of roses. Marriages have their ups and downs. But Marcus and I, we were on the up. As far as Ms. Yablonski goes, I'm sure it's only a matter of time before the police find her, and when they do, we'll have her story. Then let's see who your listeners think is responsible for my husband's death."

Kit signaled me we had sixty seconds.

I asked Andrea if she had one more thing she wanted to say. "Only that I didn't kill my husband. He wasn't perfect, but I understood him, and in what may sound very strange to some, I still loved him." I wrapped the interview with Andrea's final statement and signed off, then left the studio and hurried back to my office. I wanted to call Chase.

If Chase was the *close friend* who had stopped Andrea from murdering her husband, I wanted to know why he hadn't told me. He must have been waiting by the phone. He picked up before I even heard a ring.

"Hey, Carol. Good interview. I was listening—"

"Why didn't you tell me Andrea tried to kill her husband?"

"Hold on there, Reporter Girl. That was a long time ago and—"

"And what? You didn't think it was important?" I picked up a pencil and began scratching a note to myself. I wanted to ask Andrea more about the woman who had counseled her.

"Andrea was hardly the first woman who found out her husband was cheating on her and wanted to kill him. It's not an unusual reaction."

I bit down hard on the pencil to keep from screaming. "But she didn't just try to kill her husband, Chase, she tried to hire someone to do it for her. A woman. And not just any woman, but a woman who counseled her and who she thought might be the type of person to do such a thing. What if there's a connection?"

"Not every person who's ever been approached about a contract slaying's connected. It's not like there's a 1-800 number for it."

I tossed my pencil across the desk. The man was driving me nuts. "I don't agree. I think Andrea knows Mustang Sally, and I think at one time Andrea wanted Sally to murder her husband for her."

"Carol, hold on. I don't know anything about Andrea ever trying to arrange a hit on her husband. Yes, she bought a gun. She told me she wanted to shoot him, but I talked her out of it. And far as Mustang Sally goes, if she knew her back then, she's never mentioned her to me or anything about a contract. But go ahead and ask her yourself."

"Oh, believe me, I plan to."

# CHAPTER 25

After hanging up on Chase, I tried Andrea Reddings' number. The call went immediately to voicemail, and I left a message. But I didn't hold out a lot of hope she'd return my call. Andrea didn't strike me as the type of woman who'd avail herself to idle chitchat. She had allowed me to use her to get what word she wanted out, but until she needed me again, I doubted I'd hear back.

Even so, I must have checked my voicemail a dozen times, running back between news breaks in the studio to my office to see if just maybe Andrea Reddings had returned my call. She hadn't. But later that afternoon, when I was in the studio, a story came across the wire that so surprised me I nearly stumbled in my delivery.

*This just in...Police have arrested A-Ava...Ava Yablonski, the former girlfriend of LA Stars owner Marcus Reddings, as she waited to board a private jet at an airport in Palm Springs this afternoon. Also taken in for questioning was her travel companion, Ralph Watson, a maintenance man for the apartment building where Ms. Yablonski lives. The two have been the subject of a massive search surrounding the murder of Marcus Reddings.*

As soon as I finished my broadcast, I returned to my office and placed the call. If the story of Ava Yablonski's arrest was already on the newswire, I knew the police would have also alerted Ms. Reddings. And this time, I was confident she would want to talk.

A youthful female voice answered. Her demeanor was most professional. I assumed her to be an assistant.

"Reddings' residence. May I ask who's calling, please?"

I introduced myself and explained I was calling from KNST News and Sports Talk radio, and Ms. Reddings and I had talked earlier that morning.

"Please allow me to see if Ms. Reddings is available."

There was a long silence before Andrea came on the line.

"You don't give up easily, Ms. Childs. I assume you've called back to ask if I've heard the news?"

"I have, and I was hoping I might be able to get a statement from you."

"And what would you like me to say? That I'm not surprised? I gave you that much this morning."

"How about something else? Ralph Watson, maybe. He worked as a maintenance man for the apartment building where Ava Yablonski lived, a building you and your husband own. Do you think she hired him to push your husband off the balcony?"

"Ms. Childs, I don't believe the police make arrests without some form of evidence."

"Then you do believe there's a connection?"

"Would it surprise you to know I've had evidence all along that shows Ava Yablonski has been involved with Ralph Watson while simultaneously carrying on an affair with my husband?"

I was beginning to think there wasn't much Andrea Reddings didn't know about her husband or his affairs. But I decided to keep that to myself.

"How?" I asked. "How did you know?"

I imagined her grinning confidently with the phone to her ear.

"I had the security tapes from outside Ms. Yablonski's apartment pulled. The tapes show that Mr. Watson made numerous visits—all hours of the day—to the apartment when Ms. Yablonski was home, and again the day Marcus was murdered. They show him entering her apartment shortly before Marcus arrived. And believe me, there were no maintenance reports filed to back up any of these visits. I'm quite certain the police will find he was lying in wait."

"That sounds pretty damning."

"I'm not a fool, Ms. Childs. When you have as much to protect as I do, you cover your bases. Now, unless there's something else you called to ask about, I'm afraid I'm very busy. I've my husband's memorial to plan."

"Actually, Ms. Reddings, there is." I cleared my throat and went for it. "I was hoping we might talk about something else or someone really. Someone I think you might know or did know in the past."

"And whom might that be?"

"The woman you said you tried to contract to kill your husband."

"You mean Sally?"

My hand gripped the receiver so tight I thought I might break it. "You know her?"

"Ms. Childs, I'm hardly prepared to have this conversation on the phone. But if it'll help to convince your listeners I'm not responsible for my husband's death, perhaps you'd like to come by, and we can chat quietly about my past. Inquisitive as you are, I doubt you'll have any trouble finding the address."

The address for the Reddings' residence was a matter a public record. Not at all difficult to find. In addition to its listing with the Los Angeles County Recorder's Office, it was on every Star Sighting Map in LA, Marcus Reddings, owner of the LA Stars. What made it unique, however, was that there were addresses in Los Angeles for the rich and famous, and then there are *addresses*. By that, I meant some of them were beyond believable. The Reddings' estate, located just north of Beverly Hills, was in an area known as Billionaire's Row. And the home itself, if one could call it that, was more like an eighteenth-century French chateau, hidden behind twenty-foot, ivy-covered walls. Decorative iron gates with a coat of arms featuring an angry lion made it more like an embassy than a private residence. Miraculously, the gates swung open, as though some magic eye knew who I was and had seen me approach.

Inside the gates, I parked my Jeep in the circular drive between what I guessed to be an eighteenth-century fountain with a life-sized statue of Venus de Milo surrounded by jets of spewing water and a huge stone gabled entry to the front door. Obviously, the Reddings weren't concerned about the California drought. I rang the bell. A soft mellow tone, like elegant Tibetan wind chimes, sounded, and moments later, an elderly gentleman answered. He looked like he could have come directly from central casting, gray hair and dressed in a three-piece suit with tails. I didn't think people still had butlers, but there was no denying his position.

Without waiting for me to introduce myself, I was asked to follow him. We walked down a long vaulted corridor with statues and works of art and into the parlor, a stately looking room with an ornate wood ceiling, paned-glass windows, and paneled walls. I had once visited Hearst Castle and learned that William Randolph Hearst had raided Europe's best castles to furnish his home. I wondered if the Reddings had done the same.

"Would you be in need of anything, Ms. Childs? Coffee? Tea?"

"No," I said. "But thank you."

He nodded politely and said Ms. Reddings would be along shortly before leaving the room.

I took a seat in one of the wingback chairs in front of a large, pane glass window overlooking a well-manicured backyard with another fountain and more marble statues and waited. On the table beside me, a small antique clock began to chime. Three p.m. It wasn't more than six or seven inches high and no bigger than the palm of my hand, but with its delicate cloisonné finish and gold enamel leafing, it was too stunning to resist. I picked it up. The inscription on the bottom read, *To Andrea, love Marcus, for old times' sake.*

"Nice, isn't it?" Andrea entered the room from behind me.

Startled, I placed the clock back on the table and started to stand.

"Please, don't. Sit." She waved a thin arm above her head as she approached. Her hair, swept up in a French twist like a silver helmet, didn't move.

In person, Ms. Reddings was older and smaller than I expected. Reed-thin with crepe paper skin. She walked with a slight bend, her shoulders slightly forward, but with the steely determination of a woman not to be messed with.

"That little bauble there," she said, pointing to the clock on the table, "was a gift from Marcus, for our tenth anniversary. The man could be very generous when it suited him. Particularly when he was feeling guilty. Let that be a lesson to you. You should always keep your men feeling guilty."

I didn't say anything.

"Go ahead, look around. I have a house full of expensive apologies from all over the world."

Even to my untrained eye, I could recognize the treasures. A Degas, a Remington bronze, and above the mantel, a painting by Peggy Hopper, a serene beach scene with a reclining native girl with lei in her hair beneath swaying palm trees.

"That there," she said pointing to the painting, "is one my favorites. He bought that for me along with a little island retreat I used to visit. But you're not here to talk about my collectibles, are you? You want to know about Sally."

"I do."

"Then why don't we start with you telling me how you knew?"

"I didn't. I took a chance. The night you called the station about Marcus' death, there was another caller right after you. She had called once before, and I didn't put a lot of stock in what she was saying. I thought she was some late-night crazy. But then she said something that really threw me." I paused and looked directly into Andrea's eyes, my hands gripping the sides of the wingback chair. "She said you were right about the contract killings. She said some women needed her help. And that's why they had their own special court of appeals. I told her I didn't understand, and she said, 'but *Ms. Reddings does.*' Those were her exact words. 'Ms. Reddings does.'" Andrea glanced out the window, and I continued. "At first, I dismissed it. Like I said, crazy, right? But then this morning, when you were on the air again, you mentioned something about asking a woman you had gone to for counseling for help. Specifically, you said you wanted to contract with someone to kill your husband. I put two and two together and took a guess. I'm hoping I'm not wrong."

"I'd say it was a lucky guess, Ms. Childs." Andrea went over to the bar, opened a crystal decanter, and poured herself a glass of scotch.

"You want one?"

"No, thank you."

"Ms. Childs, before we go any further, you need to understand, this meeting between us is strictly off the record. If you report *anything* about what I'm about to tell you, I'll make you look like a fool. And more importantly, you'll never work in this town again. You understand?"

I nodded. With Andrea's money and power, the right word from her and my career would be dead.

"Say it."

I raised my hand like I was about to take a pledge. How many times did I have to promise never to breathe a word about Sally? Since first learning about the woman, my job had been threatened twice, once by DJ and now her.

"I promise," I said. "This is off the record. Not a word."

Andrea took a sip from her glass, then put it down on the bar, her eyes never leaving mine.

"It was several years ago. I'd had it with Marcus, his controlling nature, always telling me he was right and I was wrong, that I was too sensitive. Not to mention his philandering. I was reeling from his latest affair. Finally, I decided I needed to do something about it. I could have gone anywhere, but in the midst of my depression, I found this online self-help group. Quite frankly, I liked the anonymity of it. I'd come to think of myself as a mentally and emotionally abused wife, and I didn't like it." Andrea paused and took another sip of her drink.

"Surprised?" Her eyes searched the room like she didn't expect me to believe someone so well-heeled could possibly feel trapped in an abusive relationship. "It's not just the poor and downtrodden, Ms. Childs. Women of all breeding and walks of life can find themselves trapped with an abusive partner."

I shifted in my chair and told her I'd covered enough stories to know she was right. That I'd dealt with high-profile Hollywood agents who wanted to bury stories about their client's bad behavior, and how both the police and the media were often encouraged to lose track of reports that showed certain high-profile personalities in a bad light.

"Then I suspect you'll understand why I felt safe within this group. Nobody knew my name, and I never knew theirs. I would have been humiliated if they did. Eventually, I was invited to join with several of the women for an in-person, semi-private session. It was there that I met a woman who introduced herself to me as Sally. I have no idea if that's her real name, but it's the name she used." Andrea took another sip of her drink and stared out the window. "She explained to me she was part of a secret panel of women. She called it a tribunal, some type of high court, whose job it was to review select cases of women in crisis and offer to help those chosen to find a better life."

"Did you understand what it was she was talking about? What her solution was?"

"It didn't take much to figure it out. Most of the women in the group were desperate to escape their situation. Some had started over so many times, they were ready to give up. In each of their cases they had been stalked, and when they were found, the abuse would begin all over again." Andrea went back to the bar and refilled her glass.

"These other women Sally talked about, the ones on her secret panel, did you ever meet them?"

"No." Andrea shook her head. "My case, as awful as it was, didn't qualify for the type of help the group passed out." Andrea took a sip of her drink. "I'm afraid Sally didn't have a lot of patience for me. She said I had put myself in my own sad situation, and if I wanted out, she saw no reason I couldn't leave. I had the money. I had the means. I'd obviously chosen to stay. And that was my problem." Andrea twisted the glass in her hand.

"You sound angry."

"Angry?" She laughed. "I was furious. I'd never been turned down for anything in my life. I remember when I left that night I swore if Mustang Sally wouldn't kill Marcus, I would. That's when I called your boyfriend, Chase."

"He's not my boyfriend, Ms. Reddings. He's—"

"A friend?" She winked at me and took another sip of her drink. "With benefits, perhaps?"

"No." I shook my head adamantly. Not that the thoughts hadn't crept across my mind, but I wasn't about to admit to them. Not in the middle of a case with so much at stake. "It's a professional relationship. Nothing more."

"Too bad. Chase is a good man. I don't mind telling you if I were thirty years younger..." She raised a brow suggestively. "Well now, I suppose that doesn't concern you. What does is that I offered him all kinds of money to take care of Marcus for me. But he refused."

"After that, you never saw Mustang Sally again?"

"Technically, that would be correct. I didn't ever see her again, but I have been in touch with her." Andrea paused and glanced out the window, then back at me as though she were evaluating what she was about to say. "You have to understand, Ms. Childs, no one had ever talked to me like that. Most people wouldn't dare. But I couldn't put Sally and the stories I had heard out of my mind. After a while, I decided she was right. Horrible as things were with Marcus, I was living the life I'd chosen. Marcus didn't deserve to die because I didn't want to be married to him anymore. The truth is I liked being Mrs. Marcus Reddings."

The surprise must have registered on my face. Andrea took stock of my reaction. She walked to the chair opposite me and sat down.

"The difference is, Ms. Childs, I had choices. Most of the other women I'd met didn't. Finally, it seemed to me if Sally couldn't help me, maybe I could help her."

"How?"

"Money, Ms. Childs. It may be the root of all evil, but it's the bedrock of many a charity, mine included."

"And Sally's one of your charities?"

"I didn't think the woman had anything but an old car and the clothes on her back. For all I knew, she could've been living in her car when we met. I simply made sure her coffers were full when she needed them."

"Then you must know how to get hold of her."

"It's not like I can pick up the phone and call. In fact, I haven't spoken to Sally in years. And I know the cell number I had for her back then wouldn't be working. Not anymore. She used disposable phones with a different number each time. Mustang Sally was as much an abused victim as those she helped. She was afraid of being found. The woman has as many enemies as she has friends."

"But if she's one of your charities, you must have a way of getting in touch with her."

"That doesn't mean I know where she lives. My guess would be below the grid. What I do know is that she has—or had—a son. An adult child, if you know what I mean. He was what we used to call developmentally challenged. He was with her that day we met, went everywhere with her."

"But even not knowing where or how she lives, you're still able to funnel money to her?"

"Giving money, Ms. Childs, is never a problem. You'd be amazed at the number of ways people can launder money without anyone knowing."

I sat back and crossed my arms.

"How do you do it?"

"Every month, on the eighth, I put a bag of small bills together and leave it in a post office box that both she and I have a key to. Simple as that. I own the box. She picks up whatever is in it. Nobody questions it. People in my position seldom have their mail delivered to their homes."

"And you know what she uses the money for?" I said.

"I've never asked. I assume she uses it to help with her day-to-day expenses."

"It helps finance a murder-for-hire program."

"A necessary evil, Ms. Childs. And from your questions, I can see you've already spent time investigating. So I don't need to tell you the police can't stop these men. As far as I'm concerned, the money goes to helping women start over. Find a new life, go back to school, pay attorney fees, buy groceries. Whatever they need."

"I'm not naive to what you're saying, Ms. Reddings. I know the police can't do much to help an abuse victim. But I am concerned about Sally. She's called the radio station on more than one occasion, and not just my show. It's as though she's had some kind of mental break. She's starting to share about who she is and what she does."

"That's not good, Ms. Childs. Not at all."

"No. It's not. And if she continues, someone is going to get wise to what she's all about. Which is why I have to find her and fast. As you say, Sally's got enemies, and I'm afraid time's running short."

Andrea glanced out the window, a look of concern on her face. Then, standing up, she reached for a small butler's bell on the table between us.

"I'm afraid there's nothing more I can tell you. I've already told you more than I should."

She rang the bell, and I stood up.

"But if you know anything, anything at all that might help—"

"Ms. Childs, I will do what I can from my end to find Sally. But you need to know, if my name is connected to this in any way, it won't bode well for you. You understand me?"

I stood up and nodded. "Believe me, you're not the first person to tell me that."

"Good. Then I think we're done here. The butler will show you out."

# CHAPTER 26

Halfway down the drive from the Reddings' estate, with the view of the chateau still in my rearview mirror, my cell phone rang.

Before I could even say hello, Chase asked, in a very know-it-all kind of way, how it had gone with Andrea. "She have anything to say about Sally?"

I bit my tongue. I had told Chase I planned to talk to Andrea, but I certainly hadn't shared with him that I'd gone to see her. "What, are you following me?" I asked.

"Don't have to. Tyler told me. I called to get some information about the station, and he mentioned you'd gone to visit with her."

I exhaled like I was breathing fire. How many times did I have to tell Tyler not to share my itinerary with anyone, particularly Chase?

"But tell me, I can't wait to hear how right I was about Andrea. That she doesn't know Mustang Sally and never did."

I fought back the urge to tell him differently. "You're right. She wasn't much help."

I wasn't about to share with him what Andrea had told me about Sally. I was beginning to feel what information I had concerning Mustang Sally was mine and mine alone. And whatever information Chase had, at least what I could get from him, was mine too.

"Well, don't feel too badly there, Blondie. I've got something."

"On Sally?" My hands clutched the steering wheel.

"Sure do. In fact, I think I figured out where she's hiding. Just a matter of time now."

"Really?" I glanced at the clock on my dashboard. It was four fifteen, and I needed to be back at the station in time for the five o'clock news. Only a miracle would allow me enough time to head Chase off if what he was telling me were true. "How much time?"

"Aren't you going to ask me how I did it?"

I relaxed and eased my foot off the accelerator. If Chase wanted to impress me with his investigative techniques, I felt certain Mustang Sally wasn't in any immediate danger of being picked up.

"If you promise not to call me Blondie again, sure. Spill the beans. How did you find her?"

"I've been listening to your station nonstop. Like you do the police scanners. I kept thinking if old Sal had called twice maybe she'd call again. And that's when I heard her. No denying that voice. No other like it. Heard her midday during the Dr. Sam Show." Chase paused, like I should be putting two and two together, but so far nothing was ringing any bells.

"Go on."

"He was talking about the West Nile Virus outbreak and how it's pretty much under control. Then Mustang Sally called in and said she didn't think so. That her son was dead because of it. And you know what that means?"

"No. I'm not sure I do." I wasn't getting the significance of how Sally's call to Dr. Sam had revealed her location. But it was clear to me Chase thought he had something and was compiling information about her as fast as I was. Or maybe faster.

"It means," he said, "if Sally's able to hear the station during the day and at night, she's gotta be living within the station's primary daytime signal area. If she weren't, she'd never have heard Dr. Sam's show in the afternoon and called in. The station's daytime signal wouldn't have reached her." Chase paused like he expected me to start jumping up and down.

"And?"

"And I started thinking. If Sally's son died of West Nile Virus, she had to be living in an area where there were a lot of mosquitos. All the cases so far have been reported in wide open spaces where there's standing water and horses. Which means she's living in a rural setting, somewhere within the station's daytime signal area. That narrows the search down big time. It's like she's living in our own backyard." I had to admit that was pretty good detective work. KNST's nighttime signal was three times bigger than the daytime signal and covered most of southern California. The FCC restricted the daytime signal to a much smaller footprint.

"All right, but the daytime signal is still huge. Better than twenty-five hundred miles. Everything from north of the valley to the Pacific Palisades. How could you possibly know exactly where she is?"

"Because when I was talking with Tyler I asked him to email me a map of the station's signal area, and then I did a small overlay map showing where all the West Nile victims had died. I'm figuring she's holed up somewhere in the Antelope Valley, just north of the city. Maybe in one of those little no-tell motels or a guesthouse out behind somebody's ranch."

"Nice," I said.

"Won't take long now. All I've got to do is match up the map with my social media contacts—those I asked to call into your show the first time—and see who lives out that way. Then I can start canvassing the area. Want to join me?"

# CHAPTER 27

"Absolutely. When you've got Mustang Sally in your crosshairs, count me in. I want to be there."

I couldn't think of a better response. If Chase was right, I had to find a way to stop him or at least to slow him down. But right now I was thirty minutes away from my five o'clock newscast, and I needed to hurry back to the station. With no time to talk, I suggested we catch up later and hung up the phone.

I was almost through KNST's security gates when my reporter's bag began to buzz like a rattlesnake on the seat next to me. Only this time, it wasn't my cell phone, but Jennifer's. I forced myself to focus. Aside from me, there were the only two people who had Jennifer's number. Mustang Sally and Jennifer's fiancé, Jason. If it was Mustang Sally, it could only mean one thing. Sheri had succeeded in posting Jennifer's message in the Butterflies' chat room, and Mustang Sally was responding.

I pulled into the parking lot, reached into my bag and fumbled for the cell. The Caller ID was blocked. But the message was clearly from Sally. *We have a meeting with the tribunal. Tomorrow Night. UCLA. The old Medical Center. West Wing, Room 518. Come alone. 9 p.m.*

I placed Jennifer's cell back on the seat beside me, picked up my phone, and called Sheri. I still had a few minutes before I needed to be inside the station.

"Mustang Sally just texted me. She's set up a meeting with her tribunal."

"For real? I've been posting on the website all morning. I had no idea if Sally would see it or not." The angst in Sheri's voice was palpable. "Where?"

"UCLA. The old Medical Center. Tomorrow night."

"Oh my God, Carol. That place is like a morgue."

"I can't think about that now. But you and I need to meet. Your place, tonight. If Misty hears us talking, she may leak something to Chase. Not that she'd do it deliberately, but with the way things are with her, I never know. And I'm going to need you to help me."

I threw my phone in the bag and headed into the station, my mind racing. I needed to talk with DJ as soon as possible, and I also wanted to have a serious chat with Tyler about not sharing my whereabouts with Chase. But first, I had a news update to do. I went directly to the studio.

Fortunately, a top of the hour newscast was brief. A CliffsNotes version of the day's news. At best, it was five minutes, four if there was a commercial break, and there were seldom more than five or six stories, including sound bites. I breezed into the news booth with time to spare. The computer screen on the news desk was already populated with stories Tyler had chosen in my absence. I put on my headphones and glanced through the glass into the studio. I had to forcibly lock my jaw to keep it from falling open.

Sitting next to Big John, KNST's afternoon drive personality, was Ben Silva, the impenetrable Saint Silva. With the station directive not to discuss Silva's accident, I couldn't have been more surprised if it were Mother Teresa herself.

They were in the final strokes of an interview. From what I could gather, Silva had asked for the opportunity to talk about the accident, no doubt trying to put an end to any speculation he might've been involved. His comments were focused on his wife's accountability and well-being.

John asked about the arrest.

"Something like this is always a tragedy," Silva said. "For all parties. It's unfortunate my wife chose to drive me to work that night. As I told the police, neither of us saw the young woman. All I can remember is that she darted out in front of us. We stopped and checked, but we couldn't see anything. It was pitch black. At the time, I thought my wife had just nicked the back of her bike, and that she had just picked it up and left.

"And then you went home."

"Yes. It was getting late, and my wife insisted we go back to the house and I take her car to work. She returned with my car, to the scene of the accident. It was then she saw the young woman's bike. It was thrown some twenty feet into the bushes, at which point she called me, and I told her to call the police."

I didn't believe a word of what he was saying. It didn't make sense someone like Silva would let his wife drive him to work, much less in his prized t-top corvette. Silva was six-two, his wife barely five feet. I doubted she could even see over the steering wheel. I couldn't prove it, but maybe Chase could. I made a mental note to mention it to him. After all, I had promised to call him back, and I was searching for a way to slow him down while I concentrated on Sally.

After I had finished my report, I went immediately to DJ's office. Her assistant, who normally guarded the door and scheduled her appointments, was gone and the door to her office was open. With no one to keep me out, I tapped lightly on the door and announced my presence.

"Ms. Presley?"

DJ smiled up at me. "Carol. Please, come in." She waved to me with the back of her hand, her long fingers fanning her face. "We've just been discussing you."

*We?*

I stepped into the office and noticed Tyler sitting on the sofa to the side of DJ's desk.

Granted, I wanted to talk to Tyler, but I was desperate to speak with DJ first, and what I needed to share with DJ was definitely not the conversation I planned to have with Tyler.

Tyler looked over his shoulder as I entered the room.

"Yes, Carol, come in. I've been telling DJ what a successful week you're having. What with that interview with Ms. Redding yesterday and your show Sunday night. Good work. Must be that new detective I asked you to work with. Things going well with the two of you?"

Nope. This was definitely not the conversation I wanted to have. DJ knew nothing of Chase. Even worse, if she thought I might have shared information about Mustang Sally with a PI, I'd be finished.

"Good." I nodded my head nervously and started to back out of the room, making excuses for interrupting them and suggesting I come back later.

DJ stood up, her eyes pinned to mine. "No. Please. Stay. I do need a word with you, and Tyler was just leaving."

Tyler got up and high-fived me on the way out. After he had left, DJ asked me to close the door.

I leaned back against it with my hands behind me. "I've made contact with Sally. I'm meeting her tomorrow night."

"Are you going to need any help?" DJ reached into her desk and took out a small pad of paper.

"No. I'm sure it'll be fine. I've arranged to pick her up for coffee. When I do, I'll bring her to you."

I wasn't about to share with DJ the truth about how I'd managed to arrange a meeting with Sally. While I hadn't shared DJ's secret, I feared telling her anymore would reveal that I had already said too much to too many people. Instead, I let DJ assume I'd gotten lucky and Mustang Sally had called the station and suggested we meet.

"Perfect." DJ scribbled a number down on the pad and handed it to me. "This is a burner cell. I don't want anything traced to me in case things don't go down the way we've planned."

"What could go wrong?" I asked. "It's just coffee, right?"

"You don't need to worry about Sally, Carol. She'll be just fine. I'm not going to hurt her. I only want to help save Sally from herself. Call me when you've picked her up, and I'll meet you wherever you like. And remember, don't say a thing about this. Not to anyone."

# CHAPTER 28

It helped to have a best friend who grew up in Hollywood and with whom I could brainstorm things like kidnappings. Although I didn't realize how much until I arrived at Sheri's house and she explained to me the flaw in my plan.

"No way you're going to meet Mustang Sally dressed like that."

"Why? Sally doesn't know what Jennifer looks like. And I doubt she'd know me, even if I introduced myself as Carol Childs, KNST's late-night host for *The Soap Box*. You know, reporter extraordinaire." I opened my arms wide and smiled. I was feeling a bit full of myself, giddy at the prospect of kidnapping Sally and beating Chase to the punch.

"You don't get it, do you?"

We were standing in Sheri's closet, a good-sized wardrobe that ran the length of the house and was jam-packed with clothes, shoes, and hatboxes. Sheri was a clotheshorse. She had tons of designer pieces in various sizes and colors, plus a rack of costumes from her father's movies. She spun me around to a full-length mirror.

"Look at yourself, Carol. You don't exactly look like an abuse victim on the run."

I stared at myself in the mirror and pulled my hair up in a bun atop my head. Maybe a different hairstyle might help. "Abuse victims don't necessarily look abused," I said.

"Yes, but one on the run needs to appear desperate. Disheveled."

I supposed she was right. If Jennifer was any example, when I had last seen her, she appeared as though she had been sleeping in her clothes. And while I was no fashionista, by comparison, I did look a little too put together.

Sheri grabbed the collar of my coat, helped me take it off, and threw it on a lounge chair in the center of the closet.

"Try this." From the rack, she grabbed an old western duster. No doubt from one of her father's movie shoots. The long jacket looked as though it had been used in a gunfight. It included what I hoped were fake bloodstains and what was a small bullet hole in the shoulder.

I put my finger through the hole. "A little too desperate, don't you think?"

"Not if we cover it with a scarf. Maybe something like this." Sheri pulled a black knit shawl from one of the drawers beneath the rack and threw it over my shoulders. "Now kick off your shoes. You're going to need tennis shoes and not good ones. Something old, like these."

She handed me a pair of beat up old high-tops. Fortunately, Sheri and I were the same size. I may have been six inches taller, but size-wise, from head to toe, we were a match.

I slipped them on and stared at my reflection in the mirror. If disheveled or one-stop-short-of-homeless was the look we were going for, I was it.

"One more thing," Sheri said.

"What?"

"The hair. We need to change it."

From the top of the shelf, Sheri pulled down a hat box full of wigs and tossed a few on the floor. Blonde. Platinum. Red. Then finding what she wanted, thrust it in my direction.

"Try this."

I pushed my hair beneath a short dishwater 'do shingled in the back and longer in the front, with stringy curls to my collar. I turned and stared at myself in the mirror. I looked like I'd just come in from the rain.

From behind me, Sheri put her hands on my shoulders and pushed down.

"What?" I said.

"You need to slouch."

"Slouch?"

"Like you've got the world on your shoulders, Carol. You're

scared. Frightened. You've been running. If you're going to pull this off, you've got to embrace the role."

"What, are you directing now?" I looked at Sheri. "I'm beginning to think you missed your calling."

"Trust me. You don't grow up the daughter of a director without learning a thing or two about dressing for the part."

"Obviously not," I said. "Anything else?"

"A black eye."

"No way!" I backed up, my hands in front of my face.

"Relax. I'm not going to hit you. But you're definitely going to need it. And it's easy enough to do with makeup. You have an ace bandage at home?"

I sighed and nodded yes.

"Wrap your wrist with it. It'll look like it's sprained and they'll think he did it. We can do your makeup before you go tomorrow. "

"We?"

"I'm going with you."

There was no point in arguing. If Sally didn't want to go with me or resisted for any reason, I was going to need Sheri's help. On top of which, using my car was out of the question. My tomato-red jeep, with its KNST stickers on the bumper, was hardly conducive to an undercover operation. Instead, Sheri volunteered her son's car, a second-hand Range Rover that had been one of her father's cars, used to scout location shoots in the desert. Together we plotted how Sheri would go with me as far as the student café directly across from the old hospital. As a graduate of the University, I knew the campus well. From inside the coffee shop, she'd have a good view of the medical center's West Tower entrance and could wait there until I'd finished my meeting with Sally and her tribunal. The idea was that once I had wrapped things up, so to speak, I'd ask Sally to walk with me back to the car. Tell her I was worried I might have been followed and had a few questions. When Sheri saw us leave the building, she would trail us back to the parking lot. I had no idea if I'd need help getting Sally into the car, but if I did, if something went wrong, Sheri would be there to help. At least that was the plan.

# CHAPTER 29

Wednesday I felt like I had rocks in my stomach. I must have pulled Jennifer's cell from my bag at least a dozen times, checking to see if Mustang Sally had called or texted me to cancel our meeting. And every time my own cell rang I would jump, fearful it would be Chase asking if I'd heard anything from Sally, or worse, calling to tell me he had found her. I didn't want to lie to him, but what else could I do?

Finally, after procrastinating as long as possible, I picked up my office phone and called Chase. He answered, his voice upbeat like he was both surprised and happy to hear from me.

"Hey there, you actually can call back. I thought you'd lost my number."

I resisted the urge to smile. "I told you I'd call."

"You'll forgive me if I wasn't holding my breath."

I wasn't up for playing games. I didn't want to get into a discussion about our mutual hunt for Mustang Sally. Before he had a chance to ask for an update, I asked him for a favor.

"Look, I don't have a lot of time, but there's something I could use your help on."

I expected Chase to come back with some obnoxious remark about how he knew I'd finally come around. Instead, he simply replied, "Shoot. What ya got?"

I explained Silva's accident and how I couldn't believe he was innocent. That I felt certain his wife hadn't been driving the car, but that Silva had.

"Turns out, the police have charged her with manslaughter, and management has got a blackout on any employee of the station talking about it. But I was hoping—"

"That if someone was to do a little snooping around and bring something to the attention of the authorities, maybe those charges would be dropped?"

"And filed against Silva."

"Don't see why not. What's in it for you?"

"Nothing." I squeezed my eyes shut. Other than keeping Chase occupied while I meet with Sally, it wasn't a total lie. Only a convenient little white lie I hoped might help Silva's wife and buy me some time to deal with Sally.

Chase chuckled. "That's what I like about you, Carol. You're all about trying to do the right thing."

"Yeah, that's me." I tried to sound upbeat as I squeezed the handle of the phone in my hand. "Always trying to do the right thing."

Sheri and I drove down to UCLA in her son's Range Rover, exactly as planned, and separated as soon as she parked the car. Sheri went to the student café directly across from the old medical center, while I headed off to the West Tower to meet with Sally.

The Medical Center, a sixty-two-year-old superstructure, easily covered several city blocks. While still in use for classrooms, it had been declared unfit as a hospital after being damaged in the 1994 earthquake. The small entrance to the West Tower was little more than a set of double glass doors that appeared to have been added as an afterthought to allow for an additional emergency exit. Directly across from the doors was a bank of wide, steel gray utilitarian-looking elevators, the type designed for patient gurneys. The lobby was empty.

I wrapped my arms around myself and glanced at my watch: 7:55. It was still early. Perhaps Sally had intended to meet me on the fifth floor. Room 518.

I punched the elevator call button and waited impatiently. When the doors opened, a handful of students, chatting with backpacks and notebooks in hand, got off. I squeezed in and hit the button for the fifth floor. Then from behind me, I heard her voice.

"Jennifer?"

"Sally?" My voice cracked, the pitch higher and softer than normal.

There with her back against the elevator wall, shadowed in the dim light, was Sally. She wasn't at all what I expected. She was taller than me, probably close to six feet, and big, with broad shoulders and coarse, kinky gray hair she had piled in a bun on top her head. She looked to be somewhere in her mid-sixties and was wearing a London Fog raincoat and a plaid Burberry scarf wrapped high around her neck. If I didn't know better, I'd think she was an instructor, or maybe a late-night student finishing up one of the master classes offered in the building.

"Our group's upstairs. I was just coming to meet you. Are you alone?"

I nodded yes, kept my eyes on the floor, and crossed my hands in front of me, hoping I appeared as nervous and frightened as Sheri had coached me. Which didn't take a lot of acting on my part.

"We can't be too careful." I could feel Sally's eyes on me. Searching my person for some clue of who I was and what she imagined I must have been through. Then reaching for my hand, she pulled me close to her, turned my face to hers, and stared at my blackened eye. "He do this to you?"

I pulled away, covering my face with my bandaged hand. Sheri's makeup was good. How good, I didn't know. I worried being this close, Sally might see the fear in my eyes wasn't from being abused, but of her discovering my deception.

"I thought I was safe. I moved here thinking he wouldn't find me. But he did. And then he wouldn't leave me alone. He promised it'd be different this time. That he loved me, and that he had changed. That I was the only one who understood him, and we belonged together. And then it started all over again. The yelling. The threats."

I tried to recall every horrible scenario I had ever reported on or read online with what Jennifer had told me about her breakup. Jennifer's story paled in comparison, but Mustang Sally didn't know that.

Sally grabbed my hands and squeezed them between her own.

"You don't have to worry, Jennifer. Not anymore. We can stop him. But you have to trust me."

I squeaked out an "I know." And stared back down at the floor. *Sheri, you should give me an Academy Award for this.*

"This will go quickly." Sally patted my hand. "My group didn't want to meet tonight. They're nervous, and I can't blame them. Some things have happened, and it's all my fault. But I convinced them how important tonight was. We're all committed to the cause, and they're here for you."

"What happened?" I asked.

"A lot happened. Something terrible happened to someone I was trying to help, then I lost someone very close to me, and I started drinking. Something I never should have done. But you needn't worry. I'm not drinking now, and my tribunal's here for you. All you have to do is tell them your story."

I kept my eyes and head low and nodded nervously.

As the elevators doors opened, Sally gave my hand a final squeeze and waited for me to step out into the hallway. It looked deserted, lit with old neon grey-white lights, and cold. On the wall opposite us was a bulletin board cluttered with announcements and want ads. Beneath it, a trash can overflowed with coffee cups and paper products.

"Is anyone else here?"

"You mean students? No. Not now. There are a few evening classes in the building, but nothing on this floor. Just us."

With no one in sight, Mustang Sally instructed me to follow her. I was glad I'd met her in the elevator. It would've been easy to get lost. The white-tiled hallways were like a maze, spreading endlessly past empty nursing stations, closed wooden doors to what must have been patient rooms, and every two hundred feet or so, old-fashioned emergency showers with pull handles like those from some ancient teaching hospital. It seemed to go on forever, through sets of double doors into more of the same.

"We have to be very careful about where we meet. In my line of work, you can't be too cautious."

"I suppose not."

I shuffled along beside Sally. Behind which of the doors marked with caged emergency lighting had she hidden her tribunal? She must have suspected my nervousness and kept talking.

"Ironically, hiding in plain sight works best. It's why I chose the Medical Center. The campus is busy. No one's checking for student IDs, there's a number of entrances—or, in our case, emergency exits—and believe me, if anything doesn't look or sound right, we'll use them."

Then coming to a stop in front of a large door with a round portal window, she peered inside as she placed her hand on my shoulder.

"You'll be fine, Jennifer. Behind this door is a lecture hall. There's a stage in the front of the room. And a chair in the center of the stage. That's where you'll go. Once we're through these doors, you'll turn right to the stage, I'll turn left to the auditorium. The stage lights will be on so you won't be able to see me or the other women sitting with me, but you will be able to hear us."

"I don't understand. What is it you want me to do?"

Sally laughed.

"What, you have stage fright? Don't worry. This is all for your safety as well as ours. We'll ask you some questions. They'll be looking at you very carefully. Studying you and listening to your responses. When you're finished, I'll meet you back here."

"Then what?"

"Then we'll see. My guess is, given the circumstances, they'll approve an operation."

"But, they're not going to hurt him. Just convince him to leave me alone, right?"

"Jennifer, you don't need to worry about Jason. Not anymore. All you need to think about is getting on with your life."

"But Jason—"

"He's a bad man, Jennifer."

Fortunately, I didn't have to worry about protecting Jason. Jennifer had shared nothing with Sally as to his identity, and other than my seeing him with her that one time in the restaurant, I doubted I could describe him. If the tribunal's questions got too specific, I planned to steer clear of details. All I needed to do was get through the next thirty minutes and convince Sally to walk out the door with me.

"You look nervous." Sally patted me on the back.

"Shouldn't I be?"

I wasn't acting. I didn't need to. I could feel the color draining from my face. The idea of being on stage in front of a group of shadowed assassins was chilling.

"You'll be fine. Take a deep breath." I did as instructed. "You ready?"

"Yeah. I think so."

Sally was right. I couldn't see a thing from the stage. I took a seat on the chair as instructed and tried to shield my eyes from the bright lights. But the lights were aimed directly at me, blinding me to whoever was in the audience. The farthest I could see was the edge of the stage. I could hear them, mumbling, but whatever they were saying I couldn't make out.

The first question came from Sally. She asked me to state my name and share briefly who I was and where I had come from.

I repeated everything Jennifer had told me about herself. That I had grown up in the Bay area. Graduated from UC San Francisco. And met Jason while on spring break in Cancun. I started to perspire. The lights felt hot. I wasn't sure if it was nerves of the heat, but I could begin to feel myself sweat.

Then from within the yawning dark space in front of me, came a series of questions.

"And Jason. How long have you been together?"

I answered. A second, third, and fourth question followed, like rapid fire from different voices.

"Can you describe your relationship?"

"When did the abuse begin?"

"What have you done to stop it?"

Before I could answer the final question, a siren, a piercing, wailing alarm, sounded, and a white strobe light began flashing.

"What's happening?" I stood up. "Somebody tell me, what's going on?"

From the seats, I heard voices screaming. "Run! Get out. Now! Go!"

In the near blinding white light, I could see the shadows of the women, scurrying like ducklings one behind the other, toward the exit.

I yelled for Sally. "Where do I go? What do I do?"

There was no response.

Without waiting, I ran off the stage, down the stairs, and back to where Sally told me to meet her. But she wasn't there. The hallway was empty. The only sound was the warble of the fire alarm and pulsating wave-like motion of the emergency lights.

I felt my way back down the hallway, my heart racing, fearful I might be trapped. What if this was a fire? If I got stuck in this building, nobody would find me. I had to get out. But how? I was lost. How many turns down long empty corridors and sets of double doors had Sally walked me through? It was useless. Even if I could retrace my steps, I couldn't take the elevator. In a fire, an elevator was the worst of all possible choices. I needed to think clearly. There had to be a staircase somewhere. Something between the floors, not just a bank of elevators. I scanned the hallway for a sign to an emergency exit. There was nothing. Beneath the flashing light, and with my hand on the wall to guide me, I groped my way farther down the hallway. Searching. And then I saw it, at the end of the hall, a steel and concrete stairway.

I took the steps, two and three at a time. Fast as I could. Bracing myself against the railing and the cool concrete wall. Thankful Sheri had insisted I wear tennis shoes.

When I came to the first floor, a set of heavy duty steel utility doors faced me. *Please don't be locked.* With a heavy shove, I pushed them open.

Outside, the LA air never felt so good. I took a deep a breath and looked around. Surrounding me were students. They were gathered together in small groups, chatting and waiting for the all-clear. I pushed through the groups.

"Sally? Sally, where are you?"

There was no answer, only the sound of my own name coming back at me through the crowd.

"Carol?"

Sheri rushed up to me, grabbed me by the arm, and started to pull me away from the building. "Come with me. We need to leave. Quickly."

"Why? What's happened? What's going on?"

"I'll explain when we get to the car." Sheri dropped my hand. "Follow me. Hurry. We can't be seen together. Not out in the open like this."

Sheri pushed ahead of me, weaving her way through the crowd, back to the parking structure. When I got to the car, she waited for me to get in before she spoke. "Are you okay?"

"I think so. Why? What's happening?"

"Chase. That's what's happening." Sheri put the Range Rover in reverse and backed out of the parking space, her hand on my shoulder, forcing my head below the windows. "Get down, if he's still here, I don't want him to see you."

"What happened?"

"I pulled the fire alarm."

"You did that?"

"What else could I do? Chase came into the student café right after you left and when he saw me, he wanted to know why I was there and where you were."

I was beginning to feel seasick with the sharp turns Sheri was taking. I braced myself with one hand against the back of the seat and the other on the dashboard.

"What did you tell him?"

"What could I tell him? I lied and said I was meeting some doctor. That it was a setup, and I didn't want anyone to know."

I laughed. Leave it to Sheri to come up with a good excuse. "And why was he here?"

"He said he was here for a class. Some forensics pathology thing, but I didn't think so."

"Was following me?"

"I'm not sure. But when I saw him go into the West Tower, I wasn't taking any chances."

I couldn't blame Sheri, but when the alarm went off, I lost Sally and any chance of finding her. She had split, and so had her tribunal. It was as if somebody yelled fire and they all disappeared.

When we finally stopped at a traffic light blocks from the campus, I breathed a sigh of relief. Whether Chase had been following me or was there for a night class, I couldn't be sure.

"Maybe it was just a coincidence," Sheri said.

I thought about it. Chase had mentioned he was going to night school.

"Maybe, but either way—this thing with Sally tonight—it never happened. Chase never needs to know about my failed attempt to kidnap her. Far as he's concerned, I was home with Charlie and you were out on a date."

"With a surgeon," Sheri said. "If I'm going to lie, let's at least make it good."

I picked my phone and called DJ. I needed to tell her I wouldn't be delivering Mustang Sally as we planned. Her response was simple.

"Failure's not an option, Carol. You need to find her. And fast."

# CHAPTER 30

*Find her?* If only I could. For the rest of the week, I kept Jennifer's cell on my person or in front of me like a crystal ball, staring at it, hoping Mustang Sally would text back and reschedule her meeting. But there was nothing. I even tried to log onto the Butterflies chat room as Jennifer and send a message equally as urgent as the one Sheri had sent before. But still, there was no reply. And given that Chase hadn't called to give me an update on his search, I was beginning to think Mustang Sally had vanished.

The trail had gone cold.

Sitting at my desk, I went through all my notes concerning the case. My first meeting with Chase. His belief Bruno's death was connected to two others he was investigating. Sally's first call to the station. And my last meeting with Detective Riley, who had dismissed any knowledge of Sally before he committed suicide. But if Riley did know Sally, and had taken her secret to his grave, perhaps he wasn't alone. And if Chase was right, and Riley's ex-partner was the lead investigator of the other cases Chase was working, then maybe, just maybe, he would be able to tell me more about Sally. Like where she was hiding or how I could reach out to her again.

I began with a call to Sergeant Browne, who had been helpful when I needed to find the location of Riley's retirement party.

"Sergeant Browne? Carol Childs, KNST."

"Yeah, I remember. You're that girl reporter. The one who was with him when he died."

Wow. Was that how he remembered me? I hated the thought and scrambled for what to say next.

"I'm sorry about what happened. Detective Riley was a good man. In fact, that's why I'm calling. I've been thinking about him, and I wanted to get in touch with his ex-partner. I suppose it's just therapy on my part, you know being there with him at the end. I was hoping maybe I could talk to him. Thought it might help me to work through some things."

"Detective Rios. Riley and Rios. We called them, the R and R team. Rules and Regulations. Never found one they didn't try to bend. He's been taking it pretty hard himself. Might do you both good. He's around somewhere. Why don't leave your number, and I'll have him give you a call."

Detective Rios called back before lunch, and by the time I got off the phone, I no longer had an appetite.

After dispensing with the niceties, I launched into what I wanted most: information about Mustang Sally and what, if anything, he knew.

"I was hoping, Detective Rios, that you might be able to help me. Before Riley died, I asked him if he had ever heard of anyone named Mustang Sally. I asked because she's been calling the station, and I've reason to believe she was involved in Bruno Sims' murder and the deaths of several other men. Men the LAPD knew to have been serial abusers."

There was a long pause before Rios answered. And then he said, his voice deep and full of authority, "If you're asking me if I've ever heard of anyone named Mustang Sally, I'm going to tell you right now you're wasting your time."

"I don't think so. And I'm pretty sure you'd rather not have your name come out in any investigation that ties you with a group of rogue cops who looked the other way when it came to seeing justice doled out to abusers. But let me assure you, that's not the story I'm after. And for reasons I won't go into, I'm as anxious as you are that Sally stops calling the station. So for the moment, let's pretend we're after the same thing and stop playing games. Do you know where Sally is?"

Rios sighed. "I'm going to assume this is off the record? 'Cause if it's not—"

"Relax. I'm not quoting anyone here. This is just between you and me."

There was another long pause, then in the background, I heard what sounded like a door close.

"It's been a long time, Ms. Childs. And I can't say I'd undo any of the things we did. Far as I'm concerned, it was like putting a mad dog down. Our hands weren't dirty, we simply did as you said—looked the other way. But as for knowing where Sally is today, I haven't a clue. But I will say this, if she were to suddenly show up—let's say walk in the door and start telling tales—believe me, you or anyone even close to her would never know. You understand?"

"You mean she'd disappear."

"I don't think I need to spell it out for you. I'm not about to see good cops go down for doing what needed to be done."

I glanced back at my notes. I wasn't the only one searching for Sally. And if the cops who had once been protecting her found her before I did, I didn't even want to think about what might happen. I had to find another way to flush her out.

# CHAPTER 31

It wasn't until I was driving home from work and caught a station promo for my upcoming Sunday night Soap Box that I had another idea about Sally. If Chase was right and Sally was a fan, maybe I could prompt her to call my show again.

It was a long shot, but with Misty's help, it just might work.

After meeting Sally in person, it was apparent, despite the fact Sally was much heartier than Misty, that they were roughly the same age. Which meant it was likely that Sally had also been a fan of Misty's at some point. After all, Misty had been a big name in Hollywood. Years ago, her name had appeared in the newspaper almost daily. Some of it for her work with the police and the FBI concerning missing persons. But most notably because of her notoriety as Hollywood's Psychic to the Stars. As a celeb, she had appeared on numerous television and radio talk shows and even had a popular advice column in the newspaper. In a sense, Misty, in her own last century kind of way, was the equivalent of an online chat room. Counseling the broken-hearted had always been a big part of her practice.

The closer I got to home, the more the idea of using Misty to get to Sally appealed to me. If I could convince Misty to join me on the air, not only might I be able to flush Sally out and learn her whereabouts, but I also might be able to do something to address Misty's overall health issues.

Misty's state of confusion was becoming an issue. On more than one occasion, she appeared to have forgotten Charlie's name altogether and simply referred to him as *the boy*. She had started mixing words, referring to an apple as asparagus. Then last week, she had left the keys to her van in the refrigerator. My initial response had been to kid her about her absentmindedness, but now I was seriously thinking of taking the keys away.

In my frustration, I had consulted with Dr. Sam, the station's resident GP who specialized in geriatrics. He told me he was involved in a new short-term memory study at UCLA and offered to use his powers to grant her admittance should she be interested. But I knew Misty's reservations concerning traditional medical practices would make that next to impossible. But, if I were to convince Misty to come to the station to help me on the show, maybe I might get lucky and the two just might meet. It was worth a try.

When I got home, I found Misty sitting at the kitchen table with a hot pot of tea in front of her. Without hesitation, I told her about my idea to have her co-host on the Soap Box.

"We could do some promo spots. You know, something like 'the great Misty Dawn returns to the airwaves Sunday night.' How's that sound?" I danced my hands above my head. "If Sally's listening and hears you're going to be on the air, who knows, maybe she'll call in again."

Misty put her teacup down and smacked her lips. "I'll need some zinc."

"Pardon me?" *Did she not understand?*

"And a small amount of milk thistle and maybe some cilantro too. Mixed with my tea, it'll help me focus."

"Misty, did you hear me? I want you on the air with me Sunday night."

"I heard you, Carol. But for this, I'm going to need to sharpen my meditation skills. See if I can connect with Sally on a different plane. One can never be too sure about things like this. I'll have to mix up a batch tomorrow."

I reached for a glass above the bar and filled it with red wine. "Thing is, Misty, we need to chat with Tyler first to get his approval. Which I'm sure will be fine. But my time frame's a little tight. You free tomorrow?"

"If you'll agree to have Charlie drive me to the station after school, I see no reason why it shouldn't be."

"Perfect. I'll meet you in the lobby at three forty-five. But don't be late. You know Tyler, he's a stickler for schedules."

I knew Tyler would be on board with my decision. He had used Misty several years before to fill in for the station's entertainment reporter and liked her. And if all went according to my ulterior motive, Dr. Sam would be exiting the studio just as I waltzed Misty down the hall to meet with Tyler.

My plan went off perfectly.

At exactly three forty-five, I met Misty and Charlie in the lobby of the station. I suggested to Charlie that he might find a snack in the employee breakroom. Without protest, he disappeared down the hallway like a bloodhound in search of treats. Which left Misty and me to wander down the hallway just in time to accidentally-on-purpose run into Dr. Sam as he was leaving the studio.

"Misty? Misty Dawn?" The doctor stopped in his tracks, put his hands in the air, and stared at Misty like she was a rock star. "Aren't you the leading authority on southwestern herbal remedies?"

I couldn't have counted on it going better. Without waiting for her to respond, Dr. Sam took Misty's hand between his own well-padded paws and smiled. "I'm pleased to meet you. My name's Sam Willard, Dr. Willard, but people around here call me Dr. Sam."

I jumped in quickly and reminded Misty that Dr. Sam was one of our midday hosts.

"Maybe you remember Dr. Sam was who Sheri was listening to about the West Nile Virus. But lately, he's been working on a study concerning traditional versus herbal medications."

"Carol, please," Dr. Sam interrupted, "I don't want to bore you all with that now. I'm sure you're both very busy. Perhaps, if Ms. Dawn agrees, she and I might meet sometime. I'd love to know about her research. Maybe we could arrange for tea. One of your specialties, perhaps?"

Misty hunched her shoulders to her ears and smiled. "Please, call me Misty. And yes, I'd love to have tea. Carol can set something up, but you're quite right, now's not the time. As you might suspect, we're here on urgent business. I'm working a case, and I have a number of loose spirits I need to wrangle. Now if you'll excuse us, we have a meeting with the news director."

I glanced over at Sam and winked. "I'll call you then. Next week good?"

He nodded, squeezed Misty's hand, and wished her well with the wrangling of those loose spirits, then left us in the hall.

Misty linked her arm under mine, and as we continued down the hall toward Tyler's office, she whispered in my ear, "Mind you, Carol, it's always best when you meet a man who's totally smitten with you to appear busy. It makes life ever so much more interesting."

# CHAPTER 32

Sunday night I introduced Misty as my special guest and co-host for the evening. In the back of my mind, this was my last chance to do something that might attract Sally. If Sally had tuned to my show before because of the talk of relationships between men and women, with any luck, maybe she would again.

I opened, sharing with my listeners that after last week's show I had been thinking about relationships. Was love but a fleeting experience? Was marriage becoming a thing of the past? An institution best replaced by a contract for those who planned to enter into a long-term affair? After much contemplation, I said I had turned to my friend Misty Dawn, who had been responsible for giving love advice to the some of Hollywood's greatest stars. I then turned the show over to Misty and hoped if Mustang Sally was listening, I had said something to spark her interest.

"Thank you, Carol. And, yes, I did counsel some big screen names in my time, but I'm not about to name names. I was always above that kind of thing. Capitalizing on someone's pain and misfortune strictly for my personal benefit? I couldn't do that. However, I will say this, the rich and famous, their problems are frequently no different than most couples, just on a grander scale and more expensive. Beyond that, there are only three things a woman needs to understand when dealing with a man."

"Only three?" I asked half-heartedly.

"Just three," Misty said. "If a woman follows them I can guarantee she'll not only be happier with her man, but also herself."

"Sounds a little simplistic, Misty. But I'm game. What are these magic three things a woman needs to know?"

"First, women need to understand men haven't the first clue about what a woman is. Not at all. And those men who say they do are lying. Women are a mystery. I can't tell you the number of Hollywood's leading men who have told me exactly this. And this, ladies, is to our advantage. To win at love, a woman must remain mysterious."

I wanted to laugh out loud, but I resisted the urge.

"Okay, Misty, and number two?"

"When a man tells a woman something about himself, believe him." She chuckled and leaned closer to the mic. "If he says he likes to spend his weekends at the track, don't think with all your charms you're going to change him."

This time, I did laugh out loud. I couldn't help myself, and I could see I wasn't alone, the switchboard was beginning to light up. Matt, my screener, flashed me a thumbs-up sign from the control room. If nothing else, this was going to be a fun exchange.

Misty continued. "And, if he tells you he's not into children or interested in marriage, accept that's who he is. Any woman who thinks she can change a man will only end up losing herself. It's a downhill slope."

More lights joined the brigade. The board lit up like a Christmas tree.

"And three, Misty. What's your third rule?"

"Men need a cave. If your man's grumpy and retreats to his cave, leave him there. Never, ever, go after a man in a cave."

I didn't interrupt. I let Misty take the calls and sat back and listened. Perched on the broadcast stool with her headphones on, Misty was clearly enjoying herself. In the studio's low lights, I could imagine her in her prime, like a gypsy fortune teller doling out advice.

And then, five minutes before the top of the hour, Matt tapped softly on the glass and held up an erasable white board. *Sally. Line two.*

I could feel my blood pressure rising. I nodded to Misty, then covering the mic with my hand, whispered, "Let me take this next call."

"Welcome to the show. This is Carol Childs." I tried to sound upbeat. Despite the growing knot in my stomach, if this was Mustang

Sally, I needed to find a way to secure her location, something I could use later to track her down. In my friendliest voice, I added, "May I ask who's calling and where you're calling from?"

"My name is Sally. And does it really matter where I'm calling from? I have a question for Misty Dawn. I want to know what you tell a woman who loves a man so bad it hurts. Real bad."

The question stopped me. In a split second, the tenor of the show went from lighthearted laughter to a much darker space. I leaned into the mic and was about to ask again where she was calling from, but Misty raised her hand to stop me, as though she knew Sally had something else to say.

Sally continued. "The type of love where you don't know any better. You think that's how it's supposed to be, and that you can change him and make it better."

Misty turned her head in my direction. The thick cataracts on her eyes almost seemed to glow in the low light. I wasn't sure if she was staring at the wall behind me or if she was in some type of trance, getting a reading off Sally's voice.

"Love shouldn't hurt, Sally."

I didn't dare interrupt. I sat silently and waited for Sally to respond. In the background, I thought I could hear the faint sound of a foghorn. I pushed my headphones closer to my ears and strained for any ambient sound. Then there it was again. The low bellow of the horn. I glanced back to the control room at Matt and pointed to the phone. *Could he trace the call?* He shook his head. The line was blocked.

"But it does hurt," Sally said. "It can be ugly and cruel. And people can do terrible things to one another."

"No. No, Sally. Love doesn't do that." Misty reached for the mic and pulled it to her, as though she were reaching for the hand of someone she was counseling. "But sometimes, bad things happen when we confuse love with need."

"But he needed me." Sally's voice sounded strained.

"And he hurt you."

"I tried to stop it."

"You hurt him too, didn't you?" Misty paused. "Because he wouldn't stop hurting you, and someone else you loved. Am I right?"

I knew Misty was pulling from the information we'd gathered about Sally, but to those listening and maybe even a little bit to me too, it sounded as though she were doing a reading.

"He'll never hurt me again. I made sure of it. And men like him won't hurt other women either. Ever." Sally's voice was barely audible.

"And that's how you help, isn't it?" Misty said. "You help other women who don't know how to help themselves."

"I do. Just like you, Misty. I counsel them, and when my words aren't enough, my friends and I, we take care of the problem."

Matt signaled me, we were about to go to a station break. I was afraid we'd lose the call. I put my hand on Misty's shoulder and nodded to the clock.

"Sally," I stood up and grabbed the mic, "I'm so sorry, we're about to go to a commercial, but if you stay on the line, we can talk during the break. Maybe get you some help."

I paused and waited for Matt to switch off my mic and transfer Sally's call to the studio's private line. But no luck. When I picked up the phone, the line was dead.


On the way home, my cell phone rang. It was Chase.

"You did it, Carol. That was Sally. I knew you'd find a way to get her to call. Did you get a number?"

"No," I glanced over at Misty, thankful I didn't have to lie. "The number was blocked."

"Well, I've got something. A location, I'm sure of it."

"Where?" I gripped the steering wheel tighter, my heart felt like it was about to jump out of my chest. If Chase knew Sally's location, I was in trouble. "Are you sure?"

"As sure as I am the sun's coming up tomorrow. And with a little luck, you'll go out with me when this investigation's over."

"Chase," I said his name as though I were cursing. "I don't have time for this."

"Fine. You heard that foghorn in the background when Sally was talking? I must have heard it dozens of times growing up. The sound carries in the night sky. It was a dead giveaway, and to top it all off, it fits."

"How?"

"The West Nile Virus deaths, the foghorn. They all point to the South Bay. If I hadn't heard the horn, I wouldn't have known. I've been using the station's signal map to search areas north of the valley. It never occurred to me to check the areas around the peninsula. But when I heard her tonight, I remembered, there was one case of West Nile. And there are horse ranches around there too. I just didn't think it was likely. It's such a hoity-toity area, and I was looking for something more rural. But now that I heard the foghorn in the background of Sally's call, I'm sure of it. Sally's in the South Bay, down near Rancho Palos Verdes, probably not far from the water. I'm on it, Carol. We're close. I can feel it."

# CHAPTER 33

That night I couldn't get Sally's raw, raspy voice out of my head. It stuck like a needle in the groove of an old '78 LP. The sound of it skipping between the white noise, mixed with visions of Bruno's body hanging from the Hollywood Sign. Despite the fact I had taken a sleeping pill, sleep evaded me. Finally, surrendering to my angst, I crept downstairs, grabbed my reporter's bag with my computer and cell phone, and returned to my bed. I had to do something. I couldn't wait, hoping Sally would call back before Chase called to tell me he had her in his crosshairs.

I sat on my bed and opened my computer, starting with the Butterflies website. Going all the way back to Jennifer's original post about Jason and Sally's suggestion they meet in person. It reminded me of the impassioned voicemail Sally left on Jennifer's phone. I pulled the phone from my bag and replayed the message.

*My poor girl. Don't suffer alone. We can help. You'd be doing woman everywhere a favor if you did. There's a meeting Monday at The Cow's End in Venice. Eight a.m. It would be good for you to come. But, remember, come alone and no names.*

I stared at Jennifer's aquamarine phone. It would have been so simple if I could just hit the call-back button. But the message, like the one Sally had left before telling Jennifer to meet her at UCLA, had come from a blocked caller. There was no way I could respond. And, as far as meeting Sally at The Cow's End went, I wasn't certain the restaurant was still even a viable location. Sally's message was better than a week old, and secretive as the group was, I was inclined to think they would seldom frequent the same spot. What were the chances? But it beat sitting in bed and staring at a computer screen. The good news was I knew the restaurant. The Cow's End was a prime people-watching spot in Venice, just off the boardwalk. And if I left now, even with LA's bumper-to-bumper morning commute traffic, I could be there in time to scout out the location.

The Cow's End was easily identifiable. The black clapboard building with its montage of off-center geometrically designed red framed windows—the largest of which displayed a ceramic, life-sized Holstein—was a watering hole for locals and tourists alike. Outside, a couple of Harleys were parked while a crowd of beach refugees milled about, warming themselves against the cool chill of the sea air with cups of hot coffee, waiting for the first sign of sun to break through southern California's thick morning fog.

I parked my Jeep across the street and, dodging several low-flying seagulls, followed the smell of fresh coffee.

The café was jammed with what looked like regulars, gray-bearded men with ponytails, tattooed women in cowboy boots, and tourists in tennis shoes snapping photos and selfies. On the walls were old Hollywood posters and beach memorabilia commemorating the area's hardscrabble-to-hip lifestyle. I scanned those seated, searching for anyone who I thought might fit the description of a Butterfly, eliminating the single men and mixed couples. In the corner, I spotted three middle-aged women sitting at a table like they didn't want to be disturbed.

"Excuse me, I'm—" I stopped myself before blurting out Jennifer's name. "I'm looking for a group of women I was told might be meeting here."

From the center of the group, an older woman with a short salt-and-pepper crew cut smiled. "Are you a Butterfly?"

The woman speaking didn't move her head. I noticed her hands were folded neatly in front of her, immobile in her lap, like small fists. And then the wheelchair. Its presence nearly hidden by her friends on either side. The woman next to her moved her cup away. A thin straw with a lid like a sippy-cup covered the top.

"DumpedAndDepressed."

The three exchanged a look, then looked back at me. For a moment, I thought they might have recognized my voice.

"I thought DumpedAndDepressed posted she was leaving town."

"I was planning to." I glanced over my shoulder as though I was worried, then started making up what I thought they might believe. "Almost made it too. But he found me. I've been trying to reach Sally. We had a meeting set, but she canceled."

"She's not here."

The woman next to the wheelchair eyed me carefully, scanning my body as though she suspected I might be hiding a gun beneath my jacket or a cop's badge. Casually I opened my jacket so she could see I wasn't carrying. Satisfied, she glanced back at me and nodded to the other two.

"I'm NoseyNan. This here's MerryWidow," she nodded to the woman in the wheelchair, "and that's B."

B reached across the table and shook my hand. "Short for BetterLatethanNever. Why don't you take a seat? The rest of our gang should be along soon. You're a bit early, but you must know, Sally and the rest of her tribunal aren't going to be here, not today."

"You know about the tribunal?" I searched their eyes for validation.

"You might say that," Nan said.

Merry explained how she and her deceased husband hadn't been getting along. They hadn't gotten along for a long time, but he had insisted they try to make the best of it. It was the holiday season, and he convinced her he was going to make a New Year's resolution. Things were going to be better. The holiday was a huge success, with all the earmarks of a Norman Rockwell Christmas. A beautiful tree, the house decorated with popcorn streamers coming down the stairway, and a big family dinner complete with a golden brown turkey. It wasn't until afterward when Merry had gone to the attic to return the Christmas ornaments that things changed.

"As I slipped through the floorboards, on the way to breaking my neck, I knew he had planned the whole thing. Of course, he swore it was an accident. The week before Christmas he'd replaced the old floorboards in the attic and covered the area with insulation. All but the area where I had unfortunately stepped. I think his biggest surprise was that I wasn't killed."

"And you didn't tell anyone?" I asked.

"I was too afraid," Merry said.

"I never said anything either," Nan said. "I never knew what my ex might do if I did. Plus, I didn't want to worry my family. All of them had such good marriages. I didn't want anyone to know the reality of mine."

"Our stories aren't all that different," Merry said. "Fortunately for me, I found this online group, and that's where I met Sally. If I had only found her a little earlier, maybe I wouldn't have ended up in this chair."

"And she took care of things for you?" I wasn't sure how to phrase that.

"She arranged for my husband to have an accident of his own. And I'm not sorry."

"So you've kept up with her? And you've seen her again? Here maybe?"

"Sometimes." Merry nodded her head, the only part of her body that moved voluntarily. "But we don't expect her today. At least not until the dust settles."

"What dust?" I asked.

"That hit and run in Westwood a couple weeks back?" Nan's voice was barely above a whisper.

"Caty Beardsley?" The name slipped out before I realized I said it. Some stories you never forget. Caty Beardsley was one. I was in the studio the night she was killed. With a daughter only a few years younger and with the same name, it all hit a little too close to home.

"You knew her?" Nan asked.

"No. Just the name. It was everywhere in the news. Pretty young girl getting run down in Westwood like that. Awful."

"She was one of ours," B said.

"We're not supposed to use real names, but it'd be hard not to. It's okay online, but in person when we meet, it happens."

"And that poor girl. We all knew her story. Her boyfriend wouldn't leave her alone. Kept stalking her. She met with us a couple of times before Sally introduced her to her tribunal."

"But her rescue didn't go off as planned." Merry's eyes scanned the room, suspicious of anyone who might be eavesdropping.

"What happened?" I asked.

B spoke up. "Sally tried to help, but Caty's boyfriend got to her first. Maybe you heard, she died a couple days ago in the hospital."

"Yeah, but not before Sally got him," Nan said. "That body the cops found on the Hollywood Sign? He was ours."

I had to work hard not to show my surprise. "Caty Beardsley? That was her boyfriend?"

I would never have put the two together. I had assumed Caty's death was another hit and run. A young woman crossing one of LA's busy streets at night and run down by a passing motorist. It had never occurred to me there might've been a connection. I thought back to my last conversation with Sally. She had shared with me she had suffered a loss, someone she was helping. Could that have been Caty? On top of her son's death, the pain and guilt had to be unbearable. No wonder she had been calling the station. In her own way, I felt she was crying out for help.

"That man put that poor girl through hell. He used to beat her, but not so the bruises would show. And when she finally got strong enough to leave, he killed her. We all knew it. We were going to go to the hospital and stage a demonstration. Demand he be arrested. But we had no proof. Sally told us we needed to be patient. If we went public, it would have spoiled everything. Do more damage than good, and even if he was arrested, without any hard evidence, he'd be out of jail and do it again."

"That's why Sally's not here? Because Caty died?"

"There were other issues as well. Sally hasn't been herself lately. It's caused a rift in the organization. Which is why Sally and her tribunals are lying low for a while. They'll be back, but right now, it's just us Butterflies. The survivors, supporting one another best we can."

"But if it were a matter of life and death, and I had to get hold of Sally, you must know of a way? Maybe you have a number or some way to get her a message?"

The women looked at each other, then back at me. Then Merry said, "I'm sorry. If we had a number for Sally, we couldn't give it to you. Not that we wouldn't want to, but we can't be too careful. I'm sure you understand. But if you're in need of help, a place to go, we can offer you shelter."

"No. It's not shelter I need, it's Sally. She's the only one who can help me. If you see her, or if she calls, tell her DumpedAndDepressed needs her. Tell her I'm in danger. That I'm afraid something bad is about to happen. I'm desperate."

I stood up and walked out of the restaurant. Sheri would have been proud of me. I was becoming quite the actress.

# CHAPTER 34

I hoped my brief encounter with the Butterflies was enough for them to relay my message to Sally if they could. For the moment, it was the closest contact I had, and all I could do was cross my fingers and pray.

On the drive home, I took Jennifer's cell phone out of my bag and placed it on the empty seat next to me. If I could have willed it to ring, I would have. But it sat silently while my mind raced back to my brief encounter with Bruno that morning in the grocery store. *What a jerk.* If I was right, it had been less than forty-eight hours since he'd run Caty Beardsley down and left her crumpled body on the street. And by the time I met him, he was already trying to pick up some new woman. No wonder a former abuse victim like Mustang Sally had taken it upon herself to administer justice.

I could even appreciate why Sally had sympathizers like Riley, who had risked his career to look the other way. Restraining orders. Convictions. They were seldom enough to ensure a victim's safety or sanity. Wasn't that what Detective Riley was trying to tell me when he told me to leave it alone? He knew Bruno's death wasn't a suicide, but a murder. The more I thought about it, the more my sense of justice wavered.

I stopped at a red light and tuned to the station. Tyler was doing a top of the hour news update, and the story caught my attention. The LA City Council was launching a new hit-and-run alert system. Last year, the number of the hit-and-runs, including vehicles and pedestrians, had exceeded twenty thousand. Most of them had been property damage, but one hundred and forty-four of them had resulted in pedestrian deaths. Too bad such a program wasn't in place before Caty Beardsley had been hit. Perhaps if it had, things might have been different. Maybe Bruno wouldn't have gotten away with it. But then, if he hadn't, Sally might never have called the station. The light changed, and my thoughts were interrupted by the buzz of Jennifer's cell.

I pulled over to the side of the road. The caller ID was blocked. Had one of the Butterflies made contact with Sally? I swallowed hard and answered, doing my best to soften my voice and sound more like my impersonation of Jennifer.

"Hello?"

"Jennifer, I know you're worried." The voice that came back was Sally's, raw and raspy like she was straining to speak. "And I apologize for our last meeting. I'm afraid my tribunal's frightened."

"I need your help."

There was a pause. I closed my eyes and prayed she'd agree to meet me. Just one more time, that's all I needed.

Then finally, what must have been seconds but felt like forever, she said, "Saturday night. Eight o'clock. Point Fermin. The lighthouse, on the south side. There's a section for weddings marked Area Two. Make sure it's Area Two. And bring Jason with you. We'll take a little walk out on the trail, overlooking the ocean. But remember, Jennifer, tell no one where you're going."

Sally hung up, and the dial tone droned in my ear like an empty echo. But this time, rather than feeling disconnected, I felt elated. I had made contact with Sally. A surge of adrenalin coursed through my veins. Any uncertainty about what I was doing went quickly from doubt to determination. Knowing what Bruno had done to Caty, and what Mustang Sally had risked to avenge the damaged lives of people like her, steeled my nerves. I needed to save Sally. To stop her before she sabotaged herself with any more calls to the station, speaking carelessly about her mission and her tribunal. I needed to find her before Chase found her and turned her over to the police, or even worse, the police found her, and she disappeared. DJ had promised to help Sally as she had once helped her. Maybe there was a fresh start in her future. I didn't know. Only that finding Sally was no longer about saving my job. I was on a mission of justice, and nobody and nothing was going to deter me.

# CHAPTER 35

I needed to talk to DJ. Not just on the phone, but in person. Instead of choosing the freeway to drive home, I took surface streets back to the station, thinking of exactly what I could tell her and of all the things that could possibly go wrong.

The idea of meeting Sally on the cliffs above Point Fermin sent chills down my spine. The cliffs had a ghoulish history. The steep, rock-hewn embankment could be deadly. In 1929, a landslide had tumbled a neighborhood of homes into the sea. Locals referred to the area as the Sunken City. Beneath the cliffs, large chunks of concrete, now scarred with graffiti, were mixed with the rocks and the crashing surf like tombstones. A few determined palm trees that had once peacefully lined the streets shot up from beneath the rubble as though they were flowers on a grave. Like a magnet, the park drew lovers and curiosity seekers. Some who leaped to their deaths or ventured too close to the cliffs' slippery edge. Ignoring the warning signs and falling hundreds of feet below to a rocky grave.

As I pulled into the station's lot, I had one final thought. What if Sally got wise to my plan and pushed me off the cliff? Or we struggled, and I accidentally pushed her? I couldn't allow my fears to cloud my thinking. I had a job to do. And the fewer people who knew what that job was, the better. Choosing to keep a low profile, I slipped into a parking space behind the station where Tyler wouldn't spot my Jeep and glanced at my watch: 9:35. With a little luck, I could catch DJ after her Monday morning staff meeting, and nobody would know I was here.

I used the station's back entrance, carefully entering the security code so as to not set off the alarm. Then checked to make sure the hallway was empty before sneaking into one of the empty production studios. I waited there in the dark, behind the gray-tinted glass, until I saw Tyler leave DJ's office. Once he passed, I slipped down the hall, tapped softly on her open door, and peered inside. She was standing behind her desk, stacks of papers in front of her.

"DJ? You got a minute?"

She glanced up at me then to the clock. The concern on her face matched what I was feeling. Her tone was cautious. "Come in, Carol. Close the door behind you."

I took a seat in front of her desk and didn't wait to be asked why I was there. "I got a call from Mustang Sally. We're on for a meet."

DJ sat down, her eyes fixed on mine. "Go on."

"Saturday night. Point Fermin Park in San Pedro. You familiar with the area?"

"The cliffs, huh?" DJ sat back and crossed her arms. "You think she'll show up this time and not run away?"

"Hopefully."

"We can't lose her this time, Carol. We're not going to get a third chance. Somebody's going to get wise to her, and when they do—"

"I know. But I've got a plan."

DJ leaned forward in her chair and put her elbows on the desk. "All right. I'm listening."

I took my laptop from my bag and pulled up a map for Point Fermin. Placing it on the desk in front of her, I positioned it as though she were looking at the park from the street side, peering out at the ocean. Standing up, I pointed out the lighthouse in the center of the map and the two wedding areas on either side. Wedding Area One was on the right of the Lighthouse, the south side. Wedding Area Two was to the left, on the north side.

"Wedding Area One," I said, tapping the position on the map, "is where I want to meet you at exactly eight thirty." I paused, making sure she had the exact location. What I didn't tell DJ was that Sally had asked me to meet her with Jason at exactly eight o'clock at Wedding Area Two. Thirty minutes earlier. Timing was going to be imperative. I took a deep breath and continued. "I told Sally I would meet her there. And when I do, I'll tell her she has an old friend who contacted me via my show and needs her help. That friend, of course, will be you."

I looked at the map again. The distance between the two wedding areas was enough that in the dark of night we wouldn't be seen. And with a little luck, I could make this all work to my advantage. DJ thought Sally was expecting to meet me, Carol Childs. She knew nothing about my plan to assume Jennifer's identity or that I had been using Chase to help me find Sally. Or even more worrisome, that I was considering asking him to act as Jennifer's fiancé, Jason. As to how I was going to do that and keep Chase from ever seeing Sally, I hadn't a clue. But with thirty minutes to spare between meetings, I figured somehow, something would work out. One step at a time, I told myself.

"Only one problem with all this, Carol."

"What's that?" My heart felt like a giant claw was starting to squeeze it tight.

"You can't use my name. Sally won't know me as DJ."

"No?" Is that all it was? I took a deep breath and the claw squeezing my heart released. "When we met, she knew me as Doris Jean. It wasn't until later that I shortened it to DJ."

"You think she'll remember you?"

"I'm pretty sure she will."

"Good, then that's the plan. You'll meet me with Sally at Point Fermin, at Wedding Area One, on the south side of the lighthouse, at eight thirty, and I'll introduce you as Doris Jean" I pointed again to the area where we would meet. "Just make sure it's the south side."

DJ scribbled something in her notebook, then looked back at me as though she were about to dismiss me. "Anything else?"

I closed my laptop and held it in my arms against my chest. "Before we go any further, there is something I need to know."

"What is it?"

"Once I deliver Sally to you, what are you going to do? Where will you take her? I realize you think the less I know, the better, but the fact is, I'm risking something here too. If Sally escapes or something happens, there's no guarantee she's not going to start calling the station again or maybe get picked up, and suddenly I'm an accessory to a crime."

"You don't have to worry, Carol. Where's she going, it's not likely she'd escape or want to, for that matter."

"Why? Where are you taking her?"

DJ paused and put the notebook down on the desk. "There's a safe house on one of the islands in Hawaii. I won't tell you which island, only that it's in a remote location, very secure. The locals think it's a rehab facility. In truth, it's a secure complex with ten-foot walls, security cameras, and staff like that at a five-star hotel. I spent some time there when I was in hiding. You don't need to worry, Carol. She'll be well taken care of."

"How will I know she got there okay?"

DJ picked up the notebook, scribbled something onto one of the pages, then handed it to me. "This is the same number I gave you last time. You need to wait at least twelve hours, then call this number. Ask if the package Doris Jean delivered has arrived. You'll get your answer."

I stared at the number in my hand, then got up from my seat. "Okay. 'Til Saturday."

I headed to the door, and when I got there, I heard DJ. "Carol, one more thing." I turned and looked back at her. "Just so you know, I'm glad it was you and your show Mustang Sally reached out to."

"Me too."

# CHAPTER 36

I waited outside DJ's office until I was certain the hallway was clear. Per his usual morning ritual, Tyler had gone back to the newsroom and grabbed the newspaper. I watched as he headed to the men's room, then took my leave. Quietly slipping down the hallway and out the station's back door. When I got to the car, I picked up my cell and called Sheri.

"You got time for coffee? We need to talk."

"Have you forgotten?"

"About what?"

"Our coffee klatch at eleven. Did Misty forget to tell you?"

"She's been forgetting to tell me a lot lately."

"She suggested since you're home Mondays, we have coffee together. Or in her case, tea. Where are you anyway?"

"I had a meeting."

"Again?" Sheri's voice was laced with suspicion. "With Chase, perhaps?"

"No," I said, my voice grounded, warding off any further chance of suspicion. "But I am beginning to think I may need to, and soon. Sally called."

I told Sheri to meet me at my place, then hung up and placed a call to Ms. Reddings. I had promised Andrea I would let her know when I was close to making contact with Sally. If things didn't work out with DJ, I wanted a backup plan. And since Andrea had admitted she shuffled funds secretly to Sally, she seemed like a safe bet.

The phone rang several times before the housekeeper answered. "Reddings' residence. May I help you?"

I asked to speak to Andrea and was told she wasn't available. Would I like to leave a message? I did and requested she call, soon as possible.

I met Sheri on the walk as I emerged from the parking structure beneath my condo. In her hands, she had a plate of homemade blueberry muffins with a glazed streusel topping. Still warm from the oven. I took a whiff and my stomach growled. The first normal feeling I'd had all morning.

Misty was seated at the kitchen table when we walked in, a pot of freshly brewed tea in front of her. I explained we had some serious issues to discuss and she looked at me like she had done something wrong. "What's happened?"

"Sally called. She wants to meet." I didn't get into the details of how I'd received Sally's call, that would come out soon enough. But right now I needed Misty's full attention.

Sheri slipped the plate of muffins beneath my nose, then placed them on the table. "And we need to brainstorm because Chase can't know any of this."

"And you're concerned I might say something?" Misty asked.

"There are things I've been worried you might let accidently slip, It's one of the reasons, I told him I didn't want him to help with the arbor you wanted. There's so much, Misty, he can't know."

"Because if he does," Sheri said, "and Chase finds Sally, he might try to have her arrested, and Carol needs to get to her before he can do that."

"Exactly," I said.

"And you want my help?" Misty stared down at her tea, both hands on the side of the cup as though she might be trying to read the leaves.

"I don't know how else I'm going to pull this off. I'm going to need you both. There're too many moving pieces for me to handle this alone, and too many lives that depend on me getting it right."

I explained Sally's connection to DJ and how Sally had rescued her. Then I reminded Misty how Sheri and I had run into Jennifer at the restaurant in Santa Monica after Jason had dumped her.

"After that, Jennifer went home and got online for some grief counseling. And guess who she runs into?"

"Sally?" Misty continued to stare down at her tea like the answer was right in front of her.

I glanced into her cup then back at Sheri and shrugged. If Misty was reading leaves, I sure didn't see anything.

"But pretty soon, Jennifer didn't want anything to do with her. Then Sally started calling, and that's when Jennifer gave me her cell phone. And now Sally's called again and wants to meet."

"When?" Sheri asked.

"Saturday night. Eight o'clock. I'm planning to go in Jennifer's place like I did before. Only problem is, Sally's also expecting to meet Jason."

"Where?" Sheri asked.

"Point Fermin, in San Pedro."

"Why? What's she planning to do, push him off the cliffs?" Sheri wrinkled her brow.

"I think so," I said.

Misty looked up from her tea. "And you're wondering how you're going to get Chase to pretend he's Jason so Sally can see the two of you together without his ever seeing Sally?"

I grabbed a muffin and began picking at it, eating as I spoke. I was starving.

"Yes, and once I make contact with Sally at eight o'clock, I need to get her to the other side of the lighthouse where DJ will be waiting for us at eight thirty. That gives me thirty minutes to meet with Sally, have her see me with Jason or who she thinks is Jason, and then make her disappear without Chase knowing anything about it."

Misty stirred her tea. "I think you're getting ahead of yourself, Carol. Before you go any further with this idea, you need to talk to Chase."

I knew Misty was right. I had avoided the thought of sharing with Chase anything about my meeting with Sally, but now I was stuck. I couldn't ask anyone else to step in as Jason, and Chase, I knew, would be a willing decoy. The trick was, how was I going to tell him I'd made contact with Mustang Sally without revealing my plan?

Misty suggested the following: I would call Chase and explain that Jennifer, a fan, had found Mustang Sally in an online chat room and later recognized her name and very distinct voice while listening to my show. She was alarmed by Sally's suggestion—to off her fiancé—and, as a result, called me with information about a meeting she had set up.

"Not too far off from the truth," Sheri said, "but if we're talking Saturday night, you need to get on it." Sheri grabbed my bag off the floor and put it on the table. "Call him now."

"Fine." I reached into my bag and fiddled for my phone inside. I would have liked more time to think about what I was I going say, but I knew Sheri was right. I couldn't assume just because Chase wanted to find Sally as much as I did that he would be free on a Saturday night. No doubt he had other cases and *interests*. After all, I wasn't responding in typical female fashion, and he had said he was an all-American male. The man was entitled to a social life. Just not mine. Finding my cell, I smiled. Chase had called three times. If nothing else, the man was persistent. I punched redial and counted five rings before he answered.

"You sitting down?" I didn't give him a chance to say hello.

"Well, good morning to you too, Carol." I could hear the sound of running water in the background. His breathing sounded irregular like he had run to catch the phone.

"You okay?"

"I was just getting out of the shower."

"At this hour?" I checked the clock. It was already past noon.

"I went for a run."

I covered the mouthpiece and whispered to Misty and Sheri, he was in the shower. Then back to Chase, I said, "I can call you back if this is a bad time."

"What, the idea of knowing I'm standing here stark naked talking to a beautiful woman bother you?"

I had a vision of Chase dripping wet with his dark curly hair drip-drying around his broad shoulders and felt my cheeks grow warm. Misty smiled back at me like she had the same vision. I rolled my eyes and gripped the phone tighter.

"I found Mustang Sally."

"Where? When?"

"Settle down. She's fine, and she's not going anywhere. I have an appointment with her Saturday night. I thought we should grab coff—"

"Dinner," Chase said.

"Fine. But not tonight." I still had things I needed to work out in my mind and wasn't ready to have dinner with Chase. Besides, Charlie would be home tonight, and I was looking forward to a peaceful dinner with my son.

"If you're sure she's not going anywhere."

"She's not."

"Okay, tomorrow night. I hope to have news for you too. About that other matter you asked me to check into."

"Silva?" I asked.

"Maybe. I'll tell you more tomorrow night. Il Segreto. Eight p.m."


I agreed to dinner. I would have preferred to meet for coffee or maybe even a quick drink, but both Sheri and Misty thought it was necessary.

"After all," Sheri said, "you can't lure a man to his death without offering him a last meal."

"Last meal?" I threw a muffin in Sheri's direction. "Who said anything about a last meal? Chase isn't going to die. Not really. Mustang Sally just has to see him."

"And how are you going to do that?" Sheri asked. "Without him seeing her?"

Misty raised her hands and demanded silence. "Leave that to me, ladies. We'll have a better idea how to approach the subject once Carol talks to Chase. Until then, we speak of this to no one."

# CHAPTER 37

Tuesday night it started to rain, and there was a chill in the air as I pulled into the parking lot at the restaurant for my meeting with Chase. Il Segreto was an elegant dining spot located at the top of Mulholland Drive and surrounded by multimillion-dollar homes. While I appreciated that Chase had chosen a restaurant less than ten minutes from my condo, it was a far more romantic spot than something I would have chosen.

I hugged my raincoat up around my shoulders, held my purse over my head, and doing my best to dodge the rain, hurried inside. Not an easy thing to do in four-inch heels. I would have been much more comfortable in jeans and sneakers, but Il Segreto was a little black dress type of restaurant. I reminded myself my choice in clothing, a form-fitting black dress that hugged my body like I missed being hugged, was simply a matter of respecting the restaurant's upscale dress code. No matter how intimate the atmosphere or charming Chase might be, this was simply going to be a quick business dinner, nothing more.

A hostess greeted me by name and offered to take my coat, then returned to escort me to a table at the back of the restaurant. I finger-brushed my hair from my eyes as I followed her to a small table for two in front of a warm crackling fireplace. The lights were dim, the table lit with candlelight and dressed in a white linen tablecloth and heavy silver.

Chase stood up as I approached. I did an immediate double-take. He was dressed in a tie, sports coat, slacks, and a blue shirt that matched his blue-gray eyes. And he had shaved. Gone was the scruffy beard I so disliked, and in its place, a strong, handsome smile. Taking my hand, he bussed my cheek politely with a welcome kiss.

"I took the liberty of ordering you champagne."

"Chase, this isn't a—"

"Date?" Chase took my chair out from the table and waited for me to take a seat. The scent of his cologne caused my pulse to quicken. "You're absolutely right. But seeing as I have good news and you've managed to find Mustang Sally, I thought we should celebrate. As colleagues."

Chase took the seat across the table from me. The waiter, as though he had been scripted to do so, arrived and poured a glass of champagne for me and sparkling water for Chase.

"However, if you'd prefer, you can join me in a glass of something non-alcoholic. I've got it on good authority, this is a very good year."

I felt my cheeks start to tingle. Was it the candlelight or the fact Chase had shaved and was looking so handsome, sitting across the table from me in a coat and tie. Or just the fact that I hadn't dined in such a romantic setting with a man in what seemed like forever that I felt myself growing weak? Certainly, one glass of champagne wouldn't hurt, and it might help to steel my nerves.

I said, "One glass is fine. Besides, it's been a bit cold outside, and it'll help take the chill off."

"I hope so." Chase raised his glass to mine. "To our success then."

I followed suit, took a sip, and felt instantly guilty. If Chase had any idea I didn't intend for him to get within ten feet of Sally, we wouldn't be celebrating. I put my glass back down on the table and carefully navigated the conversation away from me and back to him.

"But you first. You said you had good news. And I'm hoping it's about the hit-and-run I asked you to investigate."

"It does, but you'll find out more about that tomorrow. What I will share with you is that Tyler's going to be busy trying to fill a void on the air this weekend."

"Really? You mean because Silva's been fired?"

"He will be. After I got the results of LAPD's investigation, I picked up the phone and spoke to Tyler. Thought I should give him a heads up. If all goes as planned, sometime tomorrow, LAPD will have charged your station's Saint Silva with manslaughter, along with a slew of other charges including leaving the scene of an accident and interfering with an investigation."

"Whoa." I paused a moment and thought of the implications of Silva's arrest, what it would mean to the station and to the staff.

"You were right about Silva's wife. She couldn't possibly have driven his car. Not for any distance anyway. The seat was pushed too far back for a woman her size to be comfortably driving. She might have driven it a few blocks from her house and back to the scene of the accident. But there's no way she was driving her husband to work that night."

"And you know this how?"

"The police impounded the car. The evidence was right there. Enough so anyway, they knew Silva was lying."

"So what really happened?"

"According to one of the investigating officers, who shared this with me in exchange for a little help with Silva's wife, Silva may have been drinking. His screener in the studio that night says he remembers Silva opening a bottle of scotch after he came in and taking a couple of strong hits. He also said it wasn't unusual for Silva to nurse a bottle throughout the show, but he definitely remembers thinking he was hitting it a bit hard that night."

"And Silva's wife, Martha, what did she have to say?"

"She said after dinner, her husband left for work, just like he always did. But then about ten minutes later, he returned and told his wife he thought maybe he had hit someone. More importantly, that he needed her to return to the scene and talk to the police."

"And she agreed?"

"She did what she was told. Went back to where Silva said he thought he had hit someone and, sure enough, found a body in the bushes. That's when she called the police and made up a story about driving her husband to work. Told them she thought she might have hit something or someone while driving him to work, but couldn't see anything in the dark. It was almost eleven o'clock, and Silva was worried about being late for his show. She claims he then had her drive him back home so he could take her car into work, and she could come back."

"So Silva left her, drove to the station, and never said a word about the accident?"

"Not until the police called him to report his wife had been in an accident and was at the police station."

"She confessed all this to the police?"

"Not quite. That was the help LAPD wanted. Seemed Martha was afraid to talk to the cops. Thought if her husband found out he'd be angry with her. Accuse her of disrespecting his orders. I simply introduced myself as a private investigator, a friend of the station." I rolled my eyes. "Unlike you, Carol, there are some women who do find me quite charming, and she was more than willing to talk."

Did he wink? I felt my cheeks flush. I was glad the room was dark, and he couldn't see. "I'm not even going to comment on that," I said.

"But don't worry. Tyler had no idea you turned me on to the investigation. Your name's nowhere near it, so you haven't violated any of your company's no-tell policy."

"Does this mean you're back in good with LAPD?"

"I can tell you we're no longer as estranged as we've been. The fact Riley's dead may have something to do with it, but time will tell." Chase took a sip of water. "So, how about you and your news? Tell me how you managed to make contact with the elusive Mustang Sally?"

"Right." I picked up my champagne glass, I was going to need to fortify myself for this explanation. I took a long healthy sip. "I think we need to iron out a few logistics concerning the meet. I wouldn't want Sally to slip through our fingers. It'll be dark, and if it rains, like tonight, it could be difficult."

"What are you worried about, Carol? The woman's requested a meeting with you. She's been calling the station. You've obviously hit on something with her, and she wants to talk with you in person. She's delivering herself to you. Why are you having second thoughts?"

"I'm not certain she's such a bad person, Chase. The men she murdered were all physically abusive predators. The police couldn't protect the women. Maybe what she does is necessary. I think that's what Riley was trying to tell me before he died. That's why he wanted me to stay out of it."

"That wasn't his call, Carol."

"I know, but I've been thinking, what if we didn't find her? What if Sally got away?"

"She's a vigilante, Carol. People can't take the law into their own hands. That's what the cops are for. Besides, the woman's been reaching out to you. She needs help. Why else would she agreed to meet you?"

"About that...there's something I need to explain."

The waiter interrupted me before I could go any further. He placed two menus on the table and started sharing the night's specials. I glanced at the selection. I had absolutely no interest in food, my stomach tying itself in knots. Finally, feeling I had to order something to keep Chase from suspecting something was up, I said I'd have the linguini. Chase ordered the rack of lamb and suggested we split a Cesar salad. Reluctantly, I agreed.

"So just what is it you need to explain to me, Carol?"

"It's not me Sally's expecting Saturday night, but someone else."

I gave him the revised version of how I had come to know Jennifer Lamb. Explaining she was a fan and after her fiancé had dumped her how she had found Mustang Sally's online chatroom. "Which led to their meeting, or almost meeting. They've never really met. At least not in person."

"I see. So what you're telling me is that Saturday night, Sally is expecting to meet with Jennifer for the first time."

"Right."

"And you're going to pretend to be Jennifer."

"I am."

"And if I understand this correctly, you want me to be Jason? And once Sally's convinced I'm him, we'll kidnap her and turn her over to the authorities."

I forced a smile. "Yeah, something like that." I felt my stomach churn. I hated lying to Chase, but what could I do? Without his help, I had no chance of luring Sally to the cliffs. The whole point of our meeting was for her to meet Jason. I just needed to make sure she saw me with him, and that Chase didn't see her.

"I like it." Chase picked up his water glass. "To Jennifer and Jason."

I clinked glasses with him. "To Jennifer and Jason."

# CHAPTER 38

I knew something was wrong the next morning when I pulled into the station's parking lot. DJ's green Jaguar was nowhere to be seen. Like Tyler, DJ was always at the station by the time I arrived. The two of them lived on New York time, three hours ahead of LA, making themselves slaves to corporate. I gripped the steering wheel and felt the palms of my hands start to sweat. Where was DJ? What if she had been called out of town and couldn't make Saturday night? I hurried into the station. In the background, the morning show with Kit and Carson was being piped through the hallways, and despite the early hour, a few sales people were milling about in the sales bay like it was just another day. It wasn't until I walked into the newsroom and saw Tyler's door was shut that I knew something wasn't right. Tyler's door was never closed.

A sleepy engineer sat at a desk outside Tyler's office with a newspaper spread across his belly. He looked like he had been up all night. I asked if he knew who was in with Tyler.

"No. But the boss did say when you came in to tell you he wants to talk with you. Said it was important. I was supposed to wait and make sure you got the message in person."

"Thanks," I said. I glanced back at Tyler's door. If what Chase had shared with me last night about Silva was correct, the reason for Tyler's closed door might very well be in the office with him right now, and the fireworks—if there were any—were about to start.

"You by any chance seen DJ this morning?"

"Nope." He settled back in the chair and pulled the newspaper up over his head.

So much for conversation. I grabbed an empty desk, picked up the phone and placed another call to Andrea Reddings. In the back of mind, I continued to think of her as a safe second. If something happened to DJ, I didn't want to be left wondering what to do with Sally.

The housekeeper answered exactly as she had before and with the same response. Ms. Reddings was not available. *Again?*

"May I leave a message?"

"You may, but it could be several days before Ms. Reddings is able to return your call. She's away on business, checking on some properties."

Something about the way she said, "away on business" bothered me. I asked, "Is she expected to return anytime soon?"

"I'm sorry. I'm afraid I can't answer that. Ms. Reddings doesn't discuss her schedule with me. She may be back tomorrow or next month. I never know. But as I said, if you'd like for me to take a message, I'd be happy to."

"No. That's fine. I'll catch her when she's in town again. Thank you."

Was it a coincidence or was Misty rubbing off on me? Something about Andrea's travel schedule seemed off. With her husband dead, his accused killer in jail, and a trial pending, it seemed an odd time for a business trip. What properties might she be checking where she felt compelled to stay for an extended period of time? And why now? My mind flashed on a painting I'd seen above the mantel in Reddings' estate. A serene beach scene with a beautiful native girl reclining on the sand in front of a pink stucco villa, surrounded by swaying palms and orchids. She called it one of Marcus' expensive apologies. Something he had purchased along with an island retreat. Could she be there? And if she were, might it also have been DJ's safe house? DJ had described the house as a Hawaiian villa. Was it a coincidence or a connection?

The door to Tyler's office opened, and he walked out with Silva at his side. From behind them, the station's attorney, Mr. King, appeared. It didn't take being a reporter to know that whatever had transpired inside the room wasn't good. Chase was right. Silva was out. There was no doubt about it. Silva was ashen. His normally ramrod straight posture now round-shouldered, like a drill sergeant who had just been stripped of his rank. I watched as Silva brushed his bony fingers through his thinning hair and mumbled something to Tyler. Then, with one final handshake, said goodbye. King patted Tyler on the back, then turned to Silva and escorted him out of the newsroom. I assumed King was taking him downtown where Silva would turn himself in, but the scene played out more like a prisoner being walked from his jail cell to his execution.

Tyler spotted me sitting at the desk. He waved me over, like a traffic cop. "Carol, my office. Now."

I followed him into his office.

"Silva's out. We're going to need to get something on the air for the next newscast. He's about to be charged with vehicular homicide. He came by here on his way to turn himself in this morning. Wanted to consult with the station's attorney."

"He have any comment? Anything official you'd like to have us put out?"

"Only that he's very sorry for the pain and suffering he's caused. The usual. You know what to do. Get something on the air right away and keep it simple. Meanwhile, I've got a show to fill Saturday night."

I stood up. I didn't want Tyler to think of me as a possible fill-in for Silva. Not now. And certainly not this Saturday night. I beat it down the hall and into the news booth just in time to deliver the eight a.m. top of the hour news. I led with news of Ben Silva's impending arrest.

# CHAPTER 39

By Friday morning I was getting anxious. I hadn't heard from DJ since we'd discussed our plans for Saturday, and her car wasn't in her usual space in the parking lot. When I asked her assistant where she was, Molly told me DJ had been delayed in New York due to the weather. Blizzard conditions had dumped nearly twenty-six inches of snow on the city, and all flights in and out of the area had been grounded. Travelers were advised to stay home. Only a miracle would get her home by Saturday afternoon.

"Where's she now?" I asked.

"Stuck in the airport. Been there for the last twelve hours. She said she's not leaving 'til she's got a seat. She thinks there's a chance she might be able to get a flight out late tonight or first thing tomorrow morning."

I didn't want to sound overly concerned, so I told her I was hoping DJ might have a chance to listen to my show Sunday night.

Molly shook her head. "I doubt it. Before she left, she asked me to clear her schedule. She said she wanted some personal time and would be out of earshot. She's not due back in the station for another week."

I left Molly in the hallway and hurried back to my office where I called DJ's cell. The line went immediately to voicemail. I left a carefully coded message, making certain I didn't make any reference to our plan.

"DJ. It's Carol Childs. I wanted to know how much I appreciate your support and talking to me last week. Everything's set for my show this weekend. I was hoping you might be able to tune in, but Molly tells me you're stuck at JFK. Call me if you get a chance. I'd love to chat before I go on air. Sure could use some moral support. Talk soon."

I hung up and stared at my phone. If DJ was stuck in the airport, why hadn't she picked up? What if she didn't make it back to LA in time? Now that I had set the plan in motion, what was I going to do with Sally? And an even bigger worry, what was I going to do with Chase?

I hadn't a clue how I would handle him. And right now, while DJ wasn't calling me back, Chase was. His latest request was for us to drive to Fermin Park together. He thought it might be nice and suggested we have dinner before our staged rendezvous with Sally. I definitely wasn't up for dinner. Nor was I about to sit alone in a car with Chase for an hour's drive to the park. The memory of his cologne alone had caused my mind to wander, and I didn't trust I might accidentally let something slip about DJ or Sally. Spending any more time with him than necessary was out of the question.

As for my backup plan to contact Andrea Reddings and ask for her help, that wasn't working either. She hadn't returned any of my calls, and nobody on her staff was talking. She had simply disappeared.


In the middle of the night, I got a text from DJ. I had left my cell phone on my nightstand, just in case, and when I heard it buzz, I sat up in bed like someone had fired off a gunshot. I reached for the bedside table and fumbled for my cell phone.

DJ's coded text read: Sorry for the delay getting back to you. Looking forward to your show. Don't worry, I'll be there for you. You've got this.

*I've got this?*

I stared at the text. If DJ only knew the whole of it. All the moving pieces I was still trying to finagle into place. Chase and me. Sally and me sans Chase. DJ and Sally. I lay awake the rest of the night, tying the sheets in knots. How had I'd gotten myself into such a mess? If this whole kidnapping idea didn't go down as well as DJ predicted, would the station's attorney be advising me about my rights? Would I go to jail as an accessory to a crime? Murder? Kidnapping? And what about DJ, would she walk away from me, deny she had anything to do with it? Finally, exhausted with the possibilities, I fell asleep and dreamt about Chase. He was tugging at my arm, pulling me away from the cliff's edge. I could see the rocky shore below me, the waves crashing on the rocks, the white water churning in the dark. And then in the next scene, Chase with his sucker in his mouth was turning me over to LAPD for interfering in a criminal investigation. I woke up in a sweat. From the kitchen, I could hear the sound of water running and the clanking of pots and pans. I grabbed my robe, headed downstairs, and found Misty, buzzing around like a short order cook

"Misty?" I noticed she had on a new apron and beneath it a long vintage paisley skirt I hadn't seen before. Was it my imagination or were her cheeks rosier and her eyes a little brighter? "You look nice today. Anything special going on?"

"Come sit down. I'm making eggs and bacon. Waffles too, if you like."

I looked around the room. *Where was Charlie?*

Misty answered like she had read my mind. "Your son's out checking on my van. I suggested he drive us to the park. We're going to meet Sheri and Clint down at the USS Iowa. Have you ever seen it? I thought the boys would enjoy the outing, and it's a good excuse to get everyone down to Long Beach. From there it's just a short drive to Point Fermin, where you and Sheri can split off and do your thing." She winked. "You want coffee?"

"Are you okay?" I stood at the foot of the stairs and scanned the kitchen. It was spotless. If I didn't know better, I would swear someone, other than my sixteen-year-son who couldn't pick up a bag of potato chips without being asked twice, had been assisting her in the kitchen "You sure you're not overdoing it?"

"I'm fine. In fact, I'm better than fine." Misty stood in front of the stove and turned to me. In her hand, she waved a spatula above her head. "I've seen Dr. Sam."

"Dr. Sam? I thought we were going to do tea together sometime. Maybe next week?"

"That might've been fine for you, but evidently not for him. He called the house, and when I answered the phone, he wanted to set something up. We both agreed, why wait?"

"I see. So you meet with him?"

"At my age, Carol, waiting is for those who have time. Besides, he wanted to know more about my herbs, and I invited him over to see my garden."

I took the spatula from Misty's hand. "Are you taking something?"

"Why?" She snatched the spatula back from me like a child and smiled.

"You seem different this morning. Did Dr. Sam give you something?"

Misty turned back to the stove. "If you must know, yes. He gave me some pills to help me sleep. He thought it might help with my memory. I take one of his magic pills along with my sleeping beauty tea, and it's like somebody switched off the lights. He assured me they're nothing more than a few natural herbs like what I grow. And, for what it's worth, I think I look better too. Don't you?"

Misty angled her body towards me and, taking the side of her skirt in her hand, did a small curtsy.

"New skirt?" I asked.

"No. Not new. I just remembered where I'd put it. Amazing how a good night's sleep perks one up. I feel ten years younger. Which reminds me. I thought you might like to try one too." Misty reached into the apron's pocket, pulled out a small oval-shaped purple pill, and placed it in my hand.

"Me?" I stared at the pill. Were the walls that thin she'd heard me tossing and turning? "You think I need it?"

Misty drew her lips together and shook her head. "Not you, Carol, but someone close to you." Then tapping her index finger against my heart, she smiled and waited for me to catch on.

"For Chase then?" I folded my fingers over the palm of my hand and squeezed it tight. "Misty, are you thinking what I'm thinking?"

"I don't know what you're talking about, Carol." Misty turned back to the stove, then muttered, "Unless, you're reading *my* mind.

Which could only mean you're finally beginning to understand the principles of psychic thought. The transference of an idea from one mind to another."

"You know I don't believe in that stuff, Misty. If anything, I think maybe it's more intuition." I opened my hand and stared back down at the pill. Intuition or otherwise, I had my answer. It would be easy enough to crush the capsule up and disguise it any way I wanted. "But for what's it worth, thank you. I could use a sleeping pill and some of your special tea too."

# CHAPTER 40

By the time we left for Long Beach, it had started to rain again. Misty insisted Charlie drive the van, that the experience would be good for him. I wasn't so sure that was a good idea, what with traffic and slick roads and all, but Misty assured me her hippie van had gone hundreds of thousands of miles and was immune to road hazards, man-made or otherwise. Plus, she couldn't drive, not with the pills she had been taking, and I had never driven a stick shift and taking my car was out of the question. I needed to keep a low profile, and my ten-year-old red Jeep with its KNST bumper stickers and window decals stuck out like an overripe tomato. Charlie was our only option.

Misty volunteered to ride gunshot. She and Charlie had developed a routine on their afternoon drives, and she thought I would only make him nervous sitting up front. I agreed and buried myself behind the van's small kitchen table in the back with my portable computer. I wanted to monitor the Butterflies chat room for any activity, while I referred to my notes concerning tonight's operation. I pulled up a map of the park on my computer screen and was about to review my plan when Jennifer's cell phone buzzed from within my pocket.

The sound of it so startled me that as I reached into my pocket for the phone, I nearly knocked my computer off my lap. Misty's eyes flashed back at me. *Was it Sally?* I put my finger to my lips, shook my head, and answered.

"Carol, it's Jennifer Lamb."

I had forgotten she had the number. "Are you okay?"

"I'm sorry to call on this line. I know you wanted to keep it clear for Sally, but you weren't answering your cell, and, well, it's kind of an emergency."

I exhaled while I fished inside my bag with my free hand for my own cell phone. I had turned it off to avoid any further calls from Chase. He had continued to pester me about driving to the park with him, and by now I was running out of excuses. Earlier, I had told him Sheri, Misty, and I were taking the boys to Long Beach for a family outing. That it was part of my plan to keep Charlie busy and unaware of my clandestine activities. I explained I would catch up with him in the parking lot in plenty of time for what I was now calling Operation Butterfly. But Chase was having trouble taking no for an answer. My phone registered two missed calls and a text, ending with a smiley face and the words, *See you at the park. 7:30 p.m.*

I placed my cell on the table in front of me and asked Jennifer what was wrong.

"It's Jason." she said.

"Jason?" I glanced at Misty and shrugged. "What's happened?"

"He's back."

"Back? I thought after I left your apartment you told me you were going home, back to San Francisco."

"I couldn't go. He showed up before I had a chance to leave. We talked, and one thing led to another, and...well, he said he loves me, Carol. He wants to get back together. And, I'm confused. I don't know what to do. I was hoping I could talk to Misty."

"Misty?"

"Yes. I heard her on the show with you last week. She made a lot of sense. I was hoping you could put me in touch with her."

"I can do better than that. She's here with me right now." I rolled my eyes and handed the phone to Misty.

"It's for you, Misty. You have a fan."

# CHAPTER 41

Over dinner, I apologized to Charlie and Clint for having to break up
the family outing. Our day-long adventure aboard the USS Iowa
offered everything two teenage boys could have wanted. They rang the
ship's bell, manned the anti-aircraft guns, stood behind the sixty-six-
foot-long turrets, and climbed the impossibly steep steel stairs
between decks like seamen recruits. Then, just as we were about to
order dessert, Tyler called. Or at least I feigned his call. I explained to
the boys I was needed to cover a breaking story, but I'd be back soon.
Sheri took that as her cue to volunteer to drive me since I didn't have a
car. Her car would serve as my portable dressing room. Allowing me to
change into my Jennifer costume, complete with wig and makeup,
while driving to the park. In our absence, Misty agreed she and the
boys would wander over to Shoreline Village, where they could hang
out until I was free to join them again.

Score one for the first part of my plan. The boys were taken care
of, and Charlie, thank goodness, didn't have a clue what I was about to
do, and hopefully never would.

Part two was going to be more difficult.

I knew instantly when Sheri and I arrived at the park my plan
wasn't going to work. A huge event was going on in Area Two where I
was to meet Sally. Hundreds of people were milling around. That in
itself might not have been a problem. Sally had told me she liked to
hide in plain sight, and I was counting on a crowd myself. But tonight
was different. Not only was there a crowd, but it had been raining. And
while the rain had stopped, in place of an open-air reception beneath
the stars, which would have been perfect, the caterers had set up a big

tent. And the area outside the tent was lit up like a moon launch. My idea that in the dark of night I'd be able to maneuver between Sally, a crowd of partygoers, and Chase, was fading quickly.

"This is never going to work."

"Hold on." Sheri walked ahead of me, scanning the park for a possible alternative. "How about over there? It's still part of the party area."

I followed her gaze beyond the tent and closer to the lighthouse where in the shadows a huge fig tree hugged the cliff.

Without answering, I struck out ahead of her, the cool night air in combination with the sea wind chilling my cheeks. The giant fig's branches spread several hundred feet, offering a natural shelter. I turned and looked back at the park's entrance. It was perfect. In fact, better than perfect, beneath the tree was a small picnic table. The type of place a couple who wanted to be alone might sit and gaze out at the water. The type of place I felt certain Sally would come looking for me. But best of all, from beneath the tree, I could see anyone who approached.

I bit my bottom lip and surveyed the area. Holding my hands up in front of my face, I crossed my fingers and stared up at the stars. "This just might work."

"It's going to be fine, Carol." Sheri hugged me, her cool cheek bussed my own. "And if you need help, call my cell. I'll be in the car, waiting for the all-clear."

Earlier Sheri and I had agreed that if things didn't go as expected, if Chase got wise to my plan, or DJ failed to show, I would call her cell for backup. Exactly what that might be I didn't know, but Sheri was prepared to wing it. Worst-case scenario, if Chase got to be a problem, Sheri thought she might be able to reroute him while I took care of Sally. And if DJ failed to show, Sheri said she felt certain between the two of us, we could get Sally back to Sheri's car. And, should we need to, Sheri could accommodate Sally as a houseguest until we could come up with a more permanent solution.

I took my cell from my bag and called Chase. *Time to rock and roll.* "Where are you?"

"Just pulling into the parking lot."

"Good. I'll meet you at the park entrance." I stood up and started to walk. "One small hitch, though."

I explained the party tent and how I had been forced to move our meet beyond the tent and closer to the cliffs."

"Sexy."

"Stop." I felt my heart skip a beat and looked up at the sky. I just needed to get through the night.

"You'd prefer I say, all the easier for you to push me off the cliff?"

"That's not going to happen." I started walking again.

"Just a bit of gallows humor, Carol. Don't take it so seriously. We'll be fine."

I spotted Chase's black SUV as he entered the parking lot. He waved to me as he passed beneath a streetlight and parked the car. I bit back a smile. Much as I didn't want to admit it, I was attracted to Chase. I couldn't explain it. Sheri would have summed it up as primal, strictly a physical attraction. Whatever it was, I wasn't going to let the cool night air or a full moon complicate my mission. I had too much at stake. I needed to play Sally's kidnapping through to the end without any distractions. Besides, when this was all over, it was unlikely Chase would ever want to talk to me again.

I had just about convinced myself I could separate my feelings of attraction from my professional responsibilities when Chase got out of the car. He was dressed in black jeans and a leather jacket. The moonlight reflected his shadow off the wet pavement like some key light in a dark noir movie. Dammit, Chase, why couldn't you just smoke or chew tobacco or something awful like that. Why did he have to look so damn sexy?

"I like the hair." Chase touched the wig and smiled. "Kind of cute in a waif-like sort of way."

I put my hand on my head, suddenly self-conscious of the short curls around the base of my neck. I'd forgotten to tell Chase I had intended to disguise my identity.

"It was Sheri's idea. She thought it'd be better if I looked less like myself and more like a woman on the run."

"Humph." Chase stood back, his eyes scanning me up and down. "Not bad."

I batted his shoulder with the palm of my hand, then turned and started into the park. He followed.

"Nervous?" He asked.

"Maybe." My thin windbreaker was doing nothing for the cool night air. I felt a chill run down my back. "I've never kidnapped anyone before. Have you?"

"I try not to make a habit of it." He winked and took a sucker from inside his pocket and put it in his mouth.

"You're sure you want to do this, Chase?"

"What's happening?" Chase stopped walking and took the sucker out of his mouth. "You doubting yourself?"

"No. It's just I've been thinking. You know the cops, or some cops anyway, have been covering this up for ages. And whistleblowers, Chase, they aren't popular. You bust this case wide open, and it may not come down as you hope."

"What are you? A vigilante now? I thought you were all about uncovering the truth."

"I was...I mean, I am. It's just, in my mind, there's room for doubt. Maybe some things are best left alone."

Chase put his hands on my shoulders and bowed his head to mine, his blue-gray eyes staring straight into my own. "Trust me, Carol. That's not going to happen. Now, why don't you show me to this picnic area where Jennifer and Jason are supposed to be hanging out."

Rather than brush his hand off my shoulder, I let him put his arm around me as I led the way to the big tree. I told myself if Mustang Sally were watching I needed to make it look real. But it felt good.

"Right," I said. "And to that point, I brought refreshments. Misty insisted I bring some of your favorite tea. Something to keep us warm while we wait."

In my hands, I had Charlie's small insulated lunchbox he used for school. I clung to it like a security blanket. Inside were two small thermoses, one with a red cap, the other with a blue, and a couple of chocolate brownies Sheri had made.

"Misty, huh?"

"And Sheri too. She made some of her German chocolate brownies with sea salt, but you're going to want to drink a lot of tea. They're pretty salty."

I never thought drugging someone would be quite so simple. But that was before I had learned that when it came to food, Chase was pretty much a see-it-and-eat-it type of guy. Once I had pulled Sheri's sea salt brownies from Charlie's cooler, my job was half done. Chase did as I expected. He wolfed down the brownies, saying he hadn't eaten all day long, then swigged down Misty's tea. Or what he thought was Misty's tea. Before we had left the house, I ground up the sleeping pill Misty gave me into powder and then blended it into her favorite Sleeping Beauty tea. I poured Chase's tea into the red-capped thermos and filled the other with black coffee. I'd never been a fan of tea.

We sat on the bench with our backs up against the picnic table, the ocean behind us. Chase said he wanted to be able to have a full-on view of the park.

"Like a cop in an Italian restaurant," he said, "you want your back up against the wall so you can see who comes in and what's coming at you."

I smiled and glanced at my watch. It was almost eight o'clock. Chase yawned.

"You tired?" I asked.

"Must be the sea air." Chase leaned back against the table, his arm around my shoulder. "If you don't mind, I'll just..."

# CHAPTER 42

Chase was out. His eyes closed. His chin resting on his chest. I placed my hand over his heart to check his breathing. Soft and regular, as though he were purring. I wanted to push his dark curly hair away from his face, but I didn't dare. I couldn't risk waking him. Gently, I slipped out from beneath his arm and glanced at my watch. It wasn't yet eight o'clock. In a few minutes, the Korean Bell of Friendship would ring. Hopefully between the pill Misty had given me and her sleepy-tea, the gentle hollow sound would not wake him. I scanned the park.

People were beginning to emerge from the party tent. Couples and small groups, their arms around each other, wandered over to the cliffs to enjoy the night's view. Their drunken laughter mixed with the sound of the crashing waves on the sunken city below.

Then from within the tent, a tall and broad-shouldered image appeared. At this distance, it was difficult to tell if it was a man or a woman. I watched as whoever it was put on a hat, then turned in my direction, and paused. I could feel its eyes upon me. It was as though I were its prey and we were the only two people in the park. I stood up.

*Sally?*

As the image moved forward, I moved closer to it. In the moonlight, I recognized the long knee-length trench coat. It was the same one she had worn the night we met at the university, and then I saw the Burberry scarf wrapped around her neck. Her hands were in her pockets.

We met halfway between the tent and the picnic table.

"Thank you for coming," I said.

Without a smile or any sign of recognition, she looked over my shoulder and nodded in the direction of Chase. "That Jason?"

"Yes."

"What's wrong with him? He drunk?" Her voice was raspy.

"Passed out," I said.

Sally started to move towards him. I grabbed her arm, releasing her hand from her pocket.

"Sally, wait." In the moonlight, I caught a glint of something silver. I gripped her wrist tight and refused to let go. In her hand, Sally held a small gun. Our eyes met.

"It's just a little insurance, Jennifer. You don't need to worry. I don't plan to use it. I won't need to."

"Please, we need to talk." I pulled her closer to me. "Put the gun away and walk with me. He's not going anywhere."

Sally slid the gun back into her pocket. "He's not going to change, Jennifer. Men like him never do."

"I know. I know he's not." I tried to sound desperate. I took Sally's arm beneath my own and, holding it tight, started walking towards the lighthouse. "But I want to know I'm doing the right thing. I wish I felt more certain."

"If there were another way, Jennifer, I'd tell you. But there's not."

"It's just...I'm confused."

I dropped Sally's arm and walked on ahead in silence. On my left side, lining the pathway, were a series of short concrete barriers, about two feet in height. Beyond them the cliff, jagged and unstable in appearance, and beneath it the sunken city. Yellow caution signs warned hikers of the danger. I stopped and stared out at the water.

"Do you believe in forgiveness?" I glanced back over my shoulder at Sally. She stood stoically, her arms crossed, staring out at the sea. "Because I'm not sure I'll ever forgive myself if I do this."

"I believe in justice, Jennifer. For the victims." She stepped forward until she was standing next to me.

"And the men? You never questioned what you were doing?" I turned to Sally, she stood motionless, staring out at the inky black water, the look in her eyes distant. Suddenly they snapped back at me. Cold and calculating.

"I don't think about the men. I think about the women, Jennifer. Like you, they were all abused. Stalked and tortured like animals. Terrorized. Their lives ruined. These men were never going to stop hunting them. The cops couldn't stop them. But I could."

"How did you know you'd get away with it?"

"Because we always do."

"We? You mean you your tribunal."

"And my son. At least up until recently."

Sally stared up at the night sky. In the moonlight, I could see tears forming in the back of her eyes. If I was going for a confession, this was everything I needed. But I stalled. I had a few more minutes before I dared head towards the other side of the lighthouse where DJ would meet us.

"Your son?" I asked.

"He was as much a victim as I was. Maybe worse. Brain damaged. Because I didn't escape soon enough. It was all my fault. But he's dead now."

"I'm sorry."

"Don't be. It's not your fault. It's passed, and I make it better knowing I can make a difference."

"But how? You're here alone. Your tribunal's frightened of being discovered. You told me so yourself that night at the university. You said they're frightened you've gone too far. Spoken out too often. And now it's just you. Maybe it's time to stop, Sally."

"I can't stop. I'll never stop. Besides, I have you now. You'll help me."

"No. No, Sally, I can't do this."

"Yes, you can, dear. It'll be over in a minute." Sally put her arm around my shoulder and whispered in my ear. "The man's passed out drunk, Jennifer. It'll be easy. All we have to do is walk him to the edge of the cliff and give him a little shove. And poof." With her free hand, she opened her fingers out to the ocean. "Just like that, he'll be gone. Forever."

I pulled away. Sally was insane. I could see it. Her eyes were wide and glazed with excitement.

"And what about the police, Sally? What if they don't think it was a suicide?"

"The police?" Sally laughed and reached into her pocket. My eyes glued to her hand, fearful she might take out the gun again and force me to go back with her to find Chase. She read the look on my face and smiled. "Don't worry, dear, they'll know because of this." In her hand, Sally held out a small red ball. "It's a clown's nose. A marker. We place it on the body. The cops know what it is. Or certain cops, anyway. When they find it, the powers that be within the department find a way to record the death as a suicide."

"How? How do you know this?"

"You're surprised?"

"Yes." I grabbed her hands and held them in my own, staring at the red clown's nose.

"It was the cops who suggested it. Back when I was fearful for my life and my son's, a detective told me if my husband was to meet with an accident, nobody would be the wiser. The detective was the one who suggested the clown's nose. He gave it to me. I think he was looking for something, anything, that might give me confidence. The clown's nose was probably just a coincidence. Could have been anything. He told he had recently been to the circus and was going to give it to his nephew. He thought it might serve me better. All I had to do was put it on my husband's body, and it'd be a signal. I wouldn't have to worry about being found out."

"So you murdered your husband and left the clown's nose with his body and nobody was the wiser?"

"When the cops find a body and the death isn't immediately obvious, it's usually reported as suspicious circumstances. That is until the coroner rules on the cause of death. The detective set it up so that when they passed on a body with a red clown's nose to the coroner, he'd automatically rule the cause of death a suicide. I didn't ask any more about it. It became our little secret."

"And this detective? You remember his name?"

"I'll never forget him. His name was Detective Riley. I'm afraid the whole business haunted him. In the end, it was eating away at him."

*Riley?* I turned my face away and stared out at the ocean. I didn't want Sally to see the recognition of Riley's name on my face. "You kept in touch?"

"Not often. But when a case came up he thought I might find interesting, he'd reach out to me."

"How? It's not like it's easy to call you."

Sally laughed. "That's right, you're a modern young woman, aren't you. We did it the old-fashioned way. I carried a beeper. When he wanted me, he beeped me, and I called him."

Sally started walking again. Not much farther and we'd be on the other side of the lighthouse, close to where I had instructed DJ to meet us.

"Are you trying to tell me the cops helped you choose your victims?"

"Victims isn't the term I'd use. The victims, Jennifer, are you and me. Not the men we've murdered. The cops simply aided me in finding the women who needed my help and had nowhere else to turn. That's why I started the Butterflies. Once I was free of my husband, I felt empowered, and I wanted to help other women do the same."

"But you couldn't have killed them all."

"Goodness, no. I didn't need to. Most of the women just needed counseling, and there are women on my site who do just that. Nothing more. In fact, those who didn't qualify—who weren't stalked by serial abusers—don't even know about the other half of it. It's safer that way. But for those who were, I formed my tribunal."

"And all this time the cops never interfered?"

"The cops knew exactly what we were doing. In a sense, we were all working the same cases, but from different sides. In most instances, the cops had given up. What could they do beyond issuing a restraining order or court-ordered anger management classes? And the man's family, who you'd think would do something if they knew what was happening, seldom pulled through. In truth, the women are frequently too frightened to say anything to family or friends for fear of what might happen to them or their loved ones. Once my tribunal and I found a woman willing to leave but who couldn't, we would simply fix the situation for her. Permanently."

"And you always made it look like an accident or suicide?"

"There're lots of ways to kill someone, Jennifer. Most are easy. But some were more sensational than others." Sally tucked my arm beneath hers, and we kept walking. "We did one where the tabloids thought the man had been abducted by space aliens. And another killed by wild wolves, or I think the story said a chupacabra." She stopped and patted my wrist. "Really, who'd believe such a thing?"

I closed my eyes. I remembered the headlines. Tyler had shared them with me the night of Charlie's party. Each of the murders more ghoulish than the next. Sally put her hands back in her pockets and stared out at the ocean.

"I think those two were some of our better work. Truth was, the alien story about the body being dumped from a space ship was nothing more than sensationalism. Probably 'cause the man had just come from some type of space convention, and the tabloids picked it up and ran with it. It worked in our favor, though, fabulously." Sally laughed, glanced over at me then back out at the inky black horizon.

"What happened?"

"Nothing he didn't deserve. We ran him down. Burned him a couple times with the tailpipe of the car, but aliens...aliens never touched him."

I wrapped my arms around myself and glanced down at my watch. I needed a few more minutes before we proceeded down the path to the other side of the lighthouse.

"It sounds awful, Sally, I don't think—"

"Awful? Awful is what he did to his girlfriend, Jennifer. Burning her. Threatening to run her over. We used the same method to kill him that he had used to terrorize her. You want to know what he did to her? He dropped her off on a lonely road one night in the middle of nowhere. Then followed her. Bumping her with the car's fender and burning her with the tailpipe if she didn't move fast enough. Believe me, what we did was all very justifiable. We made the punishment fit the crime. Appropriate, don't you think?"

She didn't wait for me to answer.

"And the other poor devil, the one those tabloid rags said was killed by wolves? He died at his own hands, so to speak. He trained pit bulls to fight in the arena. An inhumane and illegal act for sure. Even more so when you knew he had also threatened his wife with his dogs. We simply took dog-man and his dogs for a walk. His wife knew the command words. Attack. Release. Too bad we remembered the second word too late. But we buried him, partially anyway, so when the cops found the body, they'd know we had finished the job."

"Sally, this is crazy."

"Crazy is what happens when you live with an abuser long enough that it starts to feel normal, Jennifer. That's crazy."

I exhaled. I needed to hold it together for a few more minutes. "And how many were there altogether?"

"Does it matter?" Sally looked at me like I had asked a naughty question.

"No. It frightens me, that's all."

"Not one died that didn't free a woman of her tormentor and whose life isn't better for it." Sally glanced back behind us. "I think it's time, Jennifer. We should be getting back to your friend. You wouldn't want him to sober up and come looking for you. He might stumble too close to the cliff and fall. And where would the justice be in that?"

I glanced at my watch: 8:27. The path was still wet from the rain. Just a few more feet and we'd be directly in front of the second wedding area. *DJ. Whatever you do, don't be late.*

Sally put her arm around my shoulder, pulled me to her and whispered, her voice in my ear. "Come on, Jennifer, we need to go."

I slipped from beneath her arm and, turning toward her, grabbed both her wrists in my hands and held tight, refusing to budge. "No. No. I can't."

Sally's strength was bigger than my own, and she surprised me. Twisting her hands from my grip, she grabbed my upper arms before I could defend myself.

"Yes, you can," she said. She shook me hard.

"No! I won't." I tried to break her grip and stepped back. Nearly stumbling over the barrier between the walk and cliff's edge. Desperate, I grabbed her and held tight, my hands on her shoulders. Like two wrestlers, we held each other, pushing and pulling, refusing to let go. Until—

Sally grabbed my hair. My wig. And I let go. With one hand I tried to hold my head while I continued to push her back away from the cliff. But I wasn't strong enough. The wig came flying off. Sally let go and glared at me. "Who are you? Why are you doing this?"

I grabbed the wig up off the ground and stuffed it in my jacket pocket. I didn't think for a second Sally knew who I really was. Only that she was frightened. Years of being on the run had taught her to trust no one. And now, in her mind, those fears had caught up with her. Those enemies she feared. Who she had evaded so carefully, living below the radar, changing out her phone. I was suddenly one of them.

Panting, I held my sides, nearly doubled over trying to catch my breath. "Sally, please, I'm here to help."

"No, you're one of them. You're trying to kill me."

With a strength I hadn't expected, she came at me again. Her energy renewed. Pushing me backward over the barrier. Falling on my back, I rolled and grabbed for a rock, anything, to get my bearings. But before I could stand, Sally was on top of me. Her rough hands on the collar of my shirt, pulling me to my feet. Then pushing me backward towards the cliff's edge.

"Sally, no." My feet slipped in the mud. I glanced back, the inky black waters churning below me. "Please, stop!"

From behind her, in the moonlight, I could see DJ running towards us.

I yelled, "DJ, help! Help me!"

DJ rushed forward, jumping over the barrier wall, and grabbed Sally from behind. Despite the difference in their height, she pinned her arms behind her. Then with one well-placed kick, like a karate chop to the back of Sally's knees, Sally fell back and collapsed like a wounded animal.

The expression on my face must have registered my surprise. Short of a Bruce Lee movie, I'd never seen such moves.

DJ smiled. "Black belt. Three years in a row. Another secret I'd prefer you not share."

Sally moaned and rubbed the back of her knee. Doubled over in pain.

"You don't need to worry, Carol. She's not going anywhere."

"Probably not. But just the same." I leaned down and slipped my hand into Sally's coat pocket and retrieved the gun. I wasn't taking any chances. "I'll give you this for safe keeping, and maybe a little insurance."

DJ took the gun from my hand and shoved it in the back of her waistband. "We're not going to need it. But I could use your help getting her back to my car."

I grabbed Sally's other arm and, putting it over my shoulder, helped Sally over the barrier.

"What are you doing?" Sally sounded as though she were still in pain.

"We're helping you escape," I said.

"Who's we?"

From beneath Sally's arm, DJ said, "Me, Sally. Doris Jean. You remember?"

"Doris?" Sally straightened up and grabbed my arm for support. The recognition spreading across her face like relief. "Is it really you?"

"Yes, but we need to go."

"She's right," I said. "It's not safe for you here anymore. The cops, your tribunal, everyone's searching for you. We need to get you out of here."

Sally turned back to DJ. "You're here to help me?"

"I'm here to return the favor you did for me."

"And Jennifer?" Sally asked.

"I'll explain everything to you in the car. But we have to get you out of here, now."

Overhead the sound of helicopter blades buffeting in the wind interrupted our goodbye. I looked up and was nearly blinded by a searchlight sweeping from beneath the chopper, it's broad beam focused on the cliff in front of me.

"Something's happened." I pushed Sally into DJ's arms. "Hurry, the two of you need to go. Now!"

DJ put Sally's arm back around her shoulder and, ducking beneath the low-flying chopper, turned and hobbled as best they could towards the parking lot.

The chopper swung wide out over the ocean, its searchlight flooding the area beneath the cliff, to the sunken city, and back towards the lighthouse, and the big fig tree.

*Oh my god, Chase.*

# CHAPTER 43

I ran. The light from the sky chopper swept the trail ahead of me. The sound was deafening as the big bird swept back from out over the ocean and hovered above the party tent. It's light, like a giant white funnel, scoped the area just beyond the cliff's edge. On its perimeter, I could see the shadow of a crowd. Then as I got closer, the looks on their faces, reflected in the copter's bright light. They were ashen.

I pushed through the crowd. My hands on the shoulders of strangers, jumping and bobbing between people, trying to look over their heads. "What happened?"

"Someone jumped."

"Or fell."

Nameless voices from in the crowd hollered back.

"Who?" My heart was beating like the thrashing of the chopper's blades above me.

No one knew. I looked back at the picnic table where Chase and I had sat. Empty! The only evidence of Chase being there was Charlie's cooler, abandoned on the bench.

"Chase! Chase, where are you?" I spun around three-sixty. Searching. Yelling his name. He had to be here. Somewhere in the crowd. God, please don't let it be him. I ran back toward the party tent. He wasn't there. I turned and ran back towards the bench. And then from behind me, I heard a voice.

"Carol! Carol, is that you? Are you okay?"

From beyond the party tent, Chase came running towards me.

I rushed to him, and without thinking, threw my arms around him. Thank God he was alive. "Where were you? What happened?"

"Someone must have fallen." He put his hands on my upper arms, rubbing them up and down as he stared into my eyes. Then he shook his head, pulled me to him, and held me tight. "I thought for a minute it might have been you. I've been searching everywhere. Where were you?"

I was about to lie and tell him I had wandered toward the cliff when I heard Sheri's voice.

"Carol, I saw the chopper. Are you all right? I couldn't wait in the car any longer. I heard somebody fell. I was afraid it was you."

Chase pulled me close. The warmth of his body against mine was reassuring.

"She's fine. It was someone from the party." He nodded over to a group of partygoers huddled near the cliff. "They were a rowdy crowd. Lots of drinking going on."

I turned away from Chase and pulled Sheri to me. She was shaking uncontrollably. I tried to reassure her. "I'm fine, Sheri. Really. You don't need to worry. Everything's okay. I promise."

Then catching her breath, she straightened herself and pushed a tear away from her eye. "And did you get what you came for?"

"Mustang Sally?" Chase looked at me, I shook my head.

"No," I said. "She never showed. And I don't think she will. Not now. Not with all the cops here and the choppers in the air. I'm sure whatever happened scared her off. She's gone."

# CHAPTER 44

Chase, Sheri, and I hung around in the park until the rescue operation's retrieval of the body was complete. I think Chase wanted to make certain the body pulled from the rocks below wasn't Mustang Sally. Which, of course, it wasn't. Rather, it was exactly as Chase had predicted. One of the partygoers, a young man who'd had too much to drink, had wandered too close to the cliff's edge and fallen to his death.

I called the the station to report the accident. Tragically, the young man's death got no more than thirty seconds of coverage and was sandwiched between two other stories. That's the way it was on a busy Saturday night.

Once the body was recovered, Sheri announced she wanted to go ahead and get the kids, it was getting late. I shouldn't worry. They would caravan back to the valley. Sheri promised she would be behind Misty's van the whole way, and Charlie would be fine driving.

"But the two of you," she paused and looked at us both, "I think you might need more time together."

I was about to protest when Sheri bussed me on the cheek and whispered into my ear. "And it might be a good idea if you drove Chase's car home." Hugging me goodbye one last time, she winked at Chase and gave him a quick thumbs up sign.

"What was that all about?" Chase said.

I shook my head like I didn't know and shrugged my shoulders.

"I take it I wasn't supposed to hear that bit about you driving me home? Something you need to share?"

I winced. "You heard that ?"

"I did. But before you say anything, I think we should go back to the picnic table, pick up Charlie's cooler, and have a little chat. What do you say?" Chase grabbed my hand and led me back to the table.

Whatever warm feelings I was beginning to harbor toward Chase suddenly chilled. I sat down on the bench and grabbed Charlie's cooler, and, with both hands, clutched it against my stomach.

"You have anything left to drink in that thing?" Chase pointed to the cooler.

"Coffee, maybe," I said.

"Because that's what you were drinking, right?"

I nodded. "Yes."

"While I was drinking tea. A special tea, maybe one of Misty's specials?"

I hugged the cooler tighter. I didn't like where this was going.

"Admit it, Carol, you're busted. You set me up. Not only did you use me to attract Sally, but then you put something in my drink so you could kidnap her out from under me."

I closed my eyes and exhaled. "Fine. You're right. I did all that, and I'd probably do it again." I looked up at Chase. He was standing in front of me, scratching his head like he wasn't certain what he was going to do.

"Think about it, Chase. If there are cops who knew what Sally was doing, and she disappeared...so what? What's the crime? We didn't kill anybody. And if you found Sally and turned her in, it wasn't going to play out well for you. A bunch of cops who were keeping a secret would go down for a crime they had turned a blind eye to. Plus, who knows how many women who had been victimized would be facing criminal charges. Nobody was going to win. You certainly wouldn't. The police wouldn't embrace you for exposing their own. Why not just help her disappear?"

Chase took the cooler from me and removed the thermos with the blue cap on it. The thermos I had been drinking from. "You mind?"

"No," I said.

He sat down next to me and poured himself a cup of coffee into the thermos cap and took a sip. "You want some?"

I nodded. I was shaking from the chill in the air or was it nerves? He held the cup to my lips as I took a sip. "Thank you."

We sat silent for a moment. The park was empty. I hugged myself. The damp chill of the night air sent a shiver down my back. The sound of waves breaking on the shore beneath us.

"I have a confession to make too," Chase said.

"What's that?"

"I wasn't a hundred percent surprised."

"No?"

"When you mentioned you were having second thoughts about Sally, I knew something was up."

"But you still drank the tea."

"No. I faked it." Chase took the red-capped thermos I had given him earlier out from the cooler and opened it up, emptying the contents out onto the ground.

"But how?"

"I'm a detective, Carol. I'm supposed to know a thing or two about human nature. It didn't take much to figure out you had spiked my drink. You had two thermoses, and you kept going on about how salty Sheri's brownies were. What was I supposed to think?"

"You just went along with it?"

"I did, but what I didn't expect was for that young man to fall off the cliff. When I heard all the commotion, I was afraid something had happened to you."

"You were worried?"

"I was."

"So I guess you're going to turn me in then?"

"Nope." Chase took a sucker out from his pocket, put it in his mouth, and leaned his elbows on the table, staring out at the horizon. "The way I see it, we're even. You gave me the tip on Silva, and from that, I was able to work myself back into the good graces of LAPD. So I've been thinking, if you can break a few rules, maybe I can do the same."

"I'm not sure I understand."

"That is unless this case has you totally soured on men."

"I'm not soured on men, Chase. It's just—"

"Because I was thinking, since we have this secret between us, I might be able to convince you to break a few rules of your own. Maybe mix a little of your professional life with your personal."

"You're blackmailing me?"

"Not at all. I'm only saying that as far as Sally goes, you're right. This is just another unsolved missing person case. And the cops, as you pointed out, aren't about to investigate. You, on the other hand, you're a case I'm not about to let go of. Not unless you tell me you're absolutely not interested. And then I'd probably tell you you're lying, because of the way you get that cute, little nervous smile on your face when I get close to you." Chase gently pushed a strand of my hair behind my ear and held my head with hand.

I grabbed the sucker out of Chase's mouth. "I'll tell you what. You get rid of this damn sucker, and I might just consider it."

"Oh yeah?" Chase took the candy from my hand, tossed it over his shoulder and pulled me closer to him. "I suppose you got something else I might like just as well."

"That all depends." My eyes met his, a lightness filled my chest.

"On?"

"Whatever you're considering a suitable substitute," I said.

"How about this?" Chase took my chin in his hand and gently turned my face to his, then kissed me softly on the lips. "Suitable enough?"

I put my arm around his neck. "Do it again."

# CHAPTER 45

Sunday morning I was awakened by the sound of Jennifer's cell phone buzzing. I had left it in my bag in the bathroom and stumbled into the room to answer it, still groggy. After last night, I was no longer apprehensive it might be Sally, and since Jennifer's desperate call to me yesterday requesting she talk to Misty, I wasn't surprised when I tapped the screen and saw Jennifer had sent a message.

*You won't believe! Just wanted to share.*

Attached was a photo of Jennifer with Jason in front of a Las Vegas wedding chapel. Jennifer was holding her left hand up in front of her. Big smile on her face. On her ring finger was a large diamond. Jason appeared dazed but pleased.

I tapped in my response. *Congratulations!* Then noticed the time. It was more than twelve hours since I'd left Sally and DJ. If I were going to learn anything, now was the time. I reached back into my bag for the scrap of paper DJ had given to me. On it was the number she had scribbled, telling me to call if I wanted to verify Mustang Sally had arrived safely.

I punched in the number and waited. Finally, after several rings, a woman's voice answered. "Aloha."

*Aloha.* The greeting caught me by surprise. I paused, then repeated the message DJ had given me.

"I'm calling to inquire about the arrival of a package. I was told someone at this number could verify delivery?"

"I'm afraid, miss, I'm not at liberty to share that information. May I ask who's calling?"

I recognized the authoritative voice on the other end of the line instantly. I started to blurt out her name, then stopped myself. My voice catching in my throat. I didn't dare call Andrea Reddings by her name. Nobody in the group used names. Instead, I ignored her request and repeated the message DJ had given me.

"Can you tell me if a package from Doris Jean arrived safely?"

Her reply came sternly. "May I ask who gave you this number?"

"I'm afraid I can't tell you that."

She laughed softly. "No. Of course, you can't. We all exist in such secrecy, don't we? Although I probably wouldn't know the name of the sender if you were to tell me. Anonymity has its benefits in this business. Wouldn't you agree?"

I didn't answer.

"But your voice, miss, it's familiar. Would I be correct in assuming we know one another?"

I looked in the mirror and pushed a strand of hair behind my ear. Did I even know who I was anymore? So much had happened in the last couple of weeks, I felt as though the face staring back at me was no longer my own. In a sense, it wasn't. The world of good and evil had changed. The lines had blurred. I was no longer an innocent bystander unaware of backdoor deals and the evil doings of a crazed world. I was part of it. I had secrets. Secrets that could undo careers and lives with a slip of the tongue, and I was choosing to hold mine.

"Yes. I think we do," I said.

"In fact, wouldn't you agree, when we last met, we had a kind of understanding?"

"If you mean I could expect your help as long as your name wasn't attached to it, yes, I'd say we did have an understanding. A very good understanding."

"I imagine you're a bit surprised, finding me here, answering the phone."

"Last I heard you were off inspecting properties. Is this one?"

"You might say it's part of a charity I support. A safe house, known only to those who've had need of it."

"And how did you know to go there? Now of all times?"

"I got a call from my housekeeper here. She keeps the place up for me. Heaven knows I'm seldom around. She called to tell me she had heard from a former guest. However, I had no idea who she was. Nor did I care. What I did care about, however, was what that my housekeeper said this former guest had arranged for a VIP to visit. And I might like to be here to greet her. The name of that visitor was, as you might guess, not revealed to me. But I suspected."

"And that's why you left LA in such a hurry?"

"It was. And you'll be delighted to know, the package you called to inquire about arrived early this morning. Safe and sound."

I breathed a sigh of relief. It was behind me now. At least the physical act of helping someone elude the law was no longer something to concern me. The rest of it, helping someone who I knew was guilty of murder, would take a while to get used to. I looked back in the mirror. I was different.

"Thank you."

"Mahalo, Ms. Childs."

# NANCY COLE SILVERMAN

Nancy Cole Silverman credits her twenty-five years in news and talk radio for helping her to develop an ear for storytelling. But it wasn't until after she retired that she was able to write fiction full-time. Much of what Silverman writes about is pulled from events that were reported on from inside some of Los Angeles' busiest newsrooms where she spent the bulk of her career. She lives in Los Angeles with her husband, Bruce, and two standard poodles.

**The Carol Childs Mystery Series
by Nancy Cole Silverman**

SHADOW OF DOUBT (#1)
BEYOND A DOUBT (#2)
WITHOUT A DOUBT (#3)
ROOM FOR DOUBT (#4)

**Henery Press Mystery Books**

And finally, before you go...
Here are a few other mysteries
you might enjoy:

# TELL ME NO LIES

Lynn Chandler Willis

## An Ava Logan Mystery (#1)

Ava Logan, single mother and small business owner, lives deep in the heart of the Appalachian Mountains, where poverty and pride reign. As publisher of the town newspaper, she's busy balancing election season stories and a rash of ginseng thieves.

And then the story gets personal. After her friend is murdered, Ava digs for the truth all the while juggling her two teenage children, her friend's orphaned toddler, and her own muddied past. Faced with threats against those closest to her, Ava must find the killer before she, or someone she loves, ends up dead.

Available at booksellers nationwide and online

Visit www.henerypress.com for details

# CIRCLE OF INFLUENCE
## Annette Dashofy

### A Zoe Chambers Mystery (#1)

Zoe Chambers, paramedic and deputy coroner in rural Pennsylvania's tight-knit Vance Township, has been privy to a number of local secrets over the years, some of them her own. But secrets become explosive when a dead body is found in the Township Board President's abandoned car.

As a January blizzard rages, Zoe and Police Chief Pete Adams launch a desperate search for the killer, even if it means uncovering secrets that could not only destroy Zoe and Pete, but also those closest to them.

Available at booksellers nationwide and online

Visit www.henerypress.com for details

# KILLER IMAGE

Wendy Tyson

## An Allison Campbell Mystery (#1)

As Philadelphia's premier image consultant, Allison Campbell helps others reinvent themselves, but her most successful transformation was her own after a scandal nearly ruined her. Now she moves in a world of powerful executives, wealthy, eccentric ex-wives and twisted ethics.

When Allison's latest Main Line client, the fifteen-year-old Goth daughter of a White House hopeful, is accused of the ritualistic murder of a local divorce attorney, Allison fights to prove her client's innocence when no one else will. But unraveling the truth brings specters from her own past. And in a place where image is everything, the ability to distinguish what's real from the facade may be the only thing that keeps Allison alive.

Available at booksellers nationwide and online

Visit www.henerypress.com for details

Made in the USA
Columbia, SC
27 June 2017